O Bed! O Breakfast!

Robert Dalby

*To Cissy,
Thanks for the good ole
Natchez support!
Best wishes,
Robert Dalby*

Genesis Press, Inc

Genesis Press, Inc.
315 Third Avenue North
Columbus, MS 39701

O Bed! O Breakfast!

Copyright 2000 by Robert Dalby. All rights reserved.

This is a work of fiction. Names, characters, places, and incidents either are the product of the author's imagination or are used fictitiously. Any resemblance to actual persons, living or dead, is entirely coincidental.

All rights reserved. No part of this publication may be reproduced or transmitted in any form or by any means, electronic or mechanical, including photocopy, recording, or any information storage and retrieval system, without permission in writing from the publisher.

ISBN 1-58571-021-0

Printed in the United States of America

FIRST EDITION

Cover photos by Mark and Laurie Coffey

FOR ALL THE STRONG WOMEN
IN MY EXTENDED SOUTHERN FAMILY

ACKNOWLEDGEMENTS

Special thanks:

To Gary M. Frazier, my editor, for his unwavering support of and superb suggestions for my manuscript.

Thanks also to: Bettye and Sonny Jenkins of Hawthorne, for their help in historical research and detail; Mark and Laurie Coffey for their cover photography; Marion Alvarez Kuehnle for being there from the very beginning; Marie Knight, Ellen Hefley, Alma K. Carpenter and Baldwin Tidmore for their dependable enthusiasm; and cousin Pendleton Hyde Coleman Murphy for permission to "have fun" with her name.

O Bed! O Breakfast!

Chapter One

Mary Dell Hoskins looked up from her shrimp remoulade and gasped at the sight of the wide-bodied matron bearing down upon her table while brandishing some sort of newspaper high above her head. There was just enough time to warn her dinner partner and supervisor, Harris Lyles, who had his back to the gathering storm.

"Brace yourself. Here comes instant indigestion courtesy of Megita Larose!"

The entire white-tiled Hotel Fort Rosalie dining room perked up in the midst of buttering their rolls and sipping their cocktails as the confrontation began. Most of them knew all too well the power that Megita Pulliam Larose wielded as president of the town's Historic Preservation Committee.

"Well, isn't this just too cozy," Megita said, pushing Harris down firmly as he made a gentlemanly attempt to rise from his chair. "The director of Fort Rosalie's Tourist Bureau and his favorite account executive in cahoots over dinner." She shook the paper in their faces. "Did you two think you were going to slide this one by me and the Committee?"

Mary Dell frowned and held out her hand. "May I see whatever it is you're waving around there like a bullfighter's cape?"

Megita slapped the paper into Mary Dell's palm and nervously fingered the string of pearls dangling from the considerable shelf of her bosom. "As if you didn't know and butter wouldn't melt in your mouth."

Mary Dell displayed the front page to Harris, and they both made a face. "*The Celebrity Inquisitor*, Megita?" Harris said. "A supermarket tabloid? I had no idea you fancied them."

"Don't get smart with me, Harris Lyles. You know very well

what I'm referring to. That horrid actress with her breasts spilling out all over the front page, that Juliette Cadbury coming here to film that awful *Whispering Dixie*. I'd heard rumors she was looking for a Deep South location but never dreamed she would end up here in Fort Rosalie with that live-in lover of hers."

Harris gestured calmly in Mary Dell's direction. "You do the honors and review it with her, please."

"Your quarrel shouldn't be with the Tourist Bureau, Mrs. Larose," Mary Dell began, choosing her words carefully. "Jim Horvath and the Mississippi Film Commission lined this up for Fort Rosalie. Ms. Cadbury and her friend, Tim Reynaldo, will play the leading roles in a three-month location shoot, and, yes, as that tabloid story says, they'll be coming down shortly to inspect our bed-and-breakfasts for local accommodations during their stay."

Megita snatched the paper back, gave her a laser beam stare and wagged a finger accusingly. "That's not all it says, my girl!"

Mary Dell winced. She detested being referred to as a girl. After all, she had recently celebrated her thirty-first birthday. She had tried to be as deferential as possible to Fort Rosalie's preeminent cultural and social icon, but it was clear Megita regarded her as little more than a Tourist Bureau lackey who was utterly beneath contempt.

"You may well wonder how I stumbled upon this lamentable rag!" Megita continued. "I assure you I am not in the habit of patronizing such drivel. But yesterday my grandson, Hillman, spent the night with me and his grandfather, and I caught him reading it with his eyes bugging out over that halter top cover photo. Oh, he just thought Juliette Cadbury was such a—what was the word—oh, yes, a 'hotty.' Not that I think that's even a real word, mind you. Well, I could have

lived with that, but after I'd snatched it from him and read her views regarding everything on God's green earth, I decided that enough was enough!"

Mary Dell took a deep breath. "Meaning?"

"Meaning—anyone that says she and her unmarried lover are going to make lots of babies without benefit of marriage if they feel like it, is giving young minds like my Hillman a very irresponsible and immoral view of the real world. That is so typical of these Hollywood types, you know. So many of them feel that their great wealth insulates them from the responsibility of their actions. And my Hillman with all his hormones is presented a horrendous role-model. Where will it all end, I ask you?"

Harris took a swallow of water and stepped up to the plate. "Megita, we're very aware of that tabloid article. It was called to our attention by the Film Commission itself. I certainly agree with you that it's a rag. It's also probably very inaccurate, misleading and even untruthful regarding Juliette Cadbury's actual views on a variety of subjects. These supermarket concoctions are always getting into legal trouble misquoting people."

"Fine. Defend this creature all you like," Megita replied, thumping the paper for emphasis. "But I've come to tell you two that I will not stand idly by when she comes to town. Here's fair warning that I intend to organize my Historic Preservation Committee into a protest group. When she and that actor friend of hers come down to Fort Rosalie to inspect our bed-and-breakfasts, we will dog her every inch of the way. We will let her know that Hollywood morality is not appreciated here in Fort Rosalie, Mississippi, and perhaps she'll think twice about making that terrible *Whispering Dixie* within the confines of our beautiful and historic city."

With that, Megita turned on her heels and marched across

the dining room to a chorus of agitated whispers. Mary Dell was the first to recover from the diatribe, giving Harris a worried look. "She could be a major problem for us."

"Understatement of the year. Keeping our three beloved bed-and-breakfast owners from each other's throats was going to be difficult enough. But now this."

The confrontation with Megita had taken the edge off Mary Dell's appetite, and she toyed with her food throughout the rest of the meal. "I've been thinking," she said later as she stirred her coffee somewhat absent-mindedly. "And I don't think I'm going to tell our bed-and-breakfast owners about Megita's intentions at the briefing tomorrow. We'll be peeling them off the walls as it is when they hear the details of Juliette Cadbury's inspection tour."

"Good idea," Harris replied, reaching across the table to take her hand. "You're the only one at the Bureau I would ever have even considered for the Cadbury-Reynaldo booking."

Indeed, in the space of five years she had become the Tourist Bureau's most accomplished account executive, quickly surpassing the savvy of a handful of older and more experienced males. The gossip-prone around the Bureau, of course, were fond of pointing to the budding romantic relationship between the boss and his only female charge, but Mary Dell had definitely not slept her way to the top. To begin with, there was the matter of Harris's divorce—which had finally come through after three and a half years. True, she had fantasized about him on that first job interview, wondering what it would be like to have him frame her face with those strong hands of his, how it would feel to run her fingers through his salt-and-pepper hair, how that first kiss would taste on her lips, a mature man having his way with her.

Yet, she had wisely maintained their professional relationship right up until the time he was once again a free man.

O Bed! O Breakfast!

Yes, he was nearly twenty years older. And yes, he had reared and married off two daughters after a quarter century of marriage to his wife, Betsy. But Mary Dell had not hesitated when he had finally asked her out after the ring was off his finger. She was ready for something more than booking hotel rooms and convention space for association executives. The slim, sweet-faced brunette everyone said just lit up the Tourist Bureau morning, noon and night, was ready for some honest-to-goodness romance in her life.

On the ride back to her apartment in Harris's Buick Mary Dell was thinking out loud. "I don't think I'd better tell Juliette's personal assistant about this new development, either."

"What's her name again?"

"Heidi Pendleton," Mary Dell replied. "Or Miss Efficient, as I call her every time we hang up long-distance. She talks just like a press release all the time. 'Miss Cadbury does not want pedestrian accommodations during her upcoming stay in Fort Rosalie. Instead, she would prefer something cozy and intimate that will help immerse her in that Southern ambience she needs to bring her character, Rella Darrow, to life.' Half the time I think I'm listening to one of those computer-generated voices."

Harris snickered. "Well, I agree with you about keeping her in the dark. We can do our best to talk Megita out of this protest idea between now and Juliette Cadbury's arrival. In fact, that should be our number one priority after we brief our bed-and-breakfast owners on the inspection weekend. You've got them coming in at eleven tomorrow, right?"

Mary Dell exhaled dramatically. "Yep. That's our Ground Zero."

"So we've resorted to nuclear terminology, have we?"

They drove along in amused silence while Mary Dell quick-

ly reviewed the history of Fort Rosalie's 'terrible trio of tourism.' To say that the three owners did not get along was a gross understatement. They fought like hellions over every booking lead the Tourist Bureau sent their way, and there was no telling what they might resort to once they learned that Juliette Cadbury was willing to pay quite handsomely to reserve one of the bed-and-breakfasts for the entire three-month shoot.

"Would you like to come up for a nightcap?" Mary Dell said a few minutes later in the apartment parking lot. It was her standard-issue invitation since they had started dating, one he had yet to refuse, and it always resulted in a pleasant session of cuddling and kissing on her living room sofa. So far, they had not gone any further, but she knew that even greater intimacy was hers for the asking.

"I was thinking we ought to get a good night's sleep tonight. I mean, considering what we've got ahead of us tomorrow," he replied. The moonlight streaming through the windshield illuminated the disappointment in her face, so he reeled her in gently with those strong hands of his. "But that doesn't mean we can't take a few minutes right here on the front seat to keep the kettle simmering."

She would have chuckled at his wordplay had he not immediately covered her mouth with his, taking her breath away with the warm, lingering kiss that followed. Running Fort Rosalie's Tourist Bureau without a hiccup was not the man's only talent. He was awfully good at this kissing business, so much so that she couldn't help but wonder what the rest would be like.

"Whoa!" she said, once he allowed her to surface for some air. "I think the kettle is boiling!" Then she rested her head against his shoulder while the drumbeat in her blood gradually began to slow.

"Be thinking of some angle to present to Megita before you drift off tonight," he told her, breaking the last vestiges of the spell before they said goodnight and she finally made her getaway.

It was difficult for her to think of anything but Harris, however, as she prepared for bed. Later, under the covers, she cradled her stuffed, black-and-tan dachshund toy, which she had named Rosalie in honor of the city, and played the wedding game in her head. She just might be on course to become the second Mrs. Harris Lyles, and therein lay the quandary. For the life of her, she couldn't fathom his lengthy separation and subsequent messy divorce. Put more succinctly: what kind of fool was Betsy Lyles to let a man like this get away?

Robert Dalby

Chapter Two

Mary Dell sighed and glanced at her watch. Five minutes to eleven. Precious few minutes left until Ground Zero. She rose from her cluttered desk and moved to the window of her cozy second-story Tourist Bureau office, pulling back the curtains to monitor the arrivals of Fort Rosalie's 'terrible trio of tourism' in the parking lot below.

Predictably, the first to drive up was the snowy-haired and diminutive Miss Aimee Pierce, rumored to be nearing eighty but still in excellent health. Her Plum Cottage, decorated from stem to stern in various shades of her signature purple, was the oldest of the B&B's—up and running for forty-five years. As a result she had hosted several famous celebrities from previous Hollywood productions as far back as the '50's, including *The Horse Soldiers*, and *Raintree County*.

Next to arrive was Fort Rosalie's resident poet, the forty-ish Edding Denbo. The literary bantam rooster of the town, people called him, but it was Mary Dell's observation that he was living proof God took care of those who could not otherwise take care of themselves. Upon the untimely death of his parents in an automobile accident it had been his good fortune to inherit the family mansion, Betterslie, along with a substantial trust fund that had allowed him to summon the muse without starving to death. Although some of his poems had actually been published in academic quarterlies, he had never made a dime off his work. It had been his further inspiration to turn Betterslie into a literary bed-and-breakfast of sorts, where on any given evening spirituous liquors of every description were consumed while discussions of blank verse flew through the air.

O Bed! O Breakfast!

Last to park—in a white Rolls-Royce, no less—were Johnny and Terrelle Lurkin—*nouveau* as the Texas oil they had struck a few years back and *riche* as Croesus as a result. One fine day they had swooped down upon Fort Rosalie in their Learjet, acquired ancient and crumbling Destiny Manor for a pittance and restored it to something that belonged in a theme park rather than the Old South. And they had recently flown to Dallas in that same Learjet to pick up the only Rolls-Royce in Fort Rosalie, a Silver Seraph ordered from the factory in a color the salesman assured them was an exact match for Mississippi's opulent state flower, the magnolia.

The Lurkins were consummate lurkers, madly pressing the flesh for entry into this club, wangling an invitation to that party or ball and otherwise making social-climbing nuisances of themselves. Despite their overwhelming neediness, their Destiny Manor had become one of the town's most successful businesses in the short space of two years.

Mary Dell cocked an ear as the owners made their way along the corridor outside her office to the upstairs meeting room. They were talking excitedly amongst themselves, and for the time being, even maintaining civil tones. But she knew that would not last long. Then she took a deep breath, opened her office door and headed for the inevitable clash of wills.

It had officially begun.

Terrelle and Johnny Lurkin were the first to rush her in the meeting room, forming a perfect double team. "Oh, honey, we've just been beside ourselves waiting for the details of this booking!" Terrelle said, taking her arm and pressing up against her. "That tacky tabloid kinda leaked the news, but we want the inside scoop now!"

Mary Dell immediately had to catch her breath, since Terrelle had apparently just done twenty or so laps in her favorite perfume. Of course, it did complement perfectly the

helmet of hair she always sprayed into rigid submission, along with the palette of makeup she never failed to apply to her middle-aged face.

Johnny was an even wider load. Six foot-five, to be exact. A big pair of bear paws to grab and hold onto his prey. An off-putting habit of getting right up into someone's face just before sending out a blast of his habitual bourbon breath. Of course, he always had that native Texas enthusiasm to recommend him, including a ranch-sized smile for every stranger he met at a party or out on the street. Mary Dell actually got a kick out of the way he could work a room or a sidewalk, as long as she was able to observe the proceedings from a reasonably safe distance.

"Now, Mary Dell, we've had a sleepless night or two since that tabloid came out," Johnny told her. "I don't know how many times I called up ol' Harris Lyles to ask him if he'd tell me more, but all he'd say over and over was that we'd just have to wait for your briefing."

Mary Dell managed to wriggle out from between them with a polite smile. "Then let's take our seats and get started, shall we?" She moved to the podium and surveyed the room. Miss Aimee was already seated on the front row, hands folded primly in her lavender lap, but Edding Denbo, all five foot-four of him, was nervously pacing near the windows. Mary Dell cleared her throat to get his attention. "Please have a seat, Edding."

The mundane directive triggered one of Edding's patented monologues, which they all knew better than to interrupt. "I fail to see why the Tourist Bureau couldn't simply have sent out a memo on this booking. Or better yet, given the details over the telephone. In case you've forgotten, that's a convenient little instrument that was invented eons ago to save on gas mileage and the wear and tear of the human body. You've

O Bed! O Breakfast!

torn me away from my current guests, which on the one hand is a blessing, considering that they are hopeless trolls from some dismal manufacturing town in Ohio. I'm certain they wake up every morning to ghastly billowing smokestacks. And while I've tried to steer our conversations to matters literary as usual, all they seem to want the answers to are questions concerning the preparation of grits, okra, and other Southern food items. As if Betterslie were some gigantic prop for a 'Hee Haw' skit or a set piece from the *Grand Ol' Opry*. Their entire stay has been grievous beyond words so far, take my word."

He paused, and everyone waited to see if it was over. With Edding there was no other way to tell. He had been known to suddenly resume his verbiage like a cardiac arrest patient springing to life following a couple of hits from the crash cart paddles. After a decent length of time, Mary Dell decided to test the waters.

"Harris and I wanted to make sure nothing fell through the cracks for a booking as important as this one. In other words, no hearsay or second-hand information. We felt that a face-to-face meeting with all of you was the appropriate course of action."

"Very well," said Edding, finally taking a seat behind Miss Aimee. "But time is of the essence, and I have scads of errands to run before returning to those Ohio-ese."

Mary Dell stood up tall and gave them her trademark sweet smile. "You already know by now that Jim Horvath has awarded Fort Rosalie the three-month location shoot for *Whispering Dixie* later this fall. We were thrilled to win this one over our arch-rival, Natchez. We've lost entirely too many films to them over the years, but this time we prevailed. You also probably know that Juliette Cadbury and Tim Reynaldo will be playing the leads of Rella Darrow and Harbaugh Kinsley, and she will actually be producing the movie. Now for

the part that impacts each of you. Ms. Cadbury's assistant, Heidi Pendleton, has informed me that the actress is interested in exclusively booking a bed-and-breakfast for herself for the duration of the shoot, and she'll be flying out from California one weekend to inspect all three of your B&B's personally. Naturally, the one she selects will be the recipient of a great deal of money and publicity, so we need to check our calendars and coordinate a date with her people out in California."

Terrelle was quivering with excitement. "Oh, I still can't believe *Whispering Dixie* is really gonna be filmed here. Johnny and I both read the book when it came out, and I told him then what a surefire movie it would make, didn't I, Johnny? All those crazy characters running around apologizing for the South and everything. Didn't I say that, Johnny?"

He was eagerly nodding his big Texas head. "My sweet thing is tellin' y'all the truth."

"And they're sure to want to stay with us out at Destiny Manor," Terrelle added.

Edding noisily cleared his throat. "I beg your damn pardon."

"Let's not forget," Miss Aimee said, staring straight ahead. "I'm the one with the celebrity experience. I arranged for John Wayne to go hunting with my cousin, Hyde, when he was here for *The Horse Soldiers*. And Elizabeth Taylor and I stayed up late at night all the time talking about her various husbands when she made *Raintree County* I should think my cozy little Plum Cottage would be just the ticket for this new production."

Mary Dell was mildly amused but hardly surprised. The civility had lasted about a minute or so. "Everyone, please. We're going to be absolutely professional about this. We'll pick our weekend, she'll come down to inspect the facilities, she'll make her decision based on her Friday, Saturday, and Sunday

O Bed! O Breakfast!

stays with each of you, and that will be the end of it."

That seemed to quiet them down for a while, but Terrelle was soon frowning and raising her hand. "Who gets to host her first on Friday? I mean, there might be an advantage in making the first impression."

Mary Dell was proud of herself. She had anticipated the question and was thoroughly prepared. "On the other hand, there's something to be said for getting in the last word. At any rate, I've decided that we'll draw straws for the order and leave it at that."

"I don't mind being in the middle," Miss Aimee said. "Saturday could end up being the centerpiece of their visit, just like an enormous arrangement of beautiful flowers."

"An enormous arrangement of beautiful purple flowers, no doubt," Edding added.

Miss Aimee turned and eyed him sharply. "Say what you will with that serrated tongue of yours, Edding, but I know what I'm doing."

"She can have Saturday if she wants," Terrelle said. "But we'll gladly draw for Friday and Sunday. I was just thinking—they might want to go to church with us on Sunday. We could make a very good impression by offering to take them to church, couldn't we, Johnny? Do you think maybe they're Baptists? Reynaldo sounds Catholic, though, doesn't it?"

Edding snickered. "Trust me on this one, dear people. A sobering round of wafers and wine will not be high on the list of priorities of a fast lane, tabloid-headline making, just-living-together-for-the-helluvit Hollywood couple like Juliette Cadbury and Tim Reynaldo."

Johnny's face grew red, and murderous intent shot from his eyes. He no doubt hated being made fun of by someone who had never made a dime in his life, yet lorded it over everyone with that inflated ego of his. "You can go straight to hell

in a handbasket, Denbo!"

Edding had one of his devastating retorts ready to launch, but Mary Dell quickly stepped in as peacemaker. "Gentlemen, gentlemen! Let's please try to be civil Fort Rosalians, shall we?" She waited for their emotions to subside and then spoke slowly and calmly. "As I've said, we'll draw straws later for Friday and Sunday, since Miss Aimee has volunteered Saturday and no one seems to object." She paused again and saw that complete order had been restored. Harris had been right, of course. She was probably the only one at the Bureau who could have handled this trio under these circumstances. Most of the other account executives threw up their hands at the very mention of their names. "Very good, then. All of you quickly check your calendars and get back to me as soon as possible, and we'll take it from there. Thank you very much."

From her office window a few minutes later, she watched them all gathering in the parking lot below. She feared the worst, and the worst came to pass. Johnny and Edding resumed their earlier confrontation, and although she could not hear them, she could clearly see the rage in their faces as they spoke. Terrelle stepped in to try and separate them, while Miss Aimee looked on, worried and wide-eyed. Just as they were about to come to blows, Harris Lyles walked out and sent them to their separate corners with their tails between their legs. "Good job down there, boss," she told him when he walked into her office shortly after. "Saw it from the window. No TKO's today."

Harris laughed and moved to the edge of her desk. "And how did it go with you?"

"Oh, just a few opening rounds of shrapnel. No serious wounds, though."

"Good. I think my letting you handle it alone was best. My presence would have been distracting."

O Bed! O Breakfast!

She watched him pull up a chair with a dreamy look in her eyes. "Maybe not to them, but definitely to me."

He smiled briefly at her flirtation before quickly resuming his usual Tourist Bureau demeanor. "I have some bad news to impart. It seems our Megita telephoned Jim Horvath at the Commission bright and early this morning, ranting and raving about Juliette Cadbury's tabloid antics and the basic concept of *Whispering Dixie* being shot here in Fort Rosalie. She also gave him a blow-by-blow of her protest plans with her flock of historical hens. Needless to say, he was not amused. He then called me up to say that we'd better find some way to talk her out of all that nonsense, or he'd for damn sure cart the entire production off to Natchez."

Mary Dell contorted her face. "Oh, no! Anything but that!"

"Hey, the man knows how to plunge in the dagger and twist it."

Indeed, the rivalry between Fort Rosalie and Natchez had been simmering ever since the two had fought over the first film to do location shooting in the state of Mississippi—*In Olden Times*. The year was 1938, and in the decades that had followed, the genuflection to Hollywood had continued, with Natchez having the better of it most recently—snaring two different versions of *Huckleberry Finn,* as well as a number of Civil War epics such as *Beulah Land* and *North and South*. Now that the new millennium had arrived, Byron Cathcart's controversial novel *Whispering Dixie* was the most ambitious project to choose Fort Rosalie in quite a while, and the Tourist Bureau did not want to lose yet another one to Natchez.

"Were you able to come up with any angles to persuade Megita?" Harris said.

"Nothing outstanding," she replied, not about to divulge that she had spent most of her final waking moments the night before fantasizing about him.

"Same here. So what I thought we'd do is simply request an appointment with her at the Founders' Club and try to reason with her. Maybe play up the rivalry with Natchez. She hates losing out to them at anything."

"Sounds like a plan."

Then he rose from his chair, reached over and gently grasped her hand. All was right with her world whenever she felt the warmth from his body, from those strong hands, flowing into hers. They had definitely made a connection in recent weeks, and there was no turning back now.

"I'll try to get Megita on the phone and see what we can arrange," he said, releasing her and then heading for the door. She kept her eyes trained on those broad shoulders beneath his crisp, gray business suit until he had disappeared into the hallway. Then she plopped back down at her desk and resumed her daydreaming.

Whatever lay ahead of them with this booking and all the controversy surrounding it, they would endure together, surely emerging on the other side of it as a permanent item. They were a team now, the best the Tourist Bureau had to offer, and there was nothing they could not accomplish or solve.

O Bed! O Breakfast!

Chapter Three

Whatever Mary Dell had expected to find at the Founders' Club when she and Harris arrived a couple of days later to keep their appointment with Megita, it hardly compared to the reality. The cavernous common room of the funereal and darkly-Victorian old building was a madhouse of implausible choreography. For starters, one group of matronly and grandmotherly types in sensible shoes and support hose was busy going around in circles on the worn Persian rug, carrying homemade posters high above their heads in preparation for their duty on the sidewalks of Fort Rosalie. Another group was occupied with a low-impact aerobic routine that included marching in place while inhaling and exhaling noisily. The sentiments of these would-be picketers left no room for interpretation: JULIETTE, TAKE YOUR ROMEO AND GO HOME, one proclaimed. CADBURY AND REYNALDO, A MORAL DISGRACE, read another. SHOUT DOWN WHISPERING DIXIE—announced a third. A public relations disaster was clearly in the making.

"All right, ladies!" Megita shouted, clapping her hands together rapidly like a schoolteacher admonishing wayward pupils. "More zest, more pep, more vigor. Pick up those feet. Move those legs!" She turned briefly toward Mary Dell and Harris, who were standing nearby barely able to suppress their amusement. "I'll be with you both in just a moment." Then she authoritatively blew the whistle that was hanging around her neck. "Very good, ladies, very good. Time for our mid-afternoon casserole break. We have Vera Jean Cappelle's lovely and scrumptious shrimp and wild rice up next for sampling."

That brought down the signs, and a line quickly formed for

the kitchen. "Some of the members have been preparing casserole recipes from our *Best of Old Fort Rosalie Cookbook*," Megita explained, while leading Mary Dell and Harris into the hallway. "Of course, our cookbook has far outsold the one the Natchez ladies put out. We intend to be a well-nourished fighting unit every step of the way. We'll have none of this dropping on the picket line from a lack of energy. In fact, we have named ourselves the Casserole Patrol, taking a stand on behalf of our beloved Deep South morality and decency. Rather catchy moniker, don't you think?"

"Rolls right off the tongue," Mary Dell replied, again struggling to avoid outright laughter.

They moved from the hallway into Megita's office—a stuffy, cluttered affair with lots of framed clippings, plaques and civic awards adorning the walls. Megita wedged her girth into the chair behind her desk, while Mary Dell and Harris took their seats on a small sofa that had seen better days. That was the irony of the Founders' Club—full of wealthy, pedigreed members who nonetheless had chosen to decorate their building from floor to ceiling with leftovers and hand-me-downs—and they got away with it simply because of who they and their families were.

"Well?" Megita said, her tone at once severe and impatient.

Harris shifted his weight to avoid the lump he had just discovered beneath him and began. "I'm sure I don't have to tell you that tourism is the lifeblood of our historic little Fort Rosalie, Megita. Almost as vital to us as the Mississippi River flowing by. You also know that the Film Commission works hard night and day to publicize our state and get serious consideration from the Hollywood community."

"So Jim Horvath has told you about my little phone call to him, has he?"

"In great detail." Harris paused to gather his thoughts. He

had carefully rehearsed his approach and did not want to veer off track. With Megita, there was simply no margin for error. "It was providential that you mentioned your cookbook in the same breath as the Natchez version. I know how you feel about Fort Rosalie's rivalry with Natchez. That you feel we have far more to offer than Natchez does—"

Megita interrupted him, looking bored. "Get to the point, Harris. I assume you have one."

"My point is that Jim Horvath is threatening to cart *Whispering Dixie* off to Natchez if these protests take place. I'm sure you realize they could greatly offend Juliette Cadbury."

Megita settled back in her chair, folded hands resting atop her protruding stomach. "Perhaps it's time Miss Juliette Cadbury was offended. And it may very well be the best thing for Fort Rosalie if that horrid *Whispering Dixie* ends up being foisted upon Natchez rather than us."

"Well, I have to admit I never thought I'd hear you concede anything at all to Natchez. But back to Ms. Cadbury. We all know that the article in the *Celebrity Inquisitor* you assailed us with the other night at dinner triggered all of this. Don't you realize that most of those tabloid stories are concocted out of whole cloth? It's very likely that Juliette Cadbury never said all those things that have you and your Committee so upset."

"Where there's smoke, there's fire."

Harris steeled himself and pressed on. "Let me return to my original premise, then. Fort Rosalie depends upon tourism to make it run smoothly and to fill its coffers. Even if everything that appeared in that article were true, there is still the point that we simply cannot afford to question the private lives of the many tourists that come here to spend their down time with us. It's just none of our business to worry and fret about what goes on behind closed doors."

Megita leaned forward, narrowing her eyes. "Now you lis-

ten to me, Harris Lyles. I happen to know for a fact that this Cadbury creature is having a profound effect on the young people of this country. My grandson, Hillman, talks about her twenty-four hours a day. He alternates between using that 'hotty' word and telling me how cool she is, but there's one thing for certain. She affects his temperature around the clock, and he doesn't see a thing wrong with any of her pronouncements. I think it's way past time that someone drew a line in the sand regarding this so-called Hollywood morality."

"I appreciate all of that, but can't we look at the big picture here? Juliette Cadbury is not going to change her lifestyle because some of us out here in the hinterlands disapprove of it. Meanwhile, she's not coming to Fort Rosalie to change the way we live, either. She'll just be here for a few months to make a movie, and then she'll be gone and forgotten."

"I doubt that very much. Not with that film as her legacy," Megita said, while opening a drawer and dropping a copy of *Whispering Dixie* on her desk with a thud. "To be blunt, this novel is full of it. And any movie based on this novel is going to be full of it. Byron Cathcart spends the entire book having that Rella Darrow character apologize for the very existence of the South. He finds nothing to recommend us except his concept of shared guilt, which he mines like gold. I'm not thrilled about his viewpoint, and I'd rather the movie not be made at all, but particularly not here, and particularly not by someone like Juliette Cadbury."

Harris looked suddenly intrigued. "So this is about more than the actress, isn't it? Your hidden agenda is that you disagree with what *Whispering Dixie* has to say about the South."

"I admit it without apology. *Whispering Dixie* is a lot of politically-correct manipulation, but perhaps even more offensive are all those sexually explicit and sexually illicit passages." Megita quickly opened the book and thumbed through the pages. "Ah, here's one. I've dog-eared them all for easy reference. I quote:

> Harbaugh turned off the engine and pointed to the slumping, derelict movie screen in front of them.
> "Remember this?" he said, inching ever closer to Rella. "All that making out we did when this drive-in theater was up and running? You always remember your first time, and you were my first for just about everything. That's why I call you 'my little cherry.' First time I unhooked a bra, first time I pulled down a girl's panties, first time I wet my finger and stuck it—"
> "I get the picture!" Rella said, rolling down the window and fanning her face with her right hand. It was a hot, humid night, similar to so many from their teenaged summers when they had done everything in the back seat of his Thunderbird, including going all the way. "You want to do it here in the middle of this abandoned acre?"
> "Just for old-time's sake, my little cherry."
> She ran her tongue across her lips while she thought about it. The idea was beginning to make her wet. What the hell—she could even play one of those old movies in her head while their juices were flowing!

Megita stopped reading and looked up with disdain. "Need I read on? It goes without saying that these passages, coupled with those tabloid pronouncements, are the perfect manifesto for immorality. It's quite clear why Miss Cadbury has such an affinity for the material, since she obviously lives it on a daily basis."

Harris flashed a half-hearted smile. "Is there nothing I can say to convince you to call off these protests?"

"Nothing remotely comes to mind."

Seeing that her supervisor had struck out, a suddenly-

inspired Mary Dell decided to take her turn at bat. "Mrs. Larose, you obviously have some very heartfelt opinions about all of this, and we certainly respect that. But it occurs to me that you might end up accomplishing the very thing you're claiming to be against."

Megita cocked her broad smug face to one side. "I don't follow."

"How many times have you seen a book or movie or whatever it is bolstered by a boycott? The extra attention and publicity sometimes cause the project to succeed where it otherwise might have failed. Left alone and ignored, there's no guarantee that *Whispering Dixie* will be a success. This is no *Gone With The Wind* we're talking about here. The book had its detractors among the critics. Not to mention that you never know how the public will react to a protest like the one you're proposing. People know how off-base these tabloids are most of the time. You could end up creating a sympathetic backlash for Juliette Cadbury."

There was an encouraging period of silence. "I hadn't considered that angle." More silence. "But you're asking me to go back on my principles. The Committee has already invested its time and money, and the girls are looking forward to the challenge. Only one member of the Committee has refused to take part."

"Will you at least sleep on my observations?"

Another pregnant pause while Megita pursed her lips and furrowed her brow. "Very well. I'll run your points past the members and see what their reaction is. But don't get your hopes up." She rose and offered both of them a brief, limp handshake. "Lest you completely misunderstand me, I have nothing against Hollywood *per se*. Many productions have come to Fort Rosalie over the years and left us better off. My own dear mother, Leona, God rest her soul, even worked on the very first movie that chose Fort Rosalie—*In Olden Times*. That was back during the Depression, and she brought home some much-needed money by working as an extra. But that was a simpler era entirely. This latest project and the person behind it are in a different category altogether, and I intend to have my say."

Since that sounded like the last word on the subject, Mary Dell and Harris made their manners and headed back to the Bureau on foot. "I knew you'd be a big help," Harris said, walking along at a fast clip and looking very pleased with himself.

"You don't actually think I changed her mind, do you? You heard her say that only one Committee member refused to participate."

"But you got her to say she'd present your points to the group, and that's a lot further than I got."

"So I earned my salary today?"

"You betcha." He stopped beneath the shade of the sprawling live oaks in front of the Hotel Fort Rosalie just a half-block away from the Bureau. "What say I buy us both a little cocktail or a glass of wine before we get back to the office?"

A few minutes later they were settled in at a corner table in the hotel bar reviewing strategy. "If Megita doesn't change her mind," Harris was saying, "we at least have to convince Jim Horvath to let the inspection weekend go through. We can't just let him haul the project off to Natchez without a fight. There's always the possibility that Juliette Cadbury will find our little ol' ladies are nothing more than a small-town amusement."

Mary Dell took a sip of wine, looking skeptical. "Yeah, but those picket signs were pretty graphic. I know I wouldn't appreciate those sort of sentiments directed at me in public."

Harris was drumming his fingers nervously on the table.

"The prickly part of this whole thing is, Megita actually raises some valid issues, even if I disagree with the forum she's using to address them. Sometimes I do get the impression that a lot of the Hollywood elite think all they have to do is show up at the Oscars with a colored ribbon pinned to their tuxes and designer originals, and that justifies the excesses of any awful script that gets produced or whatever questionable lifestyle they decide to embrace. There are a lot of mixed messages coming out of Hollywood these days. Betsy and I were vigilant about what movies and TV shows we let our girls see when they were growing up." He finished off his wine and shrugged. "And I don't totally disagree with Megita about the novel. Cathcart pretty much sledgehammers the South with all that agonizing Rella Darrow does over slavery and segregation. It isn't the most positive thing that's ever been written about us."

"And yet it was a best-seller."

Harris glanced at his watch and rose from the table. "There's no accounting for tastes. At any rate, we need to get back to the office."

There were three pink message slips on Mary Dell's desk awaiting her return. She winced when she read the names above the numbers. Call Miss Aimee Pierce. Call Edding Denbo. Call Terrelle Lurkin. All three of them wanting to touch base with her on the same day, calling up within minutes of each other. What on earth could they want now? The date of the inspection weekend had been chosen quickly by the owners and approved without hesitation at the other end by Heidi Pendleton. They were now a mere one week away from the critical whirlwind tour. Edding had drawn the long straw and elected to take first crack at the actors on Friday, leaving the Lurkins with the finale on Sunday. What was there left to discuss or decide?

Mary Dell collapsed into her chair, took a deep breath and

O Bed! O Breakfast!

began to dial. She doubted very much that she would encounter any good news on the other end of the line.

Robert Dalby

Chapter Four

It was Tuesday morning in Fort Rosalie, and the entire town was excitedly preparing for the Cadbury-Reynaldo inspection tour fast approaching on Friday. Megita and the Casserole Patrol were still madly whipping up recipes and politely rehearsing their picketing after having officially refused to back down one iota, Harris was doing his best to buy time with Jim Horvath regarding their activities, and Mary Dell was getting ready to spend the entire day with the three B&B owners. The phone calls she had returned the previous Friday had resulted in the following commitments: at ten-thirty a polite little tea party with Miss Aimee at Plum Cottage; a smart luncheon around noon at Betterslie with Edding; and finally an early happy hour with the Lurkins around three at Destiny Manor.

Though the purpose of these visits largely remained a mystery, Mary Dell suspected they all just wanted to schmooze with her a little bit, maybe test the waters for any hint of favoritism and take it from there. Well, it wasn't going to do any of them a bit of good. She would just go and sip Miss Aimee's tea and eat Edding's food and have a cocktail with the Lurkins and exercise the people skills she was so famous for and that would be the end of it.

At exactly ten-twenty Mary Dell set out on foot for Plum Cottage. It was a mere three blocks away from the Tourist Bureau, and she was looking forward to the exercise. Autumn in Fort Rosalie was her favorite time of year—a curious preference considering the town's much-publicized cycles of beautiful blooms. There were whole seasons that were far more dressy and showy. The mild springtime was an explosion of

pastel azaleas, dogwood and tulip trees, while the unbearably sticky summers seemed to bring out the best in the pink, purple and white crepe myrtles, the town's gnarled street tree of choice. Nonetheless, Mary Dell preferred the way the sky looked, the way the air felt on her skin come October. There was an intensity of blue and an overall crispness that those other stretches could never quite approximate—the sun suddenly far less hostile and much more forgiving—and all of it taken together a glorious incentive to breathe in deeply and be thankful for just being alive.

She rounded the corner onto South Vidal Street, the focal point of one of the town's oldest and most distinctive neighborhoods. Here were vestiges of the Spanish Provincial settlement period, characterized by row upon row of stuccoed town houses flush with the brick sidewalk and projecting an austere, simple charm. It was Mary Dell's fantasy to save up enough money to buy one of them somewhere down the line, and she intended to step out onto the sidewalk stylishly-dressed every morning to walk the flesh-and-blood female black and tan dachshund she was going to get to replace that stuffed toy she had and all would be well with her world.

At the dead end of South Vidal stood Plum Cottage, a mid-Victorian raised cottage the Pierce family had erected on the site after one of the aforementioned town houses had burned to the ground. Like its present owner it was prim and fussy, although the green shutters and white clapboard with gingerbread filigree gracing the front porch gave no hint of the deep purple universe lurking inside.

Miss Aimee, herself, greeted Mary Dell at the front door. "Come in, my dear, come in. It's going to be just you and me today for our little party this morning. This is my Tasmania's day off."

They moved into the front parlor and settled in on one of

Miss Aimee's ponderous ball-and-claw sofas, beside which an heirloom silver tea service had been laid out before them on the coffee table. Some time ago Mary Dell had invented a phrase to describe the interior of Plum Cottage—excessively thematic. What with everything from drapes to wallpaper, rugs to vases done up in varying shades of purple, it was not unlike walking into the middle of an enormous plum pudding—an altogether lugubrious sensation. But the place and the concept had obviously withstood the test of time, so much so that Miss Aimee and Plum Cottage were virtually inseparable in the minds of the people of Fort Rosalie.

"I know you must be curious about my wanting to speak with you this way," Miss Aimee began while pouring out tea. She tended to her hostess duties and routinely inquired about lemon, cream and sugar, passed Mary Dell an antique crystal plate heaped with tiny buttered biscuits and continued. "To sum it all up, my dear, it is absolutely vital that I win this competition and get this booking."

Mary Dell swallowed a bit of biscuit and smiled. "Now, Miss Aimee, you know that the final decision is not up to me, and there's absolutely nothing I can or should do to influence the outcome."

"Oh, I realize that, dear. But it occurred to me the other day that you and I have never really gotten to know each other in all the years you've worked for Harris at the Tourist Bureau. You've mostly been a lovely voice over the phone, or a gracious presence at one of these briefings, but even when you've visited Plum Cottage on business, we've never had the chance to sit down and talk. I'd like to remedy that today."

"Well, I'd be delighted to accommodate you," Mary Dell replied. She smiled politely and sipped her tea, while maintaining a healthy sense of skepticism.

"What I really would like to accomplish here today is for you

O Bed! O Breakfast!

to discover who Miss Aimee Lorena Pierce really is. People think they know me, but they really don't. It's my fault, of course. I've led them on all these years with this eternal purple motif of mine. People think I'm crazy in love with the color, and some probably even think I'm just plain crazy, but neither is the case. To be honest with you, I've always felt that purple was just too much of a good thing as a dues-paying member of the spectrum. However, I've embraced it with a purpose in mind, and I want you to understand that purpose."

Mary Dell put down her cup, the skepticism rapidly flagging. "Please go on. I'm fascinated."

"I thought you would be. Anyway, I'm bound and determined that I shall not go to my grave without at least one soul knowing the truth about me, and I've elected you to be the one."

Miss Aimee smoothed out the cloth napkin resting on her lavender lap, daintily cleared her throat and pointed in the direction of the marble mantel across the room where several framed and faded sepia photographs were on display. "To flesh out my story, I was the eldest of four girls. My little sisters over there were all beautiful like my mother. The twinkling blue eyes, the golden hair, all very photogenic—every one of them. On the other hand it was my fate to inherit my father's coarse features." She paused to hold up her right hand. "And please don't bother to tell me what a handsome woman I am or that I've aged gracefully or any of that other poppycock people trot out at cocktail parties and social gatherings to pass the time and make themselves feel benevolent and superior. I've always known the truth about myself, and the truth is that an aged rump roast is still a rump roast."

Mary Dell made no effort to suppress her laughter. "You'll forgive me, Miss Aimee, but I never expected to be having such a meaty discussion with you."

Then it was Miss Aimee's turn to laugh—only hers was of the loud, heartfelt variety—one that sounded to Mary Dell like it had been buried deep within her psyche for a good many years. "You're a clever girl. I just knew it was the right thing to share all of this with you. Anyway, I was far from being the belle of the ball, although Mama worked overtime one year to have me named Queen of the Azalea Festival. That aside, I had other strong points. I was particularly good with numbers, and Papa used to call me his 'little mathematician' all the time. Said it wouldn't surprise him in the least if I made a success of myself someday as a businesswoman. Of course, that was not something most women aspired to in those days. Marriage and children was the ticket, as they say. But Papa's words stayed with me long after he and Mama passed away and all my sisters had married and left town with their husbands and children, leaving me the only member of the Pierce family remaining in Fort Rosalie. That's when this old spinster decided to fulfill Papa's expectations. I was going into business and make a name for myself. If I couldn't have a husband or children, I could at least leave some sort of legacy behind. That's when I decided to turn this little cottage I inherited into Fort Rosalie's first bed-and-breakfast."

"So what's the significance of all this purple?" said Mary Dell, pressing for the payoff.

"Oh, there's nothing earthshaking to reveal. I simply felt I needed a gimmick, a calculation of some sort to make the venture truly memorable. There were those who already thought I was plenty eccentric, living alone as I did, reclusive as I was. So I took their premise and expanded upon it by decorating everything inside in purple and wearing nothing but purple out in public. Of course, it meant I had to throw out some perfectly lovely things in my closet, but it was all worth it. It worked like a charm. Plum Cottage became the genteel

sideshow of Fort Rosalie, and I made plenty of money. That first decade or so, my guests usually returned for a repeat performance, particularly the ones from up north. Most of them were convinced I was some doddering old refugee from the road company of *Arsenic And Old Lace*, or some such nonsense, and to be truthful, I did nothing to disabuse any of them of that notion. I'm still playing that part to this day. Unfortunately, I've fallen upon desperate times recently."

"What do you mean?"

"I mean my finances have hit rock-bottom. Edding started my slide when he turned Betterslie into a B&B, and the Lurkins have practically done me in with that Old South version of Disneyland they run out there. I'm not getting the business I used to because, quite frankly, their gimmicks are better than mine. Believe it or not, some people actually seem to prefer all that literary foolishness Edding spews like a geyser, and I'm sure I don't have to explain the appeal of Destiny Manor's conspicuous consumption. Not to mention the inescapable fact that I only have two rooms to offer, while Edding has four and the Lurkins have eight."

Mary Dell frowned, genuinely concerned. "But we still get our fair share of inquiries about Plum Cottage at the Bureau, and we always pass them along to you. Harris considers you one of the unimpeachable standbys of Old Fort Rosalie, and he's certainly never mentioned to me that you were having any financial difficulties."

"That's because he doesn't know. No one does. I was brought up never to complain and never to air my personal business in public. At any rate, I'm not getting my fair share of bookings anymore, and if I can't get a quick infusion of cash such as this Hollywood booking would provide me, I'll have to shut my doors. I'll be out of business for good. I've been able to put off most of my creditors this long because of the family

name and who I am, but their good will can only be stretched so long and so far. I'm literally living on my reputation at this very moment. And I don't want to have to shut my doors. Not yet. I still have my health and many more years of hospitality left in me, God willing. But I have neither Edding's trust fund nor barrels of Texas oil money to come to my rescue. Therefore, hosting this Hollywood couple is a must-win situation for me. It's do or die."

Mary Dell took the time to breathe in and out, finished the last of her tea and mulled things over. "Well, I can certainly appreciate your urgency here, but I'm sure you realize that I still can't possibly take sides."

"I'm not going to ask you to. What I will ask, however, is that you consider becoming a part of the festivities here at Plum Cottage when those actors visit. I believe you and Harris had planned to do the introductions and then leave, is that correct?"

"That's all we usually do."

Miss Aimee edged forward on the sofa, her eyes glistening with excitement. "Why not stay on and eat with us that night, return for breakfast the next morning, bring your warmth and charm to the table with you, socialize with us throughout the entire affair? Harris is always saying how good you are with people, and I've seen it for myself. I've watched you circulate and smooth things over at these Bureau cocktail affairs, how you weave in and out keeping the peace, getting people to mix and mingle and have a good time. The way I see it, you'll be an asset to me and perhaps give me the edge I need to prevail. Having you around certainly couldn't hurt my chances."

"But if I did that for you, I'd have to do it for the others as well."

Miss Aimee grinned slyly, as if she were privy to some inside joke. "Oh, I happen to know that our flighty Edding will ask you to do the same for him over lunch out at Betterslie, and the same goes for those grotesque Texans as they ply you with their liquor this afternoon."

Mary Dell drew back in amazement. "Now how did you know the exact details of my day?"

"Oh, there's nothing that Edding and the Lurkins do that I don't know about. All of us have our sources, you see. We call it the servant grapevine. My Tasmania Evans rings up Edding's Eola Griffin, who then talks to her cousin, Azureen Mazique, out at Destiny Manor, and that keeps us all well-informed. Why, anytime Edding throws one of his prima donna tantrums over a line of poetry that keeps eluding him, or whenever Terrelle and Johnny get into one of their loud-mouthed quarrels over which party they ought to try and crash, you can bet I hear about it. Naturally, they know most everything about me, too, including the fact that I've run out of money. I don't expect either of them to show me any mercy during this competition. They'd like nothing better than to drive me out of business. Then they'll be able to go at each other full tilt."

The image of Johnny and Edding at each other's throats in the Bureau parking lot flashed into Mary Dell's head. What Miss Aimee had told her certainly had the ring of truth. "It appears to me that my choices will be to tag along for all of you or none of you," Mary Dell said.

"All or nothing at all, as the late Frank Sinatra once put it so dreamily way back when in my salad days—and his."

"My instinct would be to treat you all fairly, even though you hardly treat each other that way."

Miss Aimee was shaking her head. "I've always tried my best to remain civil, Mary Dell. I was brought up to be polite and ladylike under all circumstances, but, believe me, Edding and the Lurkins do sorely try the gentility of my soul at times."

They had reached a lull in the conversation, so Mary Dell checked her watch. "Oh, look at the time it's getting to be. I need to head back to the Bureau to get ready for my little excursion to Betterslie. Got to gas up the car, you know."

They rose together and walked out onto the front porch where they lingered awkwardly for a few seconds, unable to directly address what was on their minds. Finally, Miss Aimee said: "May I have your decision on my request, dear? I would very much appreciate knowing before you leave."

Mary Dell gave her a quick, impulsive hug. "Of course. I'll be happy to hang around for you, as long as you understand that I'll have to do the same for the others. In fact, Harris and I will be Mr. and Mrs. Tourist Bureau for you."

"Fair enough."

"I'd also like to thank you for sharing so much with me today. I'll keep everything you've told me in strictest confidence," Mary Dell added. "You are truly the grand lady of Fort Rosalie."

"Thank you, dear. That means a lot to me, and you're such a sweet girl to say so."

Girl. Ugh. That word again. It reminded her too much of Megita's patronizing behavior. Nonetheless, she managed a farewell smile and wave of the hand as she made her way down the flagstone walk to the small wooden gate that marked the entrance to Plum Cottage. On the way she realized she would never be able to view Miss Aimee in the same light again. The heavy veil of gossip had been lifted, and the real woman behind the mask of eccentricity had been revealed. The new Miss Aimee was much more likeable because she was now so much more accessible, so understandable. It was difficult not to empathize with her financial plight and pull for her in the competition, especially since it seemed more likely that a jet-set, high-profile Hollywood couple like Juliette

Cadbury and Tim Reynaldo would have their heads turned first by the ostentatious trappings of a Destiny Manor or perhaps even the musty patina of a rambling Betterslie before settling for quirky, cramped little Plum Cottage.

Regardless of the eventual outcome, it was now apparent to Mary Dell that she would not be able to extricate herself from the upcoming proceedings so easily. They were not going to let her get away with just making the arrangements and standing by at the Bureau while waiting for the verdict. She was to become a continuous part of the show, and she didn't see how she could say no and still maintain her exemplary reputation.

True, she had committed Harris to the proposition without consulting him, but she was certain he would go along with it. After all, they were practically Mr. and Mrs. Tourist Bureau already, weren't they?

Robert Dalby

Chapter Five

The road to Betterslie was as strange and fanciful as its owner. The southwestern corner of Mississippi in which Fort Rosalie was wedged featured significant deposits of loess soil—a dusty and rockless geological phenomenon. As a result, the region's network of pioneer trails had worn down over the centuries, exposing the gnarled roots of the ancient trees lining the sides and forming steep, tunnel-like banks along the way. In recent years many of these picturesque sunken roads had been lost to posterity forever, graded into oblivion by hungry developers bulldozing the land into lucrative suburban tracts and parcels. But Edding Denbo would have none of that. He had made no concessions whatsoever to modern engineering—fiercely maintaining his winding bit of history in its pristine state, minus the occasional load of gravel here and there to shore up bad patches borne of bad weather.

Mary Dell intensely enjoyed her jaunts to Betterslie. Still considered 'out in the country' by the residents of Fort Rosalie proper, the drive never failed to soothe her jangled Tourist Bureau nerves, transporting her back to a simpler, more peaceful place and time. She would literally inhale the scenery up until the moment she passed through those formidable front gates—savoring all the towering magnolias, the jungle-thick stands of wild bamboo mixed with dogwood and redbud, not to mention the imposing array of moss-hung live oaks, pin oaks, and other hardwoods. Then, out of nowhere, like some half-remembered dream, Betterslie would appear on the distant horizon. It was easy to understand why Edding had made a go of it all—literary motif notwithstanding. This venerable family home of his was the ordinary tourist's quintessential

O Bed! O Breakfast!

vision of the Deep South—the white-columned, Greek Revival temple, mellowed by time and set in the midst of an unspoiled, pastoral paradise.

Mary Dell had no sooner parked her car in the grandiose circular driveway than Edding's tall, long-limbed cook and housekeeper, Eola Griffin, appeared at the front door to greet her cheerfully. "You look so pretty today, Miss Mary Dell."

They exchanged further pleasantries, embracing politely, and Eola ushered her into the massive front drawing room just off the hallway to await Edding's inevitable grand entrance. Since opening Betterslie to strangers fifteen years ago, he had developed 'the entrance' into his signature gesture, and it was now as strongly identified with him as Miss Aimee's purple was with her. He always began the conceit by posing dramatically at the top of the immense grand staircase, thereafter descending at a snail's pace to milk the illusion of an Olympian god deigning to grace mere mortals below with his presence. Once he had finally reached bottom, he would briefly acknowledge his humanity with a nod of his head and a formal greeting. After that, he was off to the races with the literary theme of the day, and there was no shutting him up.

"He up to his usual tricks," Eola said, after bringing Mary Dell a glass of iced tea from the kitchen. "You know how all this go. I got y'all lunch on the stove ready to serve, and he still up there primpin' and foolin' around like some vain old maid."

Mary Dell wagged her brows and smiled. "Wouldn't be our Edding otherwise, would it?"

"You got that right." Eola winked and headed back into the hallway, turning at the last second. "Don't you worry, now. I be back after while to save you from suffocatin' in all that hot air fixin' to come outta his mouth."

"Thanks, Eola. You're a sweetheart."

Another couple of minutes passed, after which Edding finally put in an appearance at the exact moment the grandfather clock at the bottom of the stairs began proclaiming high noon with tinny fanfare. Given his propensity for entrances, exits, and hitting his marks, Mary Dell concluded it was more than likely he had deliberately waited for just such a cue. In fact, she had often wondered why he just hadn't gone the distance long before now and hired a pair of herald trumpeters. With a detached amusement she observed the predictably slow and studied descent from her vantage point beneath the drawing room chandelier, and there was a further delay when he paused beside the clock to make a last-minute adjustment to the bangs he had carefully combed forward to conceal his receding hairline, but eventually he stood before her, eyes riveted to the glass of tea she was nursing.

"Ah!" he began, foregoing any mundane greeting. "I see Eola has brought you a libation. I believe I'll make myself a midday toddy before we get started. Just a wee something for courage." He moved quickly to a portable bar cart that seemed decidedly out of place amidst the many beautiful pieces arranged around the drawing room, poured himself a vodka and rocks and immediately proposed a toast. "To the new Edding Denbo! May the fellow I formerly was, may that unfortunate fellow rest in peace!"

Mary Dell lifted her glass, took a sip and then frowned. "What are you talking about, Edding?"

With a sweep of his hand he indicated a nearby love seat, and they settled in quickly with their drinks. "I must begin by asking you a question, and I want you to be perfectly honest with your answer. None of that Tourist Bureau diplomacy Harris preaches to all his charges like a bad sermon. Agreed?"

"Agreed."

He took a generous swig of his vodka and exhaled. "How do

O Bed! O Breakfast!

you think most people in Fort Rosalie view Edding Denbo?" He studied her closely, the way the muscles of her face gave away her struggle to find the right words. "Come now, Mary Dell. You promised me honesty and the nothing-but variety of the truth. I'll say it first if it will make it any easier for you. We both know I am held up to ridicule behind the closed doors of Old Fort Rosalie. I'm considered a buffoon—and a pretentious one at that."

She agonized while nervously running her finger around the rim of her glass a couple of times. This sort of exchange went against all of her training, every last one of her social instincts. Nonetheless, she grudgingly gave in. "Well, I have heard those particular sentiments expressed from time to time. But that doesn't mean that I agree with them. There are some who consider you one of Fort Rosalie's greatest assets."

"While others consider me one of Fort Rosalie's greatest asses."

Mary Dell swallowed hard. What a day this was turning out to be! First, a surprising heart-to-heart with Miss Aimee, and now all this visceral chewing of the fat with Edding. What was coming next?

"That would not have been my choice of words," she replied, still in shock.

"Very well. Let's view it from a different angle. Although some of my poems have been published in quarterlies like the *Sewanee Review* and the *Kenyon Review*, I am certainly no Dr. Seuss, no household word. Only the elite of academia have encountered my work. Let's face it—ever since my parents left me so suddenly, I have occupied my time amusing myself by rambling around the family mansion quoting myself and other lesser literary lights to these hopeless carpetbaggers who don't have a clue. I've grown so weary of it all—it's time I settled down and took life more seriously. I've devised a plan to do so,

and you'll be the first to hear it."

Mary Dell managed a smile but was totally unprepared for this new role of priest hearing confession. She decided she was a lot more comfortable with the outrageous and preposterous old Edding. "Let's have it, then."

"I know you're surprised to hear me telling the truth about myself—I'm sure you didn't think it remotely possible. But I've never been one to lie about myself. I know I'm too short, balding, and not much to look at. In other words, if life were a game of genetic dodge ball, I'd be one of the last chosen to play. Put yet another way, if an asteroid or comet were discovered on a collision course with Earth and a manned spaceship were launched before impact containing your basic starter kit for the human race upon landing somewhere else in the universe, I'm quite positive that an obscure Southern poet like myself would never appear on the manifest."

"Oh, I think you might be underestimating yourself."

"I have in the past. But no longer. I am going to begin a new career as a serious writer, and winning this competition will act as a springboard."

"I don't follow."

"Well, it dawned on me the other day that I have my share of stories to tell as a bed-and-breakfast owner. Some of my guests have actually shown flashes of brilliance now and again. Something amusing or noteworthy has occurred upon occasion. My first thought was that a published volume of such episodes might be worth offering to the general public. Upon further review I decided that the project might need a special touch to make it truly interesting to a national audience. Enter Juliette Cadbury and Tim Reynaldo. Imagine how much more appealing my book would be were it to include a chapter detailing their stay with me here at Betterslie. Imagine what little gems I could pack into such a chapter by getting the opportunity to dish with them about their Hollywood friends and their careers. That might be just the little something extra that puts O Bed! O Breakfast! on the bestseller list. That's the working title of the book I've started, by the way. Catchy, don't you think?"

"Yes, I do. But there's something you may be overlooking."

"What's that?"

"Assuming you win the competition—suppose Cadbury and Reynaldo refuse to talk to you about their private lives? Those awful tabloids hound them unmercifully, as you know. They may not even give you permission to write about them."

He finished the last of his vodka and puffed himself up proudly. "About that, I have no qualms whatsoever. If I have one strength, it is my ability to bend words to my ultimate purpose. I'm quite positive I can convince them that appearing in my book will be the best publicity they've ever received."

Eola appeared in the doorframe, eyes narrowed and jaw set firmly. "Mr. Denbo, it way past time for me to put lunch on the table. Everything be spoiled if y'all don't come sit down right now."

"Ah, the chef has spoken. Long live the chef!" he said, and then they moved into the commanding dining room across the hall to take their seats.

After Eola had poured out water and iced tea and served a first course of tomato aspic with a dollop of paprika-sprinkled mayonnaise on top, the conversation took a surprisingly different turn. "There's another matter I wanted to broach with you today," Edding said. "It concerns my marital status and all the idle gossip that has accrued to it over the years."

The discomfort Mary Dell had experienced a few minutes earlier returned full force. "I really don't think your private life is any of my business, Edding."

"Oh, but it is. It's part of my plan to clear the air with you

about everything so that you can understand why I absolutely must win this competition."

With an overwhelming sense of resignation plus a smidgen of deja vu from the session at Plum Cottage, Mary Dell sighed softly and flashed a smile. It was going to be that sort of day, and there was nothing she could do about it but sit back and accept her customary role of sounding board.

"I know everyone thinks I'm gay," Edding continued. "But it's just not so. Oh, I realize I've brought a large part of it on myself with my behavior and all the venting and posturing I do. In a way I thought it was expected of me—playing the part of the fussy, arcane poet to the hilt. But from my vantage point it has always amounted to nothing more than good Southern theater."

He paused for a bite of aspic, giving Mary Dell a chance to reflect. Earlier in the day, Miss Aimee's behavior had also been revealed as nothing more than good Southern theater. Was that all there was to their much-heralded Old Fort Rosalie? So many people running around playing so many parts for the benefit of gawking tourists?

"The truth is," Edding added, "I like women, have always liked them and always will like them. They just don't seem to cotton to me. For a while there when I was younger, I thought that making a name for myself writing poetry might be a good way to win a girl's heart. I certainly had no classic profile or bulging muscles to offer. When it came down to it, however, I discovered that though I had a talent for words, I had no talent at all for romantic ones. No matter how hard I tried, all my verse came out clinical and cerebral, as if I were still trying to get an 'A' from some crotchety old English professor. As a matter of fact, that's who's been publishing my work in these reviews—several crotchety old English professors."

He took a sip of his tea, and Mary Dell was grateful for

another respite. It was far too much to digest all at once. For some reason she decided to focus on her aspic, desperately hoping the quivering red mass centered on its bed of lettuce would transform itself into an oracle giving her an appropriate response when the time came. But alas, nothing but silence.

Edding resumed his remarkable narrative. "To get back to the issue of women, it may surprise you to hear that I've always wanted what most men want—a wife and family. I don't want to be the last of the Mohicans out here, and I think that having a successful book published may assist me in attracting a mate to my nest. Oh, I know what you're thinking. That phraseology probably sounds very much like typical female talk to you, but here's a bulletin for you. Men have their biological clocks as well, even if they don't run around beating their breasts and tearing their hair out about it the way women do. Turning the watershed age of forty seems to have gotten my attention in some beneficial way, and I intend to act accordingly. To put it most succinctly, Edding Denbo is ready to grow up."

Suddenly Mary Dell thought of exactly the right response to his further revelations: "You are a cosmic wordsmith, Edding Denbo."

"I find that a totally appropriate description, and I thank you for it," he replied, his face beaming.

When they had finished their aspics, Eola cleared and re-entered with bowls of steaming shrimp gumbo and a plate of jalapeno pepper cornbread. "In honor of this auspicious occasion," Edding announced, rising from his chair at the head of the table, "I have something to recite."

"Lord, here it come," Eola whispered to Mary Dell as she passed by.

Edding shook his finger playfully. "I heard that, Eola. If you have something to contribute, say it aloud."

She turned, faced her employer and cleared her throat. "I was fixin' to say I hope Miss Mary Dell like swimmin' in poetry 'cause this room about to be flooded."

"And for that torrent of insight from the kitchen corner, we thank you."

"Always glad to oblige, Mr. Denbo." She gave Mary Dell a surreptitious wink and was gone.

"Eola and I practice a perverse sort of symbiosis, I will admit," he said. "But I digress. I have composed a poem which will appear as the foreword of my forthcoming book of B&B memoirs. It, too, is entitled, *O Bed! O Breakfast!* and I shall recite it for you now." He gathered himself for a few moments and began:

O Bed! O Breakfast!
How earnestly the traveler seeks you out—
The cheery warmth, the welcome rest you promise to the weary;
Then, once installed, the traveler hopes for more—
A treasured glimpse of history on the walls,
Or echoes of his family home just left behind,
One day, one night, a respite brief to ease his mind until the journey's end;
Upon such gifts as food and friendship will his changing mood depend,
Whether traveling by his lonesome or with a feisty and rambunctious brood,
The bed-and-breakfast beckons like a lighthouse to a ship upon the open sea—
For less it cannot offer,
And less it cannot be,
The sign that promises a cozy haven from the open road;
O bed! O breakfast!
One shining, solitary moment that the traveler might ease his heavy load.

O Bed! O Breakfast!

Mary Dell waited a few seconds to make sure he had finished and applauded with genuine enthusiasm. This one was a lot shorter than most of the poems she had heard him recite, and she had not had any trouble interpreting it—another plus. That flood Eola had predicted was more like an overturned pitcher of water. Under the circumstances, what was there not to like?

"I take it you approve," Edding said, resuming his seat.

"Absolutely."

"It captures the essence of the bed-and-breakfast, don't you think?"

"No question about it. It's a charming opener for your book."

"Then I have an enormous favor to ask of you."

Mary Dell put down her soup spoon and looked him straight in the eye. "I already know. You want me to be a part of your festivities and hang around when Cadbury and Reynaldo visit. Miss Aimee requested I do the same for her at Plum Cottage."

He chuckled and rolled his eyes. "I take it her little tea party went off without a hitch this morning. Let down all that white hair and rattled off the purple prose, no pun intended, of her life story, did she?"

"More or less, but it couldn't hold a candle to your revelations."

"I suppose you know all about our little network of spies now?"

"To be honest with you, I've suspected something like that was afoot for a long time. The lot of you ought to volunteer for the CIA. Let me put your mind at ease, however, and tell you that Harris and I will be here for you—as long as you understand we'll be doing the same thing for Miss Aimee and the Lurkins."

Edding toyed with his gumbo for a while, looking lost in thought and then said: "I don't know about the others, but I'm astute enough to realize that I need someone like you around to save me from stepping in it, as the saying goes. I know I've gotten away with murder, treating people the way I have all these years. Part of it was the shell I went into after losing my parents the way I did. At any rate, my social skills are practically nil as a result, and I can't afford to blow this opportunity. Now you can understand why my new career and maybe even my chances for a family depend upon my getting this booking for Betterslie. The old Edding Denbo must emerge from his cocoon of superficiality and indifference, spread his wings and take off into the mainstream of life."

Mary Dell took another deep breath and flashed back to the moment Harris had initially turned over the Cadbury-Reynaldo booking to her in his office. Because of the involvement with the 'terrible trio,' she had felt a palpable sense of doom settling around her shoulders even then, and now the pressure was quadrupling in intensity. This, before she had even gotten to hear whatever the Lurkins had up their sleeves. Thankfully, the remainder of the meal was taken up with small talk, giving her at least a fighting chance to digest her food in peace.

Later, at the front door, Edding made one last pitch. "I shall try my damnedest to be on my best behavior when Cadbury and Reynaldo visit me. But years of sacrificing tact to the art of cleverly turning a phrase will not depart without a struggle. If I can keep my privileged foot out of my incorrigible mouth, I may very well win this thing by a landslide."

On the drive back to Fort Rosalie Mary Dell tried to sort out her emotions. Suddenly, Edding was no longer the figure of fun that everyone whispered about behind his back. He had come out of the closet, in a manner of speaking, and cut the ground from beneath her feet. It was no longer possible to dismiss him as a spoiled, effete dilettante. An earnest, flesh and blood man had descended Betterslie's grand staircase today, just as a very real and interesting woman had emerged earlier from the purple haze surrounding Plum Cottage.

There were two separate agendas bidding for Mary Dell's sympathies now, both of them equally compelling: Miss Aimee's pressing financial difficulties versus Edding's bold blueprint for a new career and family. Then, a frightening thought occurred to her. What if the Lurkins were somehow able to humanize themselves, creating a third agenda that tugged at her heartstrings?

Well, so what? This was what Harris was paying her for. This was why he had turned the booking over to her. She was supposed to apply herself and keep things running smoothly without losing her objectivity. She had done it many times before, but something told her that this was going to be her sternest test yet.

Chapter Six

There was nothing remotely restrained about Destiny Manor. Like the fabled pleasure dome that Kublai Khan had once decreed in Xanadu, it glittered and gleamed, stopping just short of throwing off sparks. Even before the Lurkins' restoration it had punished the eye with its dizzying array of Steamboat Gothic colonnades, galleries, minarets and turrets—a nineteenth-century architectural style invented to pay homage to the flotilla of paddlewheelers plying the Mississippi River at that time. After the three-story monstrosity had been renovated, however, it was virtually impossible to locate even one focal point on any of its busy facades, reminding some of Fort Rosalie's more conservative citizens of a gigantic Tinkertoy experiment gone awry.

Nor was that all. Precisely at dusk an automatic lighting system faithfully performed its duties, illuminating every hedge, flower bed, bird, and squirrel scampering about in the trees with such intensity that motorists travelling along the nearest highway frequently reported UFO sightings to the Fort Rosalie police department or the Mississippi Highway Patrol.

"It landed somewhere over to the right in those woods. We could see the glow through the trees," the breathless witnesses usually insisted. By now the authorities had learned to nod a couple of times, mutter a few soothing, patronizing phrases and then quietly slip the paperwork into the Destiny Manor file after sending them on their way.

Mary Dell always came away from the place with a tension headache, and it wasn't just the gaudy design or the lighting that did most of the damage. Roaming the vast acreage—sometimes without supervision—were an assortment of such ornery flightless birds as ostriches, emus and cassowaries, augmented by a half dozen screeching peacocks who spent most of their time displaying their wares to the nearby peahens they coveted for sexual favors. It was a noisy and threatening menagerie that might have challenged the composure of the groundskeeper of Michael Jackson's Neverland Park, much less a mere account executive from the local Tourist Bureau.

Then there was the interior. With garish Easter Egg colors on the walls, gold leaf trim on all the kitchen and bathroom fixtures and polished marble and wood floors stretching to infinity, the Lurkins had satisfied the letter but hardly the spirit of the restoration guidelines set down many decades ago by Old Fort Rosalie's Historic Preservation Committee. They had managed to offend whole legions of those to the manor borne, even going so far as to install a large, heart-shaped swimming pool in the back yard to make one final, defiant display of their sudden wealth.

Taste, therefore, had been almost exclusively restricted to the food that was served on premises. In that regard Destiny Manor had no equal throughout Fort Rosalie and possibly even its bitter rival, Natchez. The Lurkins had lured a master chef—one Hans Dieterly—from one of the grand New Orleans French Quarter restaurants, and the breakfasts, brunches and dinners served to their guests were nothing short of sumptuous. It had even been suggested that the food was the main reason, if not the only reason, Destiny Manor had become such a success in so short a period of time.

"What's your pleasure this afternoon, Miss Mary Dell?" Johnny Lurkin said, leaning into her a little too closely and impinging upon her personal space. He could never seem to judge that sort of thing very well, causing people to back away from him all the time.

It was just past three o'clock, and the Lurkins had chosen Destiny Manor's rambling brick patio and some very uncomfortable cast-iron lawn furniture for their little happy hour. The peacocks were preening and screeching over by the pool that had given the Historic Preservation Committee apoplexy, and a quartet of nude, cherubic statues arranged around the cabana area were ludicrously spewing water out of their mouths, and already Mary Dell could feel that headache coming on.

"Oh, just a glass of white wine for me," she replied, still feeling full from Eola's delicious lunch.

Johnny zoomed in even closer, shaking his big head. "Come on, now, you've just gotta try one of my famous juleps. I know you work hard all day at that stuffy Bureau. This'll mellow you right on out." He jerked his head around to confront his wife.

"I assume you want one, too, sweet thing?"

"You have to ask?" Terrelle said. "Now, surely you've had one of Johnny's juleps before, Mary Dell. Oh, honey, they're just dee-lish."

The truth was that she hadn't, but she also knew they would keep at her in that relentless Texas way of theirs, so she gave the go-ahead and he retreated to the nearby alfresco bar to rattle around behind it and rustle up his specialty.

"We've given our maid, Azureen, and our chef, Hans, the afternoon off so we can talk freely and not mince any words," Johnny said while he worked. "We're just gonna cut right to the chase about why we asked you out here. We know you've already been to Plum Cottage and Betterslie today and heard what they have to say, but, honestly, we really do need your help bad." He finished stirring the juleps with a swizzle stick and then handed them around. "But first, you just take a little sip and tell me what you think. It's my own secret recipe."

O Bed! O Breakfast!

Mary Dell cautiously lifted the icy silver cup to her lips and swallowed bravely. "Delicious," she said, though her nostrils were stinging. The concoction was very long on bourbon and short on the lemon, mint leaves and simple syrup.

Johnny guffawed and continued. "Well, as I was saying—we need you to help us win this competition. I know it might seem like we have an edge with Destiny Manor being such a showplace and all, but to tell you the truth—"

The words suddenly seemed to catch in his throat, and Mary Dell was genuinely surprised. She had never seen the man look so vulnerable. Terrelle quickly stepped in as he took his seat and consoled himself with a Texas-sized swig of his julep.

"What Johnny is trying to say is that it's been very hard for us these past two years. We know what the elite of Old Fort Rosalie say about us behind our backs. We know they refer to us as 'Those Texans From Hell.' We're not clods of dirt, you know. When we first visited Fort Rosalie a few years back during one of your Azalea Festivals, we just fell in love with the place, and we vowed that if we could ever afford it, we were gonna move here and be a part of all this wonderful history and beautiful scenery." She sipped her drink and managed an ironic chuckle. "Little did we know how painful it was gonna turn out to be."

"Oh, it's been pure hell for me and my sweet thing," Johnny added, finding his voice again. "We were lucky enough one day to strike oil just outside Beaumont, and we thought all our prayers had been answered. First thing we did was charter a plane to Fort Rosalie so we could shop for one a' these houses. We needed somethin' to occupy us, since we haven't been able to have children. But we sure got more than we bargained for, I'll tell ya that."

Terrelle was shaking her lacquered head slowly. "We've

been treated just like we were so much trailer park trash by that Megita Larose and her Historic Preservation Committee. I don't envy that Juliette Cadbury coming to town with Megita and her tribe breathing down her neck. And it's not like Johnny and I didn't try our damnedest to play the game by Megita's rules. Why, in the beginning we didn't so much as sneeze out here without first asking her permission. We wanted to fit in and be good citizens, honestly we did. We wanted to do the right thing by Fort Rosalie. But it got to where no matter which little ordinance of theirs we tried to comply with, that Megita would barge in here and find another one to aggravate us with and shake in our faces. She just wouldn't let us alone. This wallpaper was too busy for that period of history, that color wasn't even around then and still didn't exist in nature, that furniture was all wrong for the house. Nothing ever pleased her. Finally, we just had our fill and said to hell with it. If this is the way it's gonna be, we'll do things the way we want. Destiny Manor's out here in the county, way outta the city limits, so they don't have jurisdiction anyway. So we up and more or less told Megita where she could put all her historical advice."

Mary Dell shuddered at that revelation. People in Fort Rosalie who got on the wrong side of Megita Larose and her sharp, unforgiving tongue usually paid a high price. In fact, during all the time she had worked at the Tourist Bureau, Mary Dell could not recall a single instance in which Megita had not gotten exactly what she wanted.

"I'm sorry you've had such a difficult time with Megita," Mary Dell said. "I've been there myself a couple of times."

Terrelle sighed, her expression a blend of contempt and disgust. "It just makes my blood boil to think about the way she's treated us. Why, if I'd known coming to live here in Fort Rosalie was gonna be this hurtful, I'd never have left our little

O Bed! O Breakfast!

hometown of Village Mills, just outside a' Beaumont. We are decent folks, Mary Dell, but no one in this town seems to be willing to give us a chance. That's why we want you to be here for us when this Hollywood couple comes for their visit. You're so well-spoken and so good with people. So much better than we are. We just know you'll help us make a good impression and maybe beat out the others. Then things might change around here for the better."

Mary Dell could not quite believe it was happening for the third time today. Revelations flying through the air and the frankest of talk cutting through facades, and her opinion of the Lurkins was shifting by the second. They suddenly seemed less obnoxious, less pushy and striving. All they really wanted was what everyone wanted out of life—what she, herself, sought in that town house and that little black and tan dachshund—a secure niche somewhere. As a result, Old Fort Rosalie now seemed a very uncharitable place to her, utterly lacking in the milk of human kindness toward these outsiders. Still, since this appeared to be a day for telling the truth, she decided not to avoid the obvious.

"The thing is, Megita and the Historic Preservation Committee aren't going to be impressed should you win the right to host Cadbury and Reynaldo. I hate to say it, but it might even set you back further. A live-in Hollywood couple like that, always making headlines in the tabloids? I'm reasonably certain that's not going to win Old Fort Rosalie over to your side. It might even be better for you in the long run if you lost."

"Oh, we realize that. Johnny and I have just about given up getting people to accept us. But if it's not meant to be, we can at least have a good time out here. If we end up hosting this Hollywood couple for three whole months, they could recommend us to their friends out there, and we could maybe get

their business, too. Why, they're all the time filming up and down the river from here to New Orleans and all around this part of the South. These actors pass this way more than you'd think. A lot of 'em show up around Mardi Gras time, too. We could have our own ongoing party with lots of fun people who don't give a hiccup how long your family has lived here or care one whit what kinda wingback chair their tush is sittin' on."

"That's certainly a different way of looking at it, I suppose," Mary Dell replied. "In any case, since I've already agreed to help out the others during the upcoming weekend, I'd be more than happy to put in an appearance for you, too."

Terrelle reached over and patted her hand. "Harris is so lucky to have you at the Bureau. We're all lucky to have you."

Johnny rose from his chair, filling his big chest with air. "Well, I feel a lot better about the weekend now. But, you know, I think the thing that gets to me the most is that these people around here seem to hold my friendly nature against me. Hell, I know I'm just a big ol' bear. Can't help it. That's the way all us Lurkins are. We come into the world that way, and that's how we go out. A man can't change his true nature, no matter how hard he tries, and if folks are gonna hold a big handshake and a big smile against ya, then you might as well go off and live in a cave."

"Oh, it's not as bad as all that," Terrelle added, waving him off playfully.

"We'll see, sweet thing, we'll see. And now, if you ladies will excuse me, I need to run to the little cowpokes' room for a minute."

When he had disappeared into the house, Mary Dell decided to seize the moment and give Terrelle the unvarnished truth. "I think you and Johnny are on to something with this concept of having a good time out here and forgetting about trying to fit in so much."

"What choice do we really have? I mean, other than to sell the place and move back to Texas. I'm sure that would make Megita happy. During one of her visits out here, she even told me straight to my face that she was positive we'd moved here just to irritate and torture her. Can you imagine the nerve?"

"Please. Forget about Megita Larose for a second. I think part of the problem is that you've been trying too hard—that's why everything has backfired on you. All the people of Fort Rosalie can see and feel is a couple of strangers desperately pressing in on them, and their natural instinct is to resist. You need to take the desperation out of it. Once you do that, I believe things will begin to fall into place for you."

"You actually think Megita Larose will ever fall in line?"

"Knowing her as I do, probably not. But I guarantee you there are others in Fort Rosalie who will respond to you if you just back off a bit and give them a chance to discover who you really are."

Terrelle managed a smile but still looked doubtful. "You probably don't know what it's like to be socially unaccepted, do you?"

Mary Dell said no and lowered her head slightly, feeling a twinge of guilt. She had never come close to knowing what it was like. She had arrived in Fort Rosalie five years ago from neighboring Wilkins County where the venerable and prominent Hoskins clan had long ruled the roost, and she had therefore found immediate acceptance among Fort Rosalie's social establishment. She had never had to prove herself in that regard.

"I thought not," Terrelle said, finishing her julep. "But I can tell your heart's in the right place with this advice a' yours. Hell, we couldn't do any worse than we're doing now."

"You could start by getting involved in one of the local charities," Mary Dell added. "Show people you're about more than just going to parties."

"That makes a lotta sense to me."

Johnny emerged refreshed and solicited another round of drinks, but Mary Dell was still fighting off a slight buzz from the first one and politely declined. "I've got to get back to the Bureau to run a few things by Harris. Delightful as all this has been out here—and let me hasten to add that I do appreciate your keeping the ostriches and emus locked in their pens today—I'm still just a working stiff."

"Speaking of ostriches and emus," Johnny said, "I bet you'll never guess why we bought 'em. It was our chef's idea. Hans said it would broaden our menu—that's exactly the way he put it. Of course, the peacocks are strictly for show, and we have no intention of chowing down on the cassowaries. But anyway, it was almost like Hans could see into the future, almost like he knew those actors would be passin' through one day. Why, just the other day he finished this article that said ostrich steaks are all the rage out there in Los Angeles because of the low cholesterol and all that, so we're gonna serve 'em to that Hollywood couple when they come. How about them apples?"

"How fortuitous and yummy," Mary Dell replied, rising from her chair and flashing a diplomatic grin. She wasn't sure she was up to eating ostrich, but then, she didn't think she could handle calamari that time she had ordered it in the French Quarter with her parents, and she had actually liked the taste and texture. Besides, with Harris by her side she was certain she could swallow anything. "We'll be looking forward to the culinary experience."

And with that she finally headed out, bringing her thoroughly hectic and surprising junket to a close.

O Bed! O Breakfast!

A half-hour later Mary Dell was back at her desk, lost in thought. So much so that she didn't even notice when Harris poked his head in the doorframe.

"What's the matter?" he said. "Didn't it go well?"

"Splendiferously. There is such a word, isn't there?" She gave him a wry grin. "I've discovered that I am the mother confessor of the entire known universe. All the great secrets have been divulged to me. If Carl Sagan had only come around to this office before he died, I could have given him all the answers."

Harris moved across the room and stood beside her with a fatherly demeanor. "Give me all the gory details."

"No, actually it went very well. They all wanted me to be a part of their festivities for the upcoming weekend. Do more than our usual perfunctory introductions and leave. They've asked me to stay and have dinner and cocktails with them, breakfast the next morning, the whole works. It appears that I am to be their social insurance for the occasion, since I agreed to the proposition three times."

"Well, you're very good at these things, and I think it's commendable that you're going the extra mile for them."

Mary Dell hesitated, then forged ahead bravely. "The truth is, we're both going the extra mile. I more or less committed you to make the rounds with me. I sort of positioned us as Mr. and Mrs. Tourist Bureau."

Harris pulled up a chair, then reached across and took her hand. "That's an intriguing image."

"Does that mean you approve?"

"I do. We'll present a more united front against Megita and her troops when the time comes."

She pulled back slightly, feeling a sense of relief. "Anything new from Horvath?"

"I'm managing to keep him at arm's length, telling him we're working hard on a last-minute compromise with the Committee."

"And are we?"

Harris cast his eyes heavenward with a sigh of resignation. "Nope. We're just trying to stall for time. Just trying to get Cadbury and Reynaldo here before he can snatch them away from us. Fortunately, Horvath stays so busy he doesn't have the time to monitor the situation minute-by-minute."

"What about Cadbury's personal assistant? You still think it's a good idea to keep her in the dark about Megita's protests?"

Harris momentarily rubbed his furrowed brow with the tips of his fingers, as if trying to dissolve all their pressing problems with one swift gesture. "We're trying to pull off one hell of a balancing act here, keeping so many different agendas at bay. The way I see it, we get Juliette Cadbury down here and let her fall in love with our facilities. What we don't do is give her a reason to back out before she even makes the trip. No, we'll take our chances explaining away Megita's activities once we've got the beautiful and bodacious Ms. Cadbury solidly on our turf."

Mary Dell rose to stretch. "Sounds doable to me. At any rate, spending the day with our 'terrible trio' has wrung me out. It's quittin' time, as they say in these parts, and I need to unwind. Any suggestions?'

"What say we start by taking a little stroll down to the river together? Then we can go for a drink at the hotel and play it by ear from there."

A few minutes later they were off to the Bluff—the popular name for the old parade grounds the Spanish had laid out alongside and two-hundred feet above the Mississippi River well over two centuries ago. In the middle of it stood the

Bandstand, a Victorian gazebo that had twice burned to the ground and been rebuilt, and they reached it just as sunset approached. At the moment there were no barge tows plying the muddy current, but there were plenty of cars, trucks and semis crossing the big silvery twin bridges high above the river a half-mile or so downstream.

"There's something I've been meaning to discuss with you," Harris began, leaning on the railing and staring across at the Louisiana horizon ablaze with gold and burnt orange. "It has nothing to do with work—it's personal. Since you and I are moving along pretty smoothly in our relationship, I wanted to give you a little insight into my separation and divorce from Betsy."

Mary Dell felt a mixture of surprise and relief. It was a subject he seemed to have meticulously avoided throughout the entire ordeal. "None of us at the Bureau ever felt it was any of our business to ask you about it while you were going through it, but I'm glad you want to share it with me now. Was it terribly messy for you?"

He kept his eyes trained on the river. "It was the worst thing that's ever happened to me. That's why it took me as long as it did to get up the courage to ask you out. I always thought Betsy and I would spend the rest of our lives together, but she had other plans. A few years back she came to me and said she needed to explore her creativity after giving up so much to raise our daughters. Next thing I know she's moved out of the house and down to Baton Rouge to be with this English professor who teaches creative writing at LSU. How and where she met him, I have no idea to this day, but I guarantee you the big attraction wasn't learning how to diagram sentences properly or look up synonyms in a thesaurus."

"You and Betsy did seem so happy when I first came to work at the Bureau."

He shrugged his shoulders, and she could sense the hurt in his gesture. "It's funny. The cliche you hear all the time is the one about the middle-aged man who leaves his wife for greener pastures or fresher sod, so to speak, but the opposite can also happen. I'm living proof. Maybe it was my fault. Maybe I'd become a very predictable, boring person to live with, working all these years at the Tourist Bureau booking B&B's and hotel rooms and planning conventions. Lots and lots of busy work—but perhaps too busy to really pay attention to Betsy."

Mary Dell had to restrain herself. His description of the job was more than accurate, but she wanted to seem supportive. "I think you may be too hard on yourself."

"Maybe. But there's a part of me that's still having a rough time accepting the divorce."

They were both facing the river now, and then it happened. The swollen sun ran along the length of the horizon like a gigantic egg yolk that had just been pricked by an invisible needle. The fiery strip of color lingered tremulously for a minute or two and then blinked out, heralding the onset of evening.

"You have to pay attention," Harris added. "Otherwise, the things you want to last forever will disappear on you in a second."

Then they turned away and headed to the hotel bar.

O Bed! O Breakfast!

Chapter Seven

Juliette Cadbury sat yawning in the back seat of the stretch limo she had rented for the Fort Rosalie weekend. The flight from Los Angeles had been delayed, causing them to nearly miss their connection in Dallas, and the chauffeur had not shown up on time once they had finally landed in Jackson, Mississippi. They were now speeding down I-55 in an attempt to keep their three o'clock appointment with the Tourist Bureau officials, but they were already running a good thirty minutes late.

"I don't think there's any way we can make up the time," Juliette said, glancing at her Rolex. "But what are those people gonna do down there in Fort Rosalie? Get mad at us and walk away?"

She tossed her voluminous, strawberry-blonde mane and stretched her shapely legs. Six million dollar legs, some had even called them. Along with her wide-screen smile and bountiful chest measurements, they had won for her an asking price per film that her acting alone had yet to justify. In the relatively short span of seven years and at the still tender Hollywood age of twenty-six, she had compiled a cinematic resumé that was the envy of many a better-established and more talented actress: three romantic comedies, three action-adventure romps, one science-fiction blockbuster and one experimental film that had won raves at Cannes and further enhanced her reputation as the A-list ingénue of choice. Her movies almost always did respectable box office—nothing yet had grossed under 50 million, one or two had hit the 100 million mark—and there was no shortage of people willing to bankroll her next project.

Unfortunately, her private life had been completely sacrificed to such dazzling fame and fortune. The tabloids, syndicated TV gossip shows and assorted paparazzi stalked her day and night, detailing her comings and goings without permission or regard to accuracy, blowing any little faux pas, gaffe or indiscretion she made way out of proportion. The late Princess Diana had endured less. What was more, she had absolutely no recourse other than to grin and bear it, trying gamely with the widest smile her voluptuous yet collagen-free lips could manage to pretend the lies and half-truths didn't matter, when in fact it was tearing up her insides to be so misquoted, misrepresented and misunderstood all the time.

At the moment, in fact, Juliette's mind was flashing back to that outrageous tabloid story that had first appeared several weeks earlier and which by now had taken on a life of its own. She had skimmed the latest installment at the airport newsstand while waiting for the chauffeur. "That goddamned miserable rag!" she blurted out, unable to contain her resentment.

"What's the matter, Jule?" said her lover, Tim Reynaldo, who was sitting next to her.

"That *Celebrity Inquisitor* story that just won't go away. They started out by saying that you and I wanted to have lots of babies out of wedlock, and now they're claiming I actually have one in the oven at this very moment. I know I should be used to it all by now, and I suppose I could sue the way Carol Burnett and lots of others have done, but they'd just be right back as soon as it was over like the flies and buzzards they are. The fact is, tabloid journalism has become an entire cottage industry, and you and I are the cottage with the white picket fence that keeps it laughing all the way to the bank."

"Most of their stories have a germ of truth buried in there somewhere. Any idea where this particular germ got started?" Tim said, giving her that wicked smirk of his, a trademark gesture that had propelled him into the celebrity spotlight—female heartthrob variety—a good five years before her arrival on the scene. And it was the combination of his spectacular tangle of dark curls, stunning tan, and fashionable stubble that had kept him on top until the two of them had met in New York on the set of the romantic comedy, *Something For Everyone,* whereupon they had promptly fallen into well-publicized lust. The tabloids had had a field day with it a year and a half ago and basically had never let up since.

"It was most likely that AFI fundraiser at the Beverly Hills Hotel in September," Juliette replied. "A bunch of us were standing around discussing the pros and cons of motherhood for high-profile celebrities. Maria Shriver and Demi Moore had just offered up their tributes to their large families and then Jodie Foster started raving about raising her little one as a single mother, so I just made an off-hand remark about my priorities being focused on my film career right now, but if I wanted to have a kid, I'd zoom right in on it without worrying about what anyone else thought. Hell, I may have even said that I didn't see a whole lot of conventional marriages in Hollywood that had worked out. Of course, there were scads of reporters mixing and mingling all around, so obviously one of them took all of that out of context and twisted it into the absurd story it's become."

Tim pressed on. "You've never been particularly careful around reporters, have you? Sometimes I think you just like to tempt fate."

"Come on, Tim. I could use a little support here. Especially with this big weekend ahead of us."

"You could have avoided all this travel and aggravation if you'd simply let Heidi here or a staff member of your brand-new production company handle these local accommodations arrangements. I'm sure Heidi here wouldn't have minded, and

we could have stayed home in Malibu and relaxed until the actual shoot."

Juliette gave her personal assistant of seven years standing a reassuring smile. The diminutive bundle of energy with the mousy pageboy cut was sitting across from them, tightly clutching her trusty clipboard. It was a prop she was never without—in fact, there were those who thought she surely slept with it—and as usual it was laden with notes, directions, schedules and other paraphernalia pertinent to the success of the weekend.

"My last name is Pendleton, Tim," Heidi said. "For the ten-thousandth time, please stop referring to me as Heidi Here."

"It's neither here nor there," he replied, obviously full of himself.

"All right, you two," Juliette said, leaning in and waving a hand between them. "Truce. I don't need you at each other's throats as usual. We've got to concentrate. I want everything about this production to be perfect, including what our daily living environment will be like. I went to a lot of trouble to get *Whispering Dixie* for us. Every actress in Hollywood was frantic to play Rella Darrow, and I had hoped by now that you'd be a little more enthusiastic about playing Harbaugh Kinsley, Tim."

"I'm working on it."

"Well, please try to work a little harder."

"Yeah, well, you know I don't travel well. Let me get a little more rest, and I'll be okay by the time we get to Fort Rosalie."

They rode along for another mile or so in silence, and then Juliette said: "Remind me again, Heidi, sweetie. What's our first B&B on the tour?"

Heidi shuffled more paper and squared her shoulders. "After we check in with a Mr. Harris Lyles and a Ms. Mary Dell Hoskins of the Tourist Bureau, we will be escorted to the antebellum mansion, Betterslie, home of Fort Rosalie's resident poet, Edding Denbo."

"Never had much use for poems," Tim spoke up, opening one eye cautiously. "Unless you want to count those dirty limericks the guys would write all the time on the bathroom walls at school. Remember the one about the little balls of—"

Heidi cut him off with her usual efficiency. "Yes, I'm sure we all remember that one. But I can assure you that Mr. Denbo's work aims a bit higher. As a matter of fact, while I was doing research for our trip at the library, I was able to locate several of his poems in a few of the literary quarterlies that have published him, and I enjoyed them very much."

"What else did we discover at the library during our research?" Tim continued, both eyes now wide-open. He pointed emphatically at the peculiar scenery passing by. For at least the last ten miles or so some voracious-looking vine seemed to have sprung up out of the earth and draped itself over everything in sight like one gigantic green blanket, even scaling telephone poles and the tallest trees to accomplish its smothering act. "For example, what the hell is that stuff? Looks like a set for some science-fiction film."

The question triggered Heidi's predictable clipboard reflex, and she immediately rifled through her notes to produce an answer. "Ah, here it is. It's called kudzu, and it's a vine that was imported from China around the turn of the century to halt erosion on hills and bluffs in this part of the South. Unfortunately, it quickly got out of control and took over the entire landscape, as you can clearly see. It's practically a predator plant—no natural enemies."

Tim was smirking again. "Sounds like an idea for a horror movie—*The Vine That Ate Mississippi*. I bet it took you an entire afternoon to look all that up in an encyclopedia."

"As a matter of fact, I did find it in an encyclopedia, but it only took a few minutes to locate. It was in the flora and fauna section of the article on the state of Mississippi."

"And naturally, you read the whole thing and took notes for your clipboard."

"Naturally."

Juliette stepped in as referee once again. "I thought you were going to try and get some rest, Tim. Now leave Heidi alone." She watched as he slid down in his seat and closed his eyes in resignation. Then she took a deep breath of contentment. "Bet-ters-lie, Bet-ters-lie." She stretched out the syllables several more times before repeating the word normally. "Don't you like the sound of that, Heidi? So European, so old-world, so romantic. And a Southern poet for a host. This is exactly the sort of input I'd hoped for during this hands-on mission. Nothing less will help me truly understand the character of Rella Darrow."

Indeed, she felt that all of Hollywood would judge her by how well she eventually did just that. She had given strict orders to her California entourage—no contact of any sort whatsoever. She had basically unplugged herself and was looking forward to the respite from her high-profile existence. Ahead of her lay three whole days without phone calls, pagers, voice mail, memos, answering machines, faxes, E-mail, taking meetings with agents and producers, powwows with Byron Cathcart over the shooting script, dealing with the press, reading the trades, enduring the Hollywood social grind or a hundred other variables. Just one delightful blur of breakfasts, brunches and dinners to eat, history and culture to absorb and love to make under the canopies of dreamy four-poster beds.

"Hand me the excerpt again, sweetie," she said, pointing to the clipboard. "I want to psych myself up for the arrival in Fort Rosalie."

O Bed! O Breakfast!

Heidi rummaged through her stack and eventually produced a photocopy of the page that had convinced Juliette to option *Whispering Dixie* and form her own production company to bring it to the screen. Whenever she got slightly antsy about the undertaking and needed reassurance, she would pull out that excerpt from the novel and take the plunge into Rella Darrow's angst-ridden universe. Well, who knew? An Oscar might even be her ultimate reward for plumbing such histrionic depths.

She put the page on her lap and read to herself for what must have been the umpteenth time:

Though Rella Darrow had climbed to the top of the Hollywood ladder and enjoyed all the creature comforts of such an existence, there was a part of her psyche that remained wounded, an oozing sore that would not heal. There was this business about her being from the Deep South.

It had first surfaced at the Miramax post-Oscar party a couple of years ago and re-emerged every now and then in her social and professional circles no matter how successful she was, no matter how many trendy causes she espoused, no matter how many politically-correct phrases she embraced to prove she was a good person after all. Among the most influential of the Hollywood Left she was still a tad suspect because she hailed from the land of slavery and segregation, even if she always seemed to be whispering the admission.

"How did you stand it down there growing up?" was among the standard questions they usually threw at her between bites of an hors d'oeuvre or sips of a cocktail at some chichi gathering. "Do you think people in the South will ever change their ways?"

There were other digs that caused her to fluctuate between guilt and embarrassment. References to lynchings, the poll tax, lunch counter sit-ins and other historical highlights of the civil rights movement—none of which she had been old enough to experience but all of which she was now held accountable for somehow.

And so she had finally gathered the courage to take a break from all the intimidation and the patronizing to go home again. They said you couldn't do that—go home again. But she needed answers, and, more than that, she needed absolution. One way or another, she wanted to be able to hold her head up high and stop whispering the word Dixie to the world in which she moved and lived.

Juliette looked up and smiled. The sentiments did not precisely mirror her own background, but she was a big star and she did hail from the bootheel of Missouri, which was more or less Southern in outlook, and she remained convinced that *Whispering Dixie* might just turn out to be the seminal film of her career—catapulting her to the very top of the A-list and validating her as a serious actress.

She glanced over at Tim and carefully studied his handsome face, amused by the way he was pretending to be asleep. She knew that he had always been lukewarm about *Whispering Dixie*, but something else had crept into their relationship lately. Her female intuition kept suggesting that he had something pressing bottled up inside of him. So far he had refused to talk about it, but maybe, just maybe, the romantic weekend in Fort Rosalie would drag it out of him.

Twenty miles or so outside of Fort Rosalie, Tim tentatively opened his eyes again. The jet lag finally seemed to be catching up with Juliette and Heidi now, as he discovered them both sagging in their seats with their eyes shut and mouths slack. It was going to be a do-or-die weekend for him, that much was clear. For while Juliette was head over heels in love with *Whispering Dixie*, he was head over heels in love with her, and he couldn't seem to get her attention long enough to really let her know just how much. She was always in some meeting or going someplace or talking to someone. It was a damned miracle, he often thought, that she carved out any time at all for their love-life late at night.

But he was bound and determined to transcend the cliché about the woman he loved. He knew that Hollywood insiders had seen her studs come and go. Juliette Cadbury had a new film and co-star, Juliette Cadbury had a new lover, so the joke went. Though he had managed to stick around well past the completion of the film they had made together, he wanted to stick around forever, and this was going to be the weekend he asked for her hand in marriage. The old-fashioned way. Ring and all. On bended knee, if necessary. He had it all planned out, romantic act by romantic act. He was going to pull out all the stops to win her over because the alternative was unacceptable. Being the butt of the tabloids week after week, month after month, was pure, unadulterated hell, and he was not going to tolerate it any longer. He had to save his Juliette from her own naked ambition. He would become the meaningful center her life had lacked up to now.

He was gazing down adoringly at her when the limo hit a rough patch on the highway and she was jerked into wakefulness in time to catch the expression on his face.

"What's with you?" she said, straightening up in her seat. "You look like you just won an Oscar or something."

The familiar smirk replaced his look of love. "Maybe I was hoping you'd win one for portraying Rella Darrow."

She slipped her arm through his and snuggled up to him.

"Well, that's what I like to hear. Sounds like you're warming up to *Whispering Dixie*, after all." She gazed out the window and frowned. "Please don't tell me that that's Fort Rosalie out there."

There was nothing remotely historical about any of what was passing by. Strip shopping centers. Fast food places. The usual suburban American sprawl. "This doesn't do a thing for me so far," she continued. "It could be anywhere in the country, except for the moss hanging on some of the trees."

Heidi took the cue and produced a city map from her stack of treasures. "Oh, we haven't gotten to Old Fort Rosalie yet. According to this, we have another three or four miles to go before we reach the Historic District."

"Ah, there's something over there," Tim said, pointing to a neon Confederate flag atop the registration building of a run-down motel. "A little bit of history beckoning to us."

"Very funny," Juliette said, giving him a playful shove.

More commercial references to the Deep South popped up here and there. Rebel Tire Store. The Stars and Bars Lounge. The Colonel's Place. The Dewdrop-Inn-On-Dixie. Mason-Dixon Brick Company.

Tim couldn't resist. "So this is what Rella Darrow feels so bad about—corny business signs."

Gradually, undistinguished suburbia gave ground to more distinctive architecture until finally they were immersed in the ambience of Old Fort Rosalie. Two-hundred and fifty years of history had put its best foot forward in the form of preservation and adaptive restoration, and the effect was charming. All the settlement patterns of the city were still well-represented: here was a block of stucco townhouses from the Spanish era; there a street that proudly displayed the Corinthian columns of the late Greek Revival period; yet another neighborhood

seemed to favor the brick and lacework balconies associated with the New Orleans French Quarter. Somehow it all worked well together, offering a startling and unique contrast to the typical American town.

"I think I'm going to like working here," Juliette said. "It's enchanting." Then she wrested the city map from Heidi and noticed the big red X drawn with a magic marker in the middle of the downtown area. "Is this the Tourist Bureau?"

"Yes. It should be in the next block on the left side of the street. Judging by the postcard Ms. Hoskins sent me, it's a big, two-story building with a row of columns across the front."

The limo suddenly slowed to a crawl, and the chauffeur lowered the partition to speak. "There seems to be some sort of congestion ahead of us, Miss Cadbury, but here comes a policeman to talk to us right now."

"You must be the Cadbury limo we've been expecting," the officer said a moment later, leaning down and squinting as he surveyed the passengers in the back seat. "Don't worry about a thing, folks. We'll get you into the parking lot of the Tourist Bureau right away."

Without further ado the man signaled with his hands, and the patrol car that had been blocking the street ahead of them moved aside to let them through. The reason for all the commotion then became all too apparent. A contingent of matronly-looking picketers had dug themselves in on the sidewalk opposite the Tourist Bureau, and they in turn had attracted a small group of gawkers and onlookers which the police had cordoned off at a safe distance.

Juliette gasped while Tim frowned at the range of judgmental references to their private life expressed on the picket signs. "What in God's name is going on here?" she said. "This is an example of that famous Southern hospitality?"

A horrified-looking Heidi quickly reviewed her clipboard

stack but came up empty. "This wasn't supposed to be on the schedule, I assure you."

Moments later the three of them stood in the parking lot face-to-face with Harris Lyles and Mary Dell Hoskins, both of whom were forced to spend most of their introduction time apologizing profusely for the protests of Megita Larose and her Historic Preservation Committee.

"If you'll just come inside for a few minutes," Harris continued, looking as ill at ease as he sounded, "we'll clear everything up and then get you on your way to Betterslie."

Juliette grabbed Tim's arm nervously as they headed into the Bureau and said: "So much for our quiet, romantic weekend, huh?"

O Bed! O Breakfast!

Chapter Eight

The air in the Tourist Bureau's first-floor conference room was thick with tension, despite Harris Lyles' most valiant attempts to placate the still-seething Juliette Cadbury. Just as his diplomatic skills were completely exhausted, however, his delegating instincts rose to the surface, and he gladly turned the floor over to Mary Dell, who quickly presided with a smile at the head of the glossy mahogany table. It was now up to her and her famous people skills to salvage the thing.

"You have our absolute assurance, Miss Cadbury, that the protests of these ladies, however unfortunate, will in no way interfere with your inspection of our bed-and-breakfast facilities. We've made extensive security arrangements with our police department to guarantee it. The pickets will not be allowed beyond the front gates of the B&B's."

But Juliette seemed inconsolable, her arms tightly folded in a defensive posture. "That's beside the point, Miss Hoskins. You have yet to explain to me what on earth my personal life has to do with historical preservation in this slackwater town. Everybody and his mother seems to be getting into the protest business these days. Can you possibly have any idea what it's like to be eternally stalked by that Gestapo with flash bulbs and deadlines otherwise known as the paparazzi? That's bad enough. But now this!"

Mary Dell shook her head sympathetically. "I'm sure it must be very difficult for you. And please. Won't you call me Mary Dell?" There was no response—just that same icy stare. Time to show the ace in the hole, the card she and Harris had agreed to play only if absolutely necessary. "Here's the bottom line. The Mississippi Film Commission wants you to be com-

pletely satisfied with your location, and even though we feel Fort Rosalie is the best choice for your shoot, we are willing to work with them to offer an alternative site for *Whispering Dixie* if all of this is just too disconcerting for you."

Juliette cut her eyes at Heidi, who was frantically taking notes, and then at Tim, who had abandoned his smirk for what appeared to be an encouraging nod, and said: "You have to understand how disappointed and irritated I am. I was hoping for a nice relaxing weekend instead of a vivid reminder of the worst aspects of my life." She unfolded her arms and exhaled. "As for the first name business—I'll call you Mary Dell, and you'll call me Juliette."

Mary Dell brightened at the slight softening of attitude. "Believe me, we can fully appreciate how disappointed you must be—Juliette. All we can ask is that you give us the benefit of the doubt and complete your tour as planned. We feel sure you'll discover our outstanding facilities are well worth the trouble." She was speaking as calmly and evenly as she knew how, sensing that this one was still hanging by the proverbial thread.

There was an awkward and discouraging silence. Surprisingly, it was Tim who broke through it. "Lighten up, Jule. We've come this far. I vote we stay and have some fun. Can't let some little ol' bluehairs bother us, can we?"

Finally, Juliette acquiesced. "All right. You still have us for the weekend as planned. But I'll reserve the right to take you up on that alternative location proposal."

Mary Dell felt a surge of relief throughout her body. "Good. Then that's all understood and settled. Meanwhile, may I suggest we proceed to your accommodations immediately so we can stay on schedule."

A veritable parade set out for Betterslie a few minutes later. A patrol car with flashing blue lights led the way, followed in

O Bed! O Breakfast!

order by Harris and Mary Dell in his Buick, the stretch limo, another patrol car and then half a dozen or so assorted vehicles belonging to Megita Larose and her vigilant, clucking flock, intent on moving their genteel protests to the front gates of Betterslie.

In the Buick, Mary Dell was comparing notes with her boss as the procession crawled along at a funereal pace attracting rubberneckers out on the sidewalks. "Well, at least I didn't have to mention the dreaded word 'Natchez.'"

"You handled it exactly right. You gave her the out she was looking for without publicizing the opposition needlessly."

"It was ever thus," she replied, playing a little game they had invented a few years back whenever they felt like gigging their hated rival. "The eleventh commandment. Thou shalt lose no business to that other historic town on the river."

They rode a block or so in amused silence, and then Mary Dell said: "I know we're off to a rocky start, but at least Juliette asked to be called by her first name there at the end. I do have to add one little note from the female perspective, however."

"And what's that?"

"That famous Tim Reynaldo smirk is every bit as potent as I'd been led to believe. Kinda makes me just a tad weak in the knees."

"You and millions of other females, apparently."

Mary Dell held an imaginary pen between her thumb and forefinger and moved it quickly across an invisible sheet of paper. "And how about that little hamster of a person taking notes all the time? I got the impression she was recording everything on that clipboard from coughing to throat-clearing, or maybe she was drawing sketches of us the way they do at those courtroom trials. I fully expected her to be Miss Efficient, but I've never seen such frantic secretarial skills in

my life."

When they finally emerged from the traffic lights of the downtown area and began picking up a little speed, Mary Dell turned her attention to the impending visit to Betterslie. "We'll have to stay on top of the situation once Edding gets his mouth moving out there. Knowing that our Juliette has such a short fuse, I can easily picture those two at each other's throats. But I've been promised a new, improved Edding for the occasion, so maybe it won't be such an ordeal after all."

Harris looked slightly puzzled. "A new, improved Edding, you say?"

"Perhaps from the moment we walk in."

It was Eola who greeted the entire company at journey's end, however. The mouths of her Hollywood guests agape, she led the way up the grand staircase to show the trio to their adjoining rooms, then rattled off a flurry of instructions Edding had left for them. They were to unpack, freshen up, change for dinner and assemble in the drawing room for drinks to await his entrance.

Then Eola returned to Mary Dell and Harris, who had been waiting patiently in the drawing room below. After serving them their glasses of wine, she said: "Mr. Denbo say to remind you not to let him step in it, Miss Mary Dell."

"I'll do my best," she replied with a chuckle.

Eola exited for the kitchen, turning in the hallway at the last moment. "He be down whenever."

Mary Dell sampled her white zinfandel and gave Harris a nudge. "Care to guess how long whenever will be?"

Everyone had assembled as ordered and had even started on a second round of drinks before the inevitable entrance actually got underway. The grandfather clock at the bottom of the stairs gave the first hint as it struck half-past the hour. That was Eola's cue to usher them all into the hallway at the exact moment Edding appeared on the landing above decked out in tux and ludicrous top hat.

"Welcome to Betterslie, my good friends," Edding proclaimed in his deepest voice while leaning over the railing. Then he began the familiar measured descent. "Welcome, welcome, welcome," he continued. Finally, he reached bottom, hung the hat on a large rack made of deer antlers and took a little bow. "I am Edding Denbo, your host, and the master of Betterslie, but you must all call me Edding."

Seemingly prompted by an invisible director, Juliette sashayed forward in her champagne-colored Escada original and theatrically offered her hand, which Edding bent low to kiss. "Of course you couldn't be anyone else but the beauteous Miss Cadbury, could you now? Delighted to have you here with us in Fort Rosalie. And may I add that in my studied opinion no director has yet done justice to your many charms. May I call you Juliette, my dear?"

"I wouldn't have it any other way, Edding."

"Ah, so we begin our tango," he replied. "Old South ambience and Hollywood glamour. Which of us do you suppose will end up dipping the deepest?"

"You do have a way with words, but let me take a stab as well," Juliette added. "In my humble opinion your home is beyond description. Such atmosphere and ambience everywhere you look, not to mention all this history to absorb. Our room, our four-poster bed, everything is just as I imagined a visit to the Deep South would be."

"You are too kind, of course. My great-great grandfather, Thomason Betters, obviously had someone as lovely as you in mind to roam these vast halls when he first built this house

back in 1838. That's his portrait over the mantel in the drawing room. I've often wished I had inherited anything of his looks—the full head of hair, the straight nose, that sturdy jaw and chin. Unfortunately, I appear to have gone swimming in a gene pool with a little too much chlorine."

"What a disarming sense of humor you have!" Juliette replied. "I could just lean down this very minute and kiss you on top of your cute little head."

Edding watched as Tim moved forward, bumping Juliette so forcefully that she almost spilled her cocktail. "And who might this gentleman be?'

"This is Tim Reynaldo," she replied. "My significant other who is experiencing an apparent rush of testosterone at the moment."

"Delighted to meet you, Mr. Reynaldo," Edding said, extending his hand. But Tim's grip was more than he had bargained for. "My, my! That's quite a handshake you have there. You'll forgive me if I extricate myself, however. I use some of these little rascals to grasp objects essential to my survival. You've no doubt heard of the opposable thumb theory?"

"I'm afraid Tim likes to do all of his own stunts," Juliette added, just as Heidi came up behind her and cleared her throat. "Oh—do forgive me, Edding. Let me introduce my personal assistant of long standing, Ms. Heidi Pendleton. The truth is, I don't know what I'd do without her."

Their eyes met, and Edding fussed with her hand just as he had with Juliette. "So you are the glue that holds our fabulous star together."

She blushed slightly but held his gaze. "I've read some of your poetry, Mr. Denbo—"

"Edding, please."

Her blush deepened. "Yes, of course. Your poems fascinate

me, Edding. I especially liked the one about the pond and all the noises. It reminded me of trying to get to sleep at summer camp when I was a little girl."

"Ah, yes!" he replied, revving up his engines. Whether any of them liked it or not, they were in for one of Edding's patented recitations. "That poem is one of my favorites as well. 'Noises, On A Summer Pond.' Your experience with it was exactly the sort I had hoped to tap into when I composed it. You are precisely the audience I had intended to reach." He paused briefly and then began in earnest:

What noises on a summer pond are these?
What singing, croaking, chirping sounds
That start at dusk and double, treble through the night;
And sometimes give young growing heads a fright
As sleep eludes them—jumbling up their dreams
With images and curious schemes that make no sense.
A symphony, cacophony so dense with texture
That it cannot be discerned by any ear but God's,
Or someone of his choosing—
Perhaps a special child somewhere who bolts upright in bed and thinks:
'I know the thousand different creatures there who speak,
Who tell me that it is not clarity they seek,
But rather harmony, an orchestra of nature meant to lull
And soothe; engendering the memories for a lifetime long—
That quintessential summer song—
Of which as years go by we all grow ever fond;'
Bewitching and beguiling noises,
Cricket, frog, cicada noises,
Buried deep within our childhood noises—
Noises, on a summer pond.

There was polite general applause, except for Heidi, who was loudly enthusiastic in her show of appreciation.

"I like it even more the way you recite it," Heidi said, still riveted to the man. "You definitely bring it to life for me."

Edding thanked her and indicated the drawing room with a sweep of his hand. "Now that we've successfully visited some of my verse, why don't we all have a seat and a pleasant little conversational session before Eola announces our feast? I can answer questions you may have about the house and furnishings, although the official tour will be given after breakfast tomorrow. You'll find that's standard procedure here in Fort Rosalie."

On the way in, Edding took Mary Dell aside briefly, whispering into her ear. "How am I doing so far?"

"Just fine," she answered discreetly. "I enjoyed your Fred Astaire impression at the top of the stairs. Or were you supposed to be Mickey Rooney? Just go easy on the sarcasm. Stay away from things like the 'opposable thumb' comment you made to Tim."

"But the brute nearly broke my hand. I don't think he particularly cares for poets."

"Never mind that. You be the bigger man and chill out. Harris and I are pulling for you all the way."

Then they joined the others who had settled around the drawing room on various antique love seats, chairs and sofas, and Edding was on the verge of trotting out his customary literary preamble to Fort Rosalie, when Juliette pre-empted him.

"Since you're the local literary figure, Edding, I'd be less than honest if I didn't say I'm very interested in hearing your opinion of *Whispering Dixie*. Would you mind sharing it with us?"

Edding was momentarily surprised but recovered quickly. "I assume you want honesty, so I shall not whisper in the manner of your heroine, Rella Darrow. I find Byron Cathcart to be an adequate writer. His prose is a bit on the dry side,

O Bed! O Breakfast!

but he does know his way around a paragraph or two. Having said that, I must also inform you that I consider the premise of his novel to be singularly mawkish and overwrought."

Juliette seemed caught off-guard by the blunt nature of his dig. "Is that because you think it hits too close to home for some Southerners?"

Edding could feel the annoyance creeping into his face. "Cathcart seems to take a perverse sort of delight in pointing his finger at the South all the way to the last page. Nonetheless, I do not accept his premise that we millennium-era Southerners cannot move on with our lives until we accept responsibility for the vanquished evils of slavery and segregation. It's a bit much to ask someone in the present day to take all that on and emerge with his sanity intact. Are today's Germans to agonize forever over the Nazis and the Holocaust, or should they get on with their lives and a new beginning for everyone? What's done is done, and I don't approve of the retrieval of guilt for social and political manipulation."

"So you're saying that Rella Darrow's personal quest is unwarranted?"

"It's an invention of a politically-correct writer. An exercise in the obvious."

The surface glow and good feeling created by the introductory pawing and gushing had quickly evaporated, and the conversation came to a dead halt. Edding gave Mary Dell an urgent glance, hoping she would come to the rescue, and her honed Tourist Bureau instincts came through for him.

"Edding, why don't you tell Juliette and Tim about your new writing project and the part you want them to play. I'm sure we'd all like to hear about it," she said.

Edding was delighted to switch gears, realizing that one of his patented verbal explosions over the subject of *Whispering Dixie* would very likely send Cadbury and Reynaldo running for cover in the Hollywood hills, and he went on at length about his plans for *O Bed! O Breakfast!*

The ploy seemed to work, as Juliette perked up considerably. "You mean you'd write an entire chapter just about us?"

"I think it would end up being the focal point of the book," Edding replied. "The details of your stay with me and anything else you cared to divulge about your lives."

But Tim sounded less than sanguine. "Now there's something that's never been done before. Somebody going on and on for pages and pages about our private lives in print."

"I understand your skepticism, considering the way you've been treated by the press," Edding began. "But *O Bed! O Breakfast!* would be an entirely different experience for you. I'll listen to your stories and report them accurately. Hearsay and gossip won't be allowed anywhere near you. Think of it as an opportunity to get the truth about yourselves out to your public once and for all."

"Amen to that!" Juliette replied.

Just then, Eola appeared in the hallway and said: "Dinner is served."

They all moved into the chandelier-hung dining room, found their assigned places around the long, formally-set table and awaited the first course, which consisted of fresh boiled shrimp in a remoulade sauce. Juliette took one bite and was beside herself.

"I simply must have this recipe, Edding. My friends out in Malibu would kill for a spicy taste like this. Do you share such requests with your guests?"

"I'm afraid that's Eola's department. You might ask her when she comes back in, but she generally guards her culinary secrets jealously."

"Oh, I wouldn't want every little detail. Just the opportunity to pick her brains for a few seconds and take it from there."

O Bed! O Breakfast!

Edding was amused as he sampled his wine. "Funny thing about my Eola. There are scads of things around here I know she'd be delighted to let you pick. For example, I'm sure she'd let you help her pick the suckers and the worms off the tomato plants when they're in season. And I know she wouldn't mind you tagging along to pick the dewberries that run along the length of her garden fence in the back where she grows all these fabulous herbs and spices that flavor her cooking. But I really wouldn't count on being able to pick her brains about her recipes. I'm fairly certain that's a place no one ever goes."

Juliette gave a polite little shrug, and the meal proceeded accompanied by occasional small talk. Then Eola cleared and brought out the main course—roasted quail stuffed with cornbread dressing, sweet potato casserole topped with pecans, fresh green beans, and buttered biscuits. Meanwhile, Juliette continued to rave over the food.

"We'd pay a small fortune out in California for down-home cuisine like this. You eat like this every day here?"

Edding patted his stomach. "I must admit I do have my skirmishes with the bulge because of Eola's good cooking."

"Oh, it might work out just about right. Rella Darrow is supposed to be a voluptuous sort of woman. Perhaps adding a few pounds here and there for the role wouldn't hurt me one bit."

Edding beamed, feeling exactly like a smug little boy who'd just found everything on his wish list under the Christmas tree. "My Eola is indeed a treasure, and she can be yours for the duration of your shoot here in Fort Rosalie. All you have to do is say the word."

Juliette smiled briefly and then put down her fork. "Forgive me, but maybe you can explain it to me so that I can understand. You keep saying 'my Eola.' It sounds so proprietary, almost like a throwback to such things as slavery. It's the sort

of thing Byron Cathcart addresses in *Whispering Dixie*. He implies that it's a residual attitude some whites still have toward blacks who work for them. Can you enlighten me?"

Edding stopped eating, fighting off the first hint of indigestion as a result of her comments. He glanced across the table at Mary Dell, who had just raised a cautionary eyebrow, and then took a few moments to consider before he spoke.

"I believe I can give a satisfactory answer to your question. When I use the term 'my Eola,' I do so with genuine pride. She takes pride in her work for me here at Betterslie, so I take pride in her. I do not mean to suggest through such an appellation that she belongs to me in any way, shape or form the way slaves once belonged to their masters. Her life and all the choices she makes are her own. I mean only that she has been an integral part of the bed-and-breakfast success we've enjoyed here at Betterslie. In addition to that, she was here for me when my parents died very suddenly and unexpectedly in a car wreck. I would have been utterly lost without her kindness. Does that explanation work for you?"

"It does, indeed," Juliette replied, looking down at her plate as if she had been reprimanded somehow.

Edding caught Mary Dell's eye and gave her a wink. The new, improved Edding Denbo he had promised her on her visit was holding his own so far. Now, if Juliette would just lay off the contentious social commentary.

Over the dessert of caramel custard, however, there was more prodding and probing. "I still can't help but be a bit curious," Juliette said. "Don't you know anyone here in Fort Rosalie who feels the same way Rella Darrow does in wanting to make amends with the past?"

Edding continued to think carefully before he spoke. "I know people who want to make amends with their own specific pasts—myself included. But that's hardly the same thing as taking on the entirety of Southern history. One is doable, the other simply is not."

Juliette was still not through. "Perhaps you're right. But there's a passage in the novel that I find particularly intriguing, and I'd like for you to address it, if you would. Rella Darrow is being put on the defensive by a fellow actor at some cocktail party, and he says something to the effect that many people who live in the Deep South apparently have no quarrel with looking backward so long as it involves things like fanlights, Doric columns, hoopskirts and other decorative reminders of the past. But ask them to look back on the dark side—on the slave trade, the Jim Crow laws, the lynchings and cross-burnings—and they quickly turn away, opting with grand relief for the present or even the future. Anything to avoid truly focusing on the price that was paid for that decorative past they worship so. Would you care to comment?"

"That's quite a passage you throw our way, Juliette. In fact, I would say you have isolated the gist of Byron Cathcart's charges against the contemporary South," Edding said, diligently striving to keep the inner turmoil out of his voice. "But I do think I can answer that particular diatribe of his in this way. There is nothing intrinsically untoward about maintaining our links to the past through the restoration and celebration of the buildings and trappings that have managed to survive the passage of time. We do more than shore up walls and floors and ceilings when we honor the dwellings of our ancestors, whoever they were, wherever they came from and whatever their shortcomings. We shore up our own souls and psyches and bravely assign meaning in the face of so much that is unknown and uncertain in this mysterious progression we call life. At the same time we should never attempt to sweep the grave injustices of the past under the rug. We must roundly condemn and lament them, but trudging around with

bowed heads today because they once existed does nothing but exalt and encourage the cultivation of victimhood, and the payoff for that is only increased bitterness between the races."

"Well, that was quite a mouthful," Juliette said, gazing down at her custard and smiling playfully. "And so is this delightful-looking concoction. You've given me quite a bit of food for thought tonight, Edding. I promise to sleep on your words and resume this dialogue tomorrow."

Over after-dinner drinks in the drawing room Edding felt completely in command of his guests and the proceedings, and he noticed that even Tim seemed to have warmed to him.

"That's one helluva staircase you got out there, Edding. Kinda reminds me of the one Rhett Butler climbed that time he carried Scarlett up to ravish her in the bedroom. I was thinking of sweeping my Jule here off her feet that same way tonight, but naturally I don't want to get a hernia. Think I could pull it off?"

Edding swirled his snifter of Courvoisier and laughed. "I have no idea what the weight limit is for scurrying up the staircase on the way to ravishment. The heaviest thing I ever took upstairs was a novel manuscript of mine some New York editor had just rejected with the snippiest, nastiest letter ever transcribed in the annals of literature. That was a few years back, but I do recall that I felt I was carrying up the weight of the world."

Juliette gave Tim a disdainful stare. "You are not going to haul me up that staircase tonight, Tim Reynaldo."

"Ah, come on, Jule. Let's do the thing up right. I'll haul you up the stairs to that nosebleed bed, and then we'll have some fun."

"It's called a four-poster."

"It's a Mallard piece," Edding added. "All of my beds are Mallard's work."

O Bed! O Breakfast!

Tim gulped the last of his brandy and grabbed Juliette's arm. "Then let's go give ol' Mallard a test drive, shall we? It's been one hellaciously long, jet-lag of a day."

Juliette actually seemed to be blushing but managed a perfunctory smile. "Tim and his stunts again." She rose, made her manners in an extravagant display of gushing worthy of a post-Oscar bash at Spago or something akin, and the two of them were off to the bedsheets.

Then Edding turned to Mary Dell and Harris. "Well, how do you think it all went?"

"I couldn't have written a better script for you to follow," Mary Dell said, giving him a quick hug. "All that controversy dragged out into the open, and you handled it like an ambassador to the United Nations."

"Yes, it was very impressive," Harris added, shaking his hand.

"To be completely honest, I even surprised myself a little," Edding said, showing them to the front door with a mesmerized Heidi in tow. "Perhaps wonders will indeed never cease. Now we'll expect you both for Eola's breakfast around nine-ish. Don't you dare be late."

Finally, Edding and Heidi were left alone. It had not escaped him that she had not taken her eyes off him all evening. He halfway suspected that she was the reason he had managed to remain so calm and even-tempered throughout Juliette's provocative meanderings, and he could hardly wait to explore the situation further.

"Would you care for another nightcap?" he said, boldly slipping his arm around her narrow waist. "Or have you had sufficient for the evening?"

"More than sufficient. My head is practically swimming in brandy now."

They moved together into the drawing room and plopped

down on a love seat. "There's a poem I've had in my head for many years now," he began. "I've never written it down, but I'd like to share it with you tonight, if I might. The truth is, I was beginning to think you, or someone like you, would never show up to hear it."

She nestled up against him and hooked her arm through his. "You know, this is almost like when I was a little girl and my mother read to me from *Uncle Wiggly's Storybook*. You have my undivided attention, Edding Denbo."

"The poem is as yet untitled, but that will surely come." He stared straight ahead, aligning himself mentally with the portrait of his ancestor, Thomason Betters, across the room.

A man is like a lion when he totals up his life—
He wants to walk the earth again,
If through a brand-new pair of eyes and in a different-fitting skin;
He wants his roar to echo still when he has breathed his last,
And though the time will come when he can feel that moment fast approaching,
Yet calmly will he lay his cracked and weary bones to rest upon a grave of fallen twigs
And earth—
If he has seen and also known the birth of those who follow,
Of those who run and romp and nip the muzzles of their mates as he has done,
And wander through the nights and bask in waving weeds beneath the golden sun;
A man is like a lion,
And yet a lioness must favor him to stow his seed within her secret place,
And give his countenance another chance in time—
Another striving face.

O Bed! O Breakfast!

Edding turned away from the portrait to find Heidi gazing up at him adoringly. Mission accomplished.

"And am I to become your lioness?" she said.

He leaned in, gently grazing her cheek with his lips and making a soft guttural sound in his throat. "I gently roar my approval." Then he rose and offered his hand. "May I now show you to your room?"

She did not hesitate, rewarding him with her brightest smile. "I think I'd rather you showed me to yours."

He took a deep breath, expelling years of frustration and longing, and they started the long climb in lock-step. "Then up, up and away to our nosebleed bed, as Mr. Reynaldo put it," he said. Halfway there, he stopped and turned to her. "Are you absolutely certain this is what you want, my dear? We don't have to rush things, you know. I want to respect your sense of propriety."

She started laughing—softly at first, then uncontrollably.

"Did I say something funny?"

"No, no. It's just me. This image formed in my head of me ripping all the sheets out of my clipboard, tearing through them and tossing them high in the air, watching them flutter down like so many autumn leaves. That's just so unlike me—making a mess in my head. It means that for once in my life I'm not going to be concerned with being so damned organized. I'm just going to be spontaneous and let the chips fall where they may. You'd have to know me better to realize how humorous it all is."

Edding felt like he had just conquered the world. "Be that as it may—tonight, I suspect, we shall both let go of the past."

On the ride back to Fort Rosalie, Mary Dell was wrinkling her nose in smug satisfaction. "I've never seen Edding so calm and restrained, but I think he had a little extra incentive in the person of Heidi Pendleton. I wouldn't be at all surprised if something serious develops between those two, possibly even tonight."

"No way," Harris said, shrugging his shoulders at her. "He was just flattered that she liked his poetry. It's that monumental ego of his. Everybody in Fort Rosalie knows he's not interested in women."

Mary Dell thought it over briefly and decided that Edding wouldn't mind, that it was time to share her insights with her boss. "Everyone is wrong. He told me himself on that visit I made that he wanted to marry and settle down. I know his public image doesn't fit the private reality, and he acknowledges that it's mostly his fault. But he assured me that he's very interested in women, and I have no reason to doubt his word at this point. You'd have to be blind to ignore the fact that he and Heidi were definitely in each other's faces all night. If it wasn't the real thing, it was acting every bit as worthy as the stuff Juliette and Tim keep churning out."

Harris drove on in silence for a mile or so and then said: "Well, I guess I stand corrected. Maybe I've been guilty of some tabloid thinking myself."

"Living on surface impressions is the easiest way to go. The path of least resistance. But it frequently prevents us from digging down and doing the work we're supposed to do with each other."

He did not answer, so she kept turning those last words over and over in her head right up until the moment he drove into her apartment parking lot and shut off the engine. For lack of anything better to say, she made small talk. "We made a good team this evening."

"No. You did all the work keeping Edding on track. I saw

how you did it with all those subtle facial expressions and body language. Great stuff, and I know he appreciated the help."

"Miss Aimee and the Lurkins are going to have to go some to stay in this competition. Juliette seemed completely sold on the cuisine, and I think she rather enjoyed all that verbal sparring with Edding."

"The woman definitely likes to argue, that's for sure."

They quickly ran out of observations on the evening at Betterslie and were suddenly left with a deafening silence. Mary Dell decided that the time had come to discuss the next level of their relationship.

"A minute or so ago when I mentioned digging down and doing the serious work people need to do with each other, I wasn't being abstract, you know. I intended some reference to us," she explained. "Where do you see our relationship going? For instance, can you envision us as, let's say, Mr. and Mrs. Tourist Bureau down the road?"

Harris stared straight ahead into the windshield for a while, his brow deeply furrowed. Then the muscles of his face relaxed, and he turned to her with a smile. "That's someplace I think I'd like to go. I think that's why I asked you out in the first place. The truth is, I miss being married."

"That's a confusing answer," she replied, letting her slight sense of disappointment show through. "Because it could be interpreted as meaning you miss being married to Betsy."

"Let's don't discuss Betsy. Let's just allow this forty-eight year-old warrior to heal up a bit more, shall we?"

Mary Dell decided to back off quickly. She had seen for herself the pain he had projected when they had briefly discussed the separation and divorce that evening at the Bandstand. "No problem. Would you like to come up for the usual nightcap on the sofa?"

"You bet," he said, winking at her. "Soft, warm and cuddly with you is just what I need to get me up to snuff."

Mary Dell was unable to drift off easily that night after they had finally called it quits and Harris had left. They had gone at it hot and heavy on the sofa, stopping short of sleeping together. She was the one who had put on the brakes, and he had gone along with it without pressing her too much. That aside, she was certain that Harris was the man to take her to the next level. Here was someone with an exquisite sense of timing and the experience and maturity to bring it all together for her—a woman so mired in routine, so long overdue.

Still, it had become increasingly obvious to her that there were some issues to be resolved before her dream of Mr. and Mrs. Tourist Bureau could become a reality.

O Bed! O Breakfast!

Chapter Nine

A patch of Fort Rosalie's brilliant autumn sunshine streamed through the window in Juliette's bedroom and fell across the mattress, spotlighting her face. From somewhere beneath the surface of her dreams Hollywood's darling recognized her cue and sprang instantly to life. She sat up in bed blinking and remembering, then smiling and sighing. What on earth had come over her Tim? He had been insatiable the night before, reminding her of that mind-bending first week they'd spent together in New York on the set of *Something For Everyone*. Of course, it wasn't like he hadn't warned her.

"Okay, my precious Jule," he had told her, climbing up stark naked on his knees into the four-poster and eyeing her, stalking her like a hungry animal. "You shoudda let me work off some of this energy by hauling you up that staircase. But since you didn't, you're in for it now."

He was more than true to his word, bucking and heaving and kneading and probing, and then holding her close to him afterwards, stroking her tenderly as if some terrible catastrophe might separate them at any moment. She had to admit, it was a welcome change. He had been so disinterested in *Whispering Dixie* as a project, but perhaps this meant he was coming around.

She glanced his way and watched him sleeping. He had to be exhausted, frazzled to the core, poor stud. After all, they had made an impossible jumble of the covers and filled the room with their musk in managing to do it three times during the night.

Then she remembered. She had some important reconnaissance ahead of her. Taking care not to wake him, she

slipped out of bed, threw on her robe and slippers, attended to a few essentials in the bathroom and then made her way down the staircase to Betterslie's enormous kitchen.

"Good morning, Eola," she said, standing in the doorframe and inhaling the heavenly breakfast aromas. "Or do you prefer Mrs. Griffin?"

"Good mornin' to you. Mr. Denbo, he the one put on airs all the time, not me. Eola suit me just fine." She flashed a smile while shuffling sausage patties around in her blackened skillet with a spatula.

Juliette pointed to a pot of coffee on one of the burners. "May I?"

"The cups, they over there in that right-hand cabinet. You just help yourself while I keep my eye on what I got on the stove. Got water boilin' for grits, and some biscuits like we had last night bakin' in the oven."

"I hope you don't mind my visiting with you while you work," Juliette said, retrieving the cup and pouring the coffee. "I know how territorial most cooks are. You just say the word, and I'll scoot."

"Oh, you don't bother me. Mr. Denbo, he always in here rantin' and ravin' 'bout somethin'. I just pretend to listen while I do my work 'til he finish bouncin' things off the wall. Truth is, he just like to hear hisself talk, but I cut him some slack 'cause of the way he lost his parents."

Juliette blew across the surface of her coffee to buy herself some time. She wanted to approach the thing just the right way. After a cautious sip or two, she finally had the sequence worked out.

"Edding told me last night you've never shared your recipes with anyone. I can easily understand why. Your food is world-class delicious."

Eola continued her work while humming something sooth-

O Bed! O Breakfast!

ing and nebulous, turning down the heat on the sausages and pouring a measuring cup of grits into boiling water. Finally, she said: "Thank you for the kind words. Mr. Denbo, he absolutely right. I don't share my recipes with nobody. Oh, I did try once. Offered 'em every one to my daughter, Alice. But she say, 'Mama, I love to eat, but I hate to cook. I'm gonna hire me somebody to do my cookin' when I get married.'" She chuckled and stirred the grits with a big slotted spoon. "My Alice, she as good as her word, too. She and her husband, Charlie, they live in a fine house over there in Atlanta and they doin' real well. He sell stocks and she teach in college. But she go right out and hire herself a woman to cook and clean. You know, that tickle me every time I think about it."

Juliette put down her coffee cup to concentrate on the payoff. "Well, delicious as they are, it wasn't your recipes I really wanted to discuss with you. Do you know anything at all about the movie I'm going to be making down here?"

Eola stopped stirring for a moment and tilted her head. "Mr. Denbo mention it here in the kitchen a few times. Hope you don't mind me sayin', but I don't think he favor it all that much."

"No. I got that impression last night at dinner. I think it's the subject matter that makes him feel a bit uneasy, perhaps because of his ancestors. The woman I'm portraying wants to make amends for some of the injustices of the past here in the South, and I was hoping you could help me understand her motivations a little better. Maybe you could tell me what it was like to be living down here during the time of the Jim Crow laws and segregation. Would you mind sharing any of that with me?"

Eola stared down into the pot of bubbling grits for a while. Then, just when it appeared she either had nothing to say on the subject or wanted to avoid it completely, she opened up the flood gates. "I had my fifty-sixth birthday last month, but what I still remember most like it was yesterday is they was places I couldn't go and things I couldn't do when I was growin' up. Thought things would always stay that way, too. Then some people in Alabama and Atlanta and Little Rock and places like that, they start stickin' they necks out and takin' chances. I remember wantin' to do things like they showed 'em doin' on TV. Sittin' at lunch counters and marchin' on courthouses. But my Mama say: 'Wait and see how it all turn out, Eola. Wait and see if anything change here in Fort Rosalie.' She think I might get hurt if I act up like the TV folks. She just want us to wait it out and see if they was anything to it after all the shoutin' and the siccin' dogs and the hosin' people with water was through." Eola stirred more vigorously as the grits began to thicken, then bent down to open the oven and check on her biscuits.

An impatient Juliette pressed on. "Things did change, didn't they?"

"Oh yes, they change," she replied, straightening herself up and returning to the grits and sausages. "Not too damn fast, though. Oh, this place took down they 'colored only' sign and that place finally let us come in the front, but they didn't hurry up to do it like they lives depend on it. Some took they own sweet time. But we finally got to the front of the bus and down from the balcony in the movie theater, and they was places we could go now and things we could do 'cause some people did stick they necks out."

"Do you ever regret that your mother kept you from being one of the ones who stuck their necks out?"

Eola briefly busied herself draining the sausages on a paper towel, laying them out neatly, and finally said: "In my opinion, not everybody meant to stick they necks out. They's a place for people who just wait and pray, and I was pretty good

at doin' both."

Juliette watched her shifting things to platters and puttering around the kitchen with ease and precision. "You seem so at peace with everything. So happy. This isn't just an act for us tourists, is it? You know, part of your job description."

Eola laughed. "They's not enough money in the world to keep me from bein' who I am. I do what I do 'cause I like it—no other reason. As far as the money go, my daughter, Alice, got herself two degrees from college on what I save outta what Mr. Denbo pay me over the years and what his parents pay me before that. No, I got no complaints, and what you see is what you get."

"But what about all the terrible things that have happened to people down here in the South over the years?"

Eola did not hesitate, continuing to smile. "Some things that happen did hurt my heart. You just cain't be human and deny that. But terrible things, they happen to people everywhere, not just here in the South. You can even read about 'em in the Bible. I know it sound strange to say, but sometimes I think it supposed to be like that. Like we meant to learn from fixin' up all the terrible things that happen. I never was one to think we all put here to live in a perfect world. You got to pay a price for livin,' otherwise you not livin' at all."

Juliette finished her coffee and quickly reviewed Cathcart's insistent themes in her head. "So you can honestly say you like living here in Fort Rosalie?"

"Never lived anyplace else. Never even tried to move. Got a little place in town I call home in addition to my own room out here, even though my Alice all the time sayin' I should quit my job and come live with her in Atlanta in that big ol' house she got. But I like to work, like to keep busy, so as long as I got my health, I think I be stayin' on here with Mr. Denbo a while longer. He a lonely, restless soul that need somebody to

look after him, you know."

"Well, I thank you for the coffee and the conversation," Juliette said, trying to fight off her feelings of disillusionment and disappointment. She had wanted, even fully expected, some sort of embittered explosion from the servant corner regarding the so-called 'Southern Condition' outlined in *Whispering Dixie* but instead had been presented a classic case of shrewd adaptation, adjustment and eventual acceptance by a woman who clearly knew who she was and what she wanted out of life. Edding's description of Rella Darrow's quest as a somewhat hollow, politically-correct exercise began to resonate with her more strongly now.

Juliette trudged up the staircase lost in thought but quickly came to at the sight of Heidi in her nightgown slipping out of Edding's arms in front of his door and scurrying down the upstairs hall to her own bedroom, completely unaware that she was being observed. In a morning filled with unexpected revelations, here was yet another.

"Guess who spent last night together—I mean, besides us?" Juliette said, entering the bedroom and climbing up into the four-poster next to her nude lover still immodestly sprawled atop the sheets.

Tim grunted a couple of times, not bothering to cover any part of his magnificent body, and propped himself up on a pillow. "Edding and our Heidi."

"You weren't supposed to get it right away."

"What? You thought I was going to say Edding and Eola?"

She made a fist and playfully pressed it against his muscular arm. "It's funny. All these years I've been comfortable thinking of Heidi as someone who was anatomically incorrect. You know, just a smoothed-over spot down there like some sort of doll. She's certainly never given me any indication she was interested in anything other than keeping track of my life

on that clipboard of hers. I'm having all kinds of trouble imagining her doing it."

"Geez, Jule. And she thinks I'm the one that doesn't give her any respect." His trademark smirk reappeared as she snuggled up against him in silent contentment.

"You were totally awesome last night," she said. "Are you by any chance up to something?"

He was smiling at the gathered tester above him. "You'll find out. Let's just say one night down, two to go."

"Hey, I'm not complaining, you understand. You just seem so enthusiastic about everything all of a sudden, particularly our bedroom activity."

This time he gave her the look that had melted so many of his female fans. "Don't worry. There's more where that came from."

When Edding greeted Mary Dell and Harris at the front door shortly before nine o'clock, the joint was jumping, as they say. Heidi was pacing around the drawing room off to the left, reciting aloud one of Edding's poems he had encouraged her to memorize. Eola was happily humming away and doing an amusing little dance step as she put the finishing touches on the place settings in the dining room. And the middle ring of the circus featured—of all things—Tim in sweatpants hauling Juliette up the grand staircase, making good on his threat the evening before to emulate one of Rhett Butler's most seminal moments.

"Come in and join the festivities!" Edding said, pointing everything and everyone out with a sweep of his hand. "Eola will have our breakfast on the table shortly."

Mary Dell waved and smiled at Juliette and Tim as the cou-

ple reached the landing above. Then they immediately started down.

"It may not be calisthenics, but it's still quite a workout!" Tim called out, sounding slightly winded. "This'll make the third time!"

"And it's going to be the finale!" Juliette added, her arms locked tightly around his neck. There was no mistaking the expression on her face. She definitely appeared to be having a good time. "I don't want him collapsing on me!"

"I think all of this bodes very well for you in the competition, Edding," Mary Dell said.

"Yes, indeed," he replied. "There hasn't been this much frenzied activity in the house since my mother made the mistake of holding cub scout meetings here when I was a little boy."

Harris laughed loudly. "Hey, add another guy sliding down the banister with a fifth of whiskey in his hand and two more swinging from the chandelier, and the place could be a dead ringer for my old college fraternity house at Ole Miss."

Then Eola joined them in the foyer, making the announcement that breakfast was served. Soon everyone was enjoying the generous spread of honeydew melon, grits, sausages, biscuits with hot pepper jelly, fresh orange juice and coffee—all of it served on exquisite Old Paris china. The conversation centered around polite small talk for a while, and then Edding finally took his eyes off Heidi long enough to engage Juliette in something more meaningful.

"You said you wanted to resume last night's discussion this morning. I believe it involved the fine points of such matters as Rella Darrow taking on the injustices of the past and so forth."

"I've had some time to consider your arguments," Juliette replied, smiling across the table at Tim, who was stoking up after his recent exertions. "And I've narrowed it down to this: what is it about the character of Rella Darrow that you find the most objectionable?"

The question caught Edding by surprise, giving him pause, but eventually he rose to the occasion. "I think the main thing is that Rella, as written, is not very strong. She's weak and vacillating whenever she's around her Hollywood friends and, therefore, in need of constant reassurance regarding her intrinsic worth as a person. She seeks validation from others rather than from looking within herself to a core of values. As such, she is well outside the tradition of strong Southern women."

Juliette looked irritated. "Why does everyone always bring up that steel magnolias bit? Like the South has some sort of monopoly on strong women."

"Perhaps not," Edding replied. "But we have more than our fair share. I think it has to do with our well-chronicled history. It's been pointed out by notables before that we're the only part of the country that's ever been occupied by a foreign army, and a case could be made that the women were left to hold down the fort while their husbands, sons, fathers, brothers, and boyfriends went off to fight a war that was surely unwinable from the very beginning. Many of those men never returned, of course, and the women had to go on without them. Furthermore, we cannot ignore the effects of the institution of slavery, itself. It was extremely disruptive to black family unity and stability. What little continuity that existed was usually provided by black women clinging tenaciously to their faith in whatever form. Whether black or white, the South has surely produced many strong women, but Byron Cathcart's Rella Darrow cannot be considered one of them."

Juliette seemed impressed, playfully spearing a sausage with her fork. "That has the ring of truth to it. So you think

Rella could use some toughening up when she's being pushed around by her Hollywood friends? Maybe she should just tell them all to go to hell."

"In my opinion that would be the first step in her makeover."

Juliette laughed brightly. "And here I was hoping I could get by with a new hairdo and a press-on nail job for her."

"If you wouldn't mind," Edding added, "I thought I'd just change the subject and brazenly ask you what you thought of my Betterslie."

"I won't mince words. It's most hospitable and comfortable in every respect, Edding. I'm overwhelmed."

After breakfast the formal tour of the house oozed with the same good feeling. Edding supplied them all with a dizzying parade of historic names, dates and styles that was met with universal awe and approval, if not total retention. Henry Clay had dined here one summer. Andrew Jackson had visited that particular fall. Those bumblebees in the four corners of that enormous rug were symbols of Napoleon Bonaparte. That seven-piece Victorian parlor suite in the drawing room was in Louis Phillipe style. The chandelier overhead was of Baccarat crystal. This particular bed featured a half-tester made of rosewood by Prudent Mallard. And on and on until every square inch of the mansion had been thoroughly reviewed over the course of a lengthy hour. Then Edding finally gave Mary Dell the floor.

"Time to pack and head for Plum Cottage," she said. "But take your time. Miss Aimee isn't expecting us until after one."

Later, the farewells at the front door were surprisingly difficult and heartfelt. Edding and Heidi were practically joined at the hip, and Juliette could not seem to let go of Eola's hand, swinging it back and forth the way schoolgirls at recess often do. Finally, Edding stepped up to bring his moment in the sun to some sort of conclusion.

"It seems our tango at last is done," he said, smiling at Juliette, while still holding onto Heidi.

"I wouldn't have believed we could cram so much into such a short period of time," Juliette replied. "I've really felt the pull of the South over the past twenty-four hours. You've given me a unique perspective on things."

As was usually the case, Edding got in the last word. "Eola and I will eagerly await your decision, and we trust it will be in our favor."

Out at the front gates of Betterslie, Megita and her Casserole Patrol had just begun the final shift of lunch. They were twenty-seven strong this bright autumn day, and the second group had just finished dining on either Bit Lacewell's vegetarian lasagna or Kittybelle Powell's ever-popular tuna and cheese tetrazzini out of Styrofoam boxes. The last hungry contingent then put down their picket signs and headed for the refreshment tables, while the group that had eaten first interrupted their ongoing bridge games behind the lines and resumed duties on the picket line. Megita had the rotation orchestrated perfectly and presided over all of it with her usual ponderous smugness.

"That's it, girls. You're doing just beautifully," she said, though she herself had yet to pick up a sign and put her own sneakers to the test.

Her second-in-command, the fawning and obsequious Vera Jean Cappelle, had just put the finishing touches on a couple of new signs and presented them to her leader for final approval. "How about these?" she said, her shoulders slumped in submission.

Megita scanned them quickly. NO RING, NO DATE, NO REASON TO CELEBRATE, one said. REAL LIFE MEANS REAL RESPONSIBILITY, MISS CADBURY! another declared. HOLLYWOOD MORALITY DOESN'T FLY IN FORT ROSALIE! yet a third offered. "These will do," she said.

Vera Jean hunched herself over even further. "Are you sure? You sound disappointed."

"They'll do, Vera Jean, they'll do. Don't make such a fuss. Go hand them out."

Megita watched as the new signs were switched out for some of the ones they had used yesterday. Then she checked her watch. Twelve-thirty. The procession ought to be heading their way any time now, and she could hardly wait, intent on erasing any trace of comfortable feelings that outrageous actress and her boyfriend might have after twenty-four hours of being stroked and catered to at Betterslie.

Vera Jean returned, inadvertently interrupting her leader's delicious machinations. "Have you eaten yet, Megita?"

"Of course. I ate with the first group," Megita said, eyeing her favorite lap dog shrewdly. Perhaps it wouldn't hurt to pet her just a bit for being such a good and loyal girl. "Thank you for asking about me, Vera Jean. I appreciate all your efforts out here on the front line."

Vera Jean's slack posture vanished, her smile so wide it bordered on the pathetic. "Oh, it's my pleasure. Why, this is the most fun any of us have had in ages, I think." Then her smile disappeared as quickly as it had arrived. "You know what I don't understand? How Poco McGill could refuse to participate in this! She was the only one on the entire Committee, too. She has no idea what she's missing."

Megita's eyes narrowed to slits. "That's just as well, Vera Jean. Poco has always been somewhat of a thorn in my side, you know. Always raising her hand and objecting to this and protesting that. I'm just as pleased she's not out here on the picket line with us. She'd be constantly running her mouth about something."

"That's true. Everyone on the Committee thinks of her as some sort of grinch."

Megita made a disdainful, snorting noise and heaved her generous chest. "I can think of other words to describe her, but since we are in polite society, I won't dare speak them out loud. Suffice it to say, Poco and I have been rivals since we were girls, and she has never gotten over the fact that I have everything she wants—family, status in the community, and so forth. It's a shame in a way—our mothers were such good friends."

Vera Jean made a clucking noise and shook her head. "Sometimes I don't understand why she just doesn't resign from the Committee."

"That," Megita said with a triumphant gleam in her eye, "is something devoutly to be wished."

Vera Jean suddenly squinted, pointing a finger excitedly at the winding road in the distance. "I just saw a blue light flashing. They're heading this way."

Megita blew her whistle a couple of times, and all activity came to an abrupt halt. "All right, girls, they'll soon be upon us. Let's all hold up those signs high and march proudly while they pass. Remember—you are taking a stand for our beloved Deep South and for decency and morality. You are doing a responsible thing here. The Casserole Patrol will win the day!"

The picketing resumed just before the lead patrol car passed through the gates. But the rest of the procession could not follow suit when the stretch limo lurched to a halt, and Juliette Cadbury erupted from the back seat, storming her way over to the picketers with her right hand raised high above her head. Tim, Mary Dell and Harris quickly emerged in pur-

suit, but it was too late to prevent a confrontation.

Megita moved forward, positioning herself between the picketers and the irate actress. "So we meet at last, Miss Cadbury. But why do you have your hand in the air like that?"

"To prove that it's just as your sign says," Juliette replied. "No ring, no date. My finger is bare. I'm not engaged to be married, but what business is it of yours? What the hell difference can it possibly make to you and all these ridiculous women? Are your lives so empty that you have nothing better to do than worry and fret about my marital status?"

Tim caught up with her and grabbed her arm, trying to pull her away. "Please, Jule. This won't help one bit."

But Juliette shook him off and stood her ground. "Answer me, whatever your name is. Answer me!"

Megita drew herself up imperiously. "My name is Megita Pulliam Larose, and I believe your marital status is our business when you trot out your views on illegitimacy as if they were the holy gospel. You Hollywood types seem to think you answer to no one and that everyone should cater to you just because you have a great deal of money to throw around. Well, we're here to take a stand. We'll be here every day of your stay, and we intend to give you a grand sendoff on Monday with a rally in front of the Tourist Bureau. Furthermore, should you elect to return to our town to actually make this horrible movie, we will resume our protests then as well."

Juliette's eyes were burning with rage. "I see you're a fan of those ridiculous tabloids. Tell me, is that the level of the reading material here in the famous Fort Rosalie?"

"You can insult us all you like," Megita replied. "But it will not deter us from our mission. Oh, by the way, when you settle in at Plum Cottage shortly, we'll have a little surprise for you."

Harris stepped in between them with his sternest expression. "Please, everyone. This kind of confrontation isn't going to accomplish anything. We have a schedule to keep. We really don't have time for this. Let's return to our cars."

Tim forcibly pointed Juliette in the opposite direction. "He's right, Jule. Let's go. Now."

Megita and Harris exchanged glances, but neither said anything as he retreated to his Buick with Mary Dell.

"We'll see all of you soon at Plum Cottage," Megita called out, clearly pleased with herself. "And thanks for dropping by."

Robert Dalby
Chapter Ten

Betterslie's front gates and the protests of the Casserole Patrol had receded from view for a good five minutes, but Juliette was still fuming in the back seat of the limo.

"I don't think I want to continue with this," she was saying. "Not if I have to put up with a steady diet of those meddling, vicious old hens."

"But why couldn't you have just stayed in the limo and ignored them?" Tim said. "Why did you have to jump out and confront them like that? You played right into their hands."

"Whose side are you on, anyway?"

"I'm on your side, of course. Or our side, I should say. We're in this together, although you don't seem to realize it half the time."

She turned and studied his face closely, surprised at the conviction in his voice. "What's that supposed to mean?"

"Nothing," he said. "I'm sorry I said it. What I really meant to say is that you've come all this way and gone to all this trouble for the project, and if you really believe in it the way you say you do, you can't let these foolish biddies shake you up. Hey, we've endured far worse than this at the hands of the press. You can't call this off right in the middle of it and let them win, can you?"

She considered carefully, letting the adrenaline in her blood subside a little, and then took a couple of deep breaths. "You're right. I can't let them get the best of me. All right, then. I'll try to get my mind on other things." She glanced across at Heidi. "Give me the inside info again on our next stop."

Heidi quickly shuffled papers and read from the clipboard.

"Pierce Cottage, or Plum Cottage as it is more popularly known, was built in 1878 by Jeshuah Pierce, a descendant of one of the pioneer families of Fort Rosalie, as a wedding present for his daughter, Mary Amelia. It is one of several houses built over the years by the Pierce family but is the only one still in the hands of one of the descendants, Miss Aimee Lorena Pierce, great-granddaughter of the original builder. The name, Plum Cottage, was informally given to the residence when the present owner decided to decorate the interior in various shades of purple, to the virtual exclusion of other colors—" She broke off, her voice catching in her throat and moisture welling in the corners of her eyes.

"What's the matter sweetie?" Juliette said, reaching across and grasping her hand.

Heidi let a couple of tears fall, then quickly smeared them across her cheeks. "I'm sorry. I didn't mean to make a scene, particularly after what you've just been through. It's just that Edding invited me to have dinner with him tonight at Betterslie, and I told him no, I had duties to attend to for you at Plum Cottage. It wouldn't be fair to abandon you at this point."

Juliette's mood lightened instantly. "You think we can't get along without you and your clipboard for one evening?"

Mutual laughter broke the tension, and Heidi said: "But what else could I tell him? It's my job. It's what I do. I can't appear to be playing favorites, can I?"

"You really want to be with him tonight?"

"More than anything."

"Then you're excused from your usual scribbling and kibitzing at Plum Cottage. Don't forget that Mary Dell and Harris will still be around. We'll have the chauffeur drive you back to Betterslie later on after we've gotten settled."

The two women managed to stretch forward just enough for

a brief hug, and Juliette was feeling better about things by the second. The ugly emotions produced by the confrontation with the Casserole Patrol were fading fast, replaced by her genuine fascination with the sudden emergence of Heidi's lovelife. It was Hollywood cute, that's what it was. Perhaps the proverbial happy ending in the works.

Juliette settled back in her seat and tried to focus on Plum Cottage. Then she remembered. That mean, bosomy woman had promised a little surprise when they arrived. What was that all about?

Mary Dell and Harris pulled up in front of Plum Cottage and sat in worried silence waiting for the stretch limo and the rear patrol car to arrive momentarily. Onlookers had somehow gotten wind of the itinerary and had already been cordoned off further down South Vidal Street, for once the Casserole Patrol had rolled in and set up shop, the sleepy little dead-end would be transformed into a full-fledged curbside asylum.

"We can't afford many more confrontations like the one at Betterslie," Mary Dell said, craning her neck for signs of Megita's troops.

Harris was checking the rear-view mirror. "That was pretty hairy. Megita at her worst."

"Frankly, I wouldn't blame Juliette for leaving town."

"Or at the very least asking that the production be moved," Harris added. "But if she doesn't bring up the subject, we won't either. Maybe we can tiptoe around and get through this."

The Casserole Patrol had not yet arrived when Miss Aimee came out onto her front porch and gestured to her guests just as the chauffeur finished parking the limo. "Come in, come

in," she called out. "We're waiting for you."

Plump little Tasmania Evans followed her out for the perfunctory introductions, and soon the Hollywood trio had been shown to their rooms to freshen up, while Mary Dell and Harris sat in the deep purple front parlor, sipping coffee and bringing Miss Aimee up to speed on the activities of the Casserole Patrol.

"Oh, dear," said Miss Aimee. "Megita certainly is feeling her oats these days, isn't she?"

"Another phrase connected with the horse comes to mind," Harris replied, and they all had a good chuckle.

Miss Aimee pointed to a large plate of finger sandwiches and deviled eggs on the coffee table before them. "A little bite or two to tide you over until our dinner tonight? Tasmania and I have something truly special planned behind those dining room doors across the hall. Now, mind you, no peeking before the appointed hour."

Mary Dell took a sandwich and marveled at the way Miss Aimee was able to slip in and out of that mental hoopskirt of hers. She was already playing it to the hilt, modulating her voice so that it alternated between endearing and tremulous, little ol' lady and faded Southern belle. Subtle distinctions all, to be sure, but it was the dependably good Southern theater Miss Aimee had promised her on her visit.

Unfortunately, Juliette, Tim and Heidi had no sooner emerged from their rooms to enjoy Miss Aimee's performance than Megita's troops finally took up their posts on the sidewalk across the street, loudly chanting the phrase, "Go home, Hollywood!"

Mary Dell winced. This was the venue that she and Harris had worried most about because of its proximity to Plum Cottage, well within earshot of the inhabitants, and Juliette moved quickly to one of the windows to take it all in.

"Our persecutors are back with their witch trial sentiments," she said, parting the lace curtain beneath the purple portieres and then turning away with a look of disgust. "I'm just curious, Miss Aimee. Just what is your personal opinion of these women and their self-righteous activism? It definitely reminds me of one of Byron Cathcart's observations—namely that the Deep South is nothing more than a matriarchy run amok."

Mary Dell caught Miss Aimee's eye, seeking to glide silent guidance across the space between them. 'Proceed with caution, please,' was the message of the moment her face conveyed.

"I'm so sorry you're having to endure this, Miss Cadbury. But please don't misunderstand. Megita Larose and her Historic Preservation Committee have certainly done wonders saving our heritage for posterity. They've stood up to and backed down many a greedy businessman who wanted to turn this antebellum mansion or that venerable block of houses into an ugly parking garage or tacky convenience store. That's how Megita amassed all her power over the years. But she's definitely off on a tangent now with these protests, and I've reached the conclusion she's doing it simply because she knows she can. There are some people who simply cannot handle power well, and Megita is one of them."

"I can certainly agree with that, and in a roundabout way, you've just confirmed Cathcart's observations," Juliette replied, peering out at the picketers again. Suddenly, she lost her composure. "Sweet Jesus! That's just we need now!"

Mary Dell joined her at the window, hoping to take control of the situation, but her heart sank when she saw what had Juliette so ticked off. A television crew had just arrived upon the scene. "It's Channel 12 from Jackson," Mary Dell explained.

O Bed! O Breakfast!

The anger Juliette had exhibited at Betterslie's front gates was clearly visible in her face once again. "So now we're going to have electronic media coverage of this garbage to boot. Do you really expect me to be able to relax and enjoy the rest of this weekend, Mary Dell?"

"But that TV crew won't be allowed anywhere near you."

"So you say." Then things went from bad to worse. "This is just too much. I think it's time we talked about that alternative location, don't you? Do you have any idea what a media zoo this town will be if the press-at-large gets hold of this?"

Harris stepped up quickly. "There's no need to take such drastic action yet. The Tourist Bureau will do everything it can to convince the ladies to back off."

"You really expect them to give up their fifteen minutes of fame?"

"If you like, Mary Dell and I will be happy to go out there right now and talk turkey to that TV crew," Harris replied. "They can suck up to Megita and her people all they want, but that'll be the extent of it. We'll definitely see to it that they don't bother you."

"Please, dear," Miss Aimee added. "Don't you worry about all that nonsense going on out there. Won't you sit down and have some tea and sandwiches?"

"Yeah, Jule," Tim said. "Let's just relax and soak in some of this wicked purple all over the walls. Can't explain why, but it's definitely giving me all kinds of devilish ideas for later on tonight."

Mary Dell and Harris headed across the street, leaving Juliette in Miss Aimee's capable, soothing hands. Halfway there, Mary Dell said: "I'm getting the distinct impression we're not going to make it through the weekend. Natchez keeps flashing on and off in my head like one of those neon signs on a fleabag hotel."

Harris kept his eyes on the TV crew, talking out of the side of his mouth. "Yep. Jim Horvath will absolutely despise any kind of TV coverage. Especially since the last thing I told him was that we more or less had this thing under control."

The first person to greet them was Megita, her tone more arrogant than ever. "Well, well, well. How do you like my little surprise, Harris?"

"How did you manage this communications coup?"

"Just one of those twists of fate, I suppose. My nephew took over as Channel 12's news director six months ago, so naturally I gave him a little call about all this. Voila! Instant news coverage! And if you and your assistant have come over to get in your two cents with the TV crew, you'll have to stand in line. Vera Jean Cappelle is going to be interviewed first, and then myself."

Harris huddled with Mary Dell for a few moments, and then introduced himself to the clean-cut male reporter who was pinning a lavaliere mike on Vera Jean's lapel. The two shook hands, and then Harris laid down the law. "The Tourist Bureau does not endorse these activities and is not interested in being interviewed officially on this matter, but I would appreciate your mentioning that Ms. Cadbury and Mr. Reynaldo are our guests for the weekend as they review our bed-and-breakfast facilities for their upcoming film. They will also be unavailable for any interviews, and we absolutely insist that you keep your distance and make no attempt to harass them in any way."

Mary Dell applauded politely, noting that the reporter suddenly looked like a freshly-scolded puppy, eyes drooping and wounded.

"Oh, no sir," the young man said. "We wouldn't do anything like that. The police over there have already warned us to stay over here on the sidewalk. We're just here to get the story from the Historic Preservation Committee angle, that's all."

Then it was time for the first interview, and Mary Dell could hardly believe her ears, soaking up every bizarre word with her mouth agape.

"We call that group of ladies seated at those card tables and those on the picket line as well, the Casserole Patrol," Vera Jean began. "We alternate who walks the picket line in sensible shoes and who dispenses these delicious lunches in the Styrofoam boxes. They contain our most outstanding casserole recipes from the *Old Fort Rosalie Cookbook*, which we have on sale at the Founders' Club and all upscale bookstores in the area. You can get their numbers from directory if you don't know who they are. Yesterday, for instance, the Casserole Patrol served up my shrimp and wild rice along with Mattie Lou Buskirk's turkey spaghetti. She uses that instead of the chicken because we all have to watch our cholesterol. You know, we even put out a low-fat version of our cookbook because so many of our husbands have heart problems. A few of us girls do, too. We never used to worry about that sort of thing, of course. In the old days it was butter in this, butter in that, butter 'til the cows came home. Oh, I think I may have made a joke!" On and on she went, wandering in and out of relevance with oblivious ease.

"Well, that was certainly a hard-hitting piece of news," Mary Dell said to Harris. "I've had about as much as I can stand. Let's head back."

Megita called out after them as they turned away. "Going so soon?"

"We've heard more than enough," Mary Dell replied over her shoulder.

"Now you be sure and tune in Channel 12 tonight around ten o'clock to hear what I have to say. I know you don't want

to miss it."

They kept on walking, shaking their heads, and Mary Dell said: "This thing with the Casserole Patrol has taken on a life of its own. It just might do us in."

Fortunately, things had calmed down somewhat back at Plum Cottage, and they found Miss Aimee sipping tea all by herself in the parlor.

"That was a close call," she said, motioning Mary Dell and Harris to join her.

"What happened after we left?" Mary Dell said.

"Well, that strapping young man, Tim, convinced Miss Cadbury to retire to their room for a little rest, if you care to read between the lines." She paused to bat her eyelashes coyly. "And that nice little secretary said something about going to her room to prepare for her evening out. Isn't she going to be joining us?"

Mary Dell explained Heidi's blossoming relationship with Edding and then added: "I've been thinking. And I've decided that we need your best Southern anecdotes more than ever tonight at the dinner table, Miss Aimee. Oscar-winning Southern theater, so to speak. It'll help take Juliette's mind off all the provocation she's endured today. We need to do everything we can to keep things light and airy."

"Oh, I'm right there with you, dear. I'll start off with the drive-up banking tale and move on to the sausages on the ceiling story. Later on during their stay, I may trot out paraphernalia from my reign as Queen of the 1937 Azalea Festival."

"Perfect," Mary Dell replied. "Weave that delicate purple web of yours, and we'll be just fine."

Over cocktails in the parlor a few hours later, Juliette had

O Bed! O Breakfast!

almost forgotten the day's altercations. Outside, the Casserole Patrol had called it quits for the day, and the romantic little nap she and Tim had taken had done wonders for her disposition. Dressed to the teeth in a shimmering, royal blue Vera Wang and her gorgeous hair piled elegantly atop her head, she was an Oscar-night vision playing to the adoring fans in the stands and the many media types stationed along the red carpet.

"I have to confess I don't actually own all these gowns—just one or two," she was saying to Mary Dell, treating her exactly like she was Joan Rivers on fashion assignment for cable-TV. "But I'm sure you've heard that the designers will let you borrow them at the drop of a hat for the publicity."

"I'd be so nervous entrusted with an exquisite gown like that," Mary Dell replied. "I'd be worried to death I'd spill something on it or snag it someplace."

"Oh, you get past all that, although I have to admit the expectations and trappings of this profession can sometimes weigh you down."

Tim stepped up in his tux, handing Juliette a fresh glass of wine. "What she really means is you just can't throw on your housecoat and run to the 7-11 for Oreos whenever you feel like it."

Miss Aimee moved to the center of the room and rang her dainty purple dinner bell. "Ladies and gentlemen, I believe it's time we all headed in to eat. I always say there's nothing like good food to bring people together. So shall we?"

Tasmania appeared in the hallway and indicated the door to the dining room that had been so jealously guarded all afternoon. When it was finally opened and everyone had entered to a chorus of oohs and ahs, Miss Aimee rang her bell again and said: "Miss Cadbury, Mr. Reynaldo, this is my interpretation of Plum Cottage as the centerpiece of your visit

here in Fort Rosalie."

Indeed, it was a literal one. She had put all her time and energy into what might have been nominated for the centerpiece of the ages. It consisted primarily of a miniature replica of Plum Cottage, about the size of a large dollhouse, with a copy of *Whispering Dixie* propped up against one wall. Surrounding that was a circle of lavender flowers of every description set in small bowls of water—orchids, lilies, pansies, mums, violets, even tulips and roses—if they came in some shade of purple or could be dyed that way, they were all part of the presentation. Completing the ensemble were a number of purple votive candles placed strategically around the room, each one delicately flickering and releasing a hint of incense into the mild evening air flowing in through the open windows.

Juliette slowly circled the table as if in a trance. "You went to this much fuss for us, Miss Aimee? Why, the workmanship on that little house is just fabulous!"

Miss Aimee fanned her face coyly with her fingers. "Oh, I mustn't fib to you, dear. Tasmania and I did put everything together, but the dollhouse was made years and years ago for all my little nieces. I wanted them to have something to play with when they visited me. You will admit, though, it certainly came in handy for this arrangement."

"It's utterly adorable. These little Fort Rosalie eccentricities and sidelights are charming beyond belief."

"Thank you, dear. I'll share more sidelights with you over dinner," Miss Aimee replied, moving to the head of the table. "So everyone please take your seat, and Tasmania will serve our first course."

Soon, they were all sampling Tasmania's cold tomato and cucumber soup out of Old Paris bowls, and Miss Aimee began her story-telling in earnest. "Fort Rosalie is nothing if not eccentric. Why, the Pierce family, itself, is a living, breathing encyclopedia of eccentricity. They say my Aunt Chlotilde inadvertently invented drive-up banking back in the 30's. She would get in her car and drive up right in front of the Bank of Fort Rosalie, stop in the middle of the street and honk the horn. While traffic backed up for blocks, some poor teller would rush out, grab her deposit, rush back in with it and return all out of breath with her deposit slip. Of course, she had so much money in the bank and was such a scion of Fort Rosalie society that both the bank and the police let her get away with it. Mind you, that was long before anyone had ever thought of actual drive-up banking, but I wouldn't be at all surprised if Aunt Chlotilde's antics were the inspiration years later for the procedure."

When the laughter around the table had subsided, Juliette said: "Now that's the kind of Southern character everyone wants to see portrayed on film. I wonder if there's a way I could get Byron to work something like that into the *Whispering Dixie* script."

"You'd have my permission, dear," Miss Aimee replied. "Oh, and there was one more thing about Aunt Chlotilde. She only made up the left side of her face whenever she drove up to the bank. Powder and rouge on the left cheek, lipstick only to the center of the mouth. Finally, someone got up the gumption to ask her why she did it, and her reply has to be the essence of Fort Rosalie eccentricity: 'Because the teller only comes up to the driver's side, I look straight ahead, and he never sees the right side of my face. No need to waste good makeup, you know.'"

"I love it!" Juliette proclaimed. "Tell us some more."

"Well, there's no more about Aunt Chlotilde, but I do have an unusual tale that involves myself and my sisters. It happened to me as a teenaged girl. My parents had gone out for the evening and left me in charge of babysitting my younger sisters as usual. Well, a girlfriend of mine telephoned, and I got caught up in our conversation. Back then in this part of the South, even having a telephone was still sort of a novelty. Meanwhile, my little sisters had disappeared into the kitchen, and I suppose I should have suspected they were up to something when things got awfully quiet. All I could hear from my vantage point on the telephone out in the hallway was an occasional giggle and a strange thudding noise every now and then. They're pushing each other down or something, I thought. But as I would discover later on to my utter horror, they had gone into the icebox and pulled out a big bowl of freshly-made sausage mix that Mama had just made up. Those little monsters had rolled the mix into scores of little balls and thrown them up on the ceiling just to see if they would stick, they explained to me. Let me assure you that every one of those horrid little balls did stick, and I got stuck with having to climb up a ladder and clean them all off after my parents got home. Needless to say, I never let my sisters out of my sight again whenever I drew babysitting duty."

Juliette was beginning to feel much better about Fort Rosalie now. The funny stories were working their magic for her, and the getaway weekend she had hoped for was beginning to materialize. Tasmania's good cooking—which consisted of fried chicken, rice with Vidalia onion gravy, corn on the cob and yeast rolls—added yet another layer of comfort. By the time dessert arrived, Juliette felt as if she had grown up in Plum Cottage.

"Ah! Pecan pie!" she exclaimed as Tasmania served her piece. "Another thousand calories for my Rella Darrow!"

When Tasmania put Tim's piece in front of him, he whispered something to her as she leaned down, and she said: "No, indeed, I won't forget, Mr. Reynaldo."

O Bed! O Breakfast!

"You and Tasmania keeping secrets?" Miss Aimee said, perking up at the exchange. "How very interesting."

"Yes, what are you up to, Tim?" Juliette added.

Tim offered one of his smirks but said nothing, and Tasmania exited shaking her head and chuckling to herself.

After dinner Miss Aimee led the way out into the hall and gave the gathering a formal tour of her celebrity gallery—a row of framed and autographed photos that had been given to her by her most famous guests.

"I think I had the most fun ever when Elizabeth Taylor stayed with me for *Raintree County*," she began. "I let her have both rooms, and she used the other one mostly for trying on costumes and asking me what I thought. She ended up letting me keep one of those beautiful antebellum skirts. I think it was the one she wore in all the scenes where she was supposed to be insane."

"Do you still have it?" Juliette said.

"Oh, yes. It's in one of my closets somewhere. Perhaps I can dig it up for you before you leave."

"That would be fabulous. Now, tell us about John Wayne over here," Juliette continued, pointing to a photo further down the lineup. "Did he actually kill that deer in the picture?"

"Indeed, he did. My cousin Hyde took him hunting one morning at his Buckhurst camp near the river, and John Wayne bagged a big buck that very day. He was very generous with the venison, too. I think everyone in the family had enough to last us for two years."

"Mucho venison from the king of macho and a period costume from an insane actress for your trouble," Juliette said, cracking a smile. "What an intriguing life you must lead as a bed-and-breakfast owner!"

"It has its drawbacks, though. It still takes money to run

one of these warm, fuzzy nests," Miss Aimee added. "And hosting you for three months would be a very welcome and very profitable pleasure for me, I can assure you."

Juliette took her hand warmly. "And I can assure you I'll give you serious consideration."

"What say we give serious consideration to retiring a little early, Jule?" Tim proposed. "It's been another long, ragged day."

Before Juliette could answer, Miss Aimee spoke up with a discernible twinkle in her eye. "Oh, yes. You young people need your rest. Go and relax and enjoy yourselves."

The evening quickly wound down. Mary Dell and Harris headed out following their prolific praise of the company and the cuisine, and Juliette found herself being steered very energetically to the bedroom by her mischievous-looking lover, while wondering once again what on earth had come over the man.

"I have a big surprise for you, Jule," Tim said, maneuvering her carefully to their bedroom closet and helping her with the Vera Wang and her undergarments. Then he sat her up straight on the edge of their big brass bed and did a slow strip tease with his tux. "We are gonna indulge in some deep purple tonight. No, not the kind that falls over sleepy garden walls, but the X-rated variety."

"What the hell are you talking about?" she said, falling back onto the purple quilt with her arms outstretched. "Umm! This feels so cool and sensual to the touch. I could stay just like this forever and not move a muscle."

"That's not exactly what I had in mind. Not by a long shot. I have other plans for you." Down to his underwear now, Tim

O Bed! O Breakfast!

bounded over to a small chifforobe in a corner of the room and opened the top drawer. "This is what I'm talking about, my precious Jule." He pulled out a jar of grape jelly and made an exaggerated display of it the way spokesmodels on TV game shows frequently do. "I had Tasmania bring this in from the kitchen for me. I just couldn't help it—it's all this purple decor that's done it to my primitive male brain."

Juliette sat up again, looking wary but amused. "And what does your primitive male brain intend to do with that jar of grape jelly?"

He shimmied out of his briefs, hooking them on his big toe and kicking them across the room, and then stood proudly naked before her. "I'm going to smear it all over your beautiful breasts and then lick both of them clean. And I do mean spotless, girl."

"You wicked, wicked little boy," she said, her face twisted into a smile. "I cannot believe you sometimes."

"You'd better believe me," he said. "Because I'm for real, and I'm for you."

Then he went to work, slathering her with jelly while she squirmed in anticipatory delight atop the quilt. It was when he diligently began to remove every trace of his mischievous scheme with his ravenous tongue that he sensed her shifting into high gear, and the lovemaking that followed was some of the best they had ever made. All she could come up with was the word 'wicked,' which she repeated breathlessly and quite often.

In the afterglow Tim stroked her hair while chuckling softly to himself. "Good move Heidi made spending the evening out at Betterslie with Edding. She wouldn't get much sleep tonight being right next door to us."

"Grape jelly," Juliette replied, shaking her head. "I still think you're up to something."

Across town in her apartment Mary Dell was sitting on the sofa with Harris, discussing the approach of the ten o'clock news on Channel 12. "Maybe they'll decide not to run it. Or maybe the TV crew had an accident on the way back to Jackson, and the footage never arrived." She picked up the remote, clicked the TV on and activated the mute button.

"What we need right now is for some honest-to-God luck to come our way," Harris replied, sipping the coffee she'd just made for them. "But then, I'm not sure I've ever really believed in luck. Do you?"

She put down her cup and gazed steadily into his eyes. "Call it luck, call it coincidence, but, no, I don't believe in it, either. I'm convinced nothing of any real importance that happens to us is an accident. Even the most horrendous things probably have a purpose we're meant to deal with and work through. I've never thought luck had anything substantial to do with my life. It's the intersection and interaction with all the other souls out there that drives everything. All our different agendas mixing and crisscrossing for better or worse, if you will. That's what makes life interesting—not necessarily fair—but interesting. Because it means we can't walk away from the blows by blaming our luck or claiming we had no input or responsibility. In a way, we're all of us responsible for everything that happens to us."

Harris quickly surveyed the room, coming to rest on the dachshund toy next to Mary Dell. "You're quite the philosopher, aren't you? The contrast is kind of amusing, though."

"What do you mean?"

"I mean stuffed animals and serious discourse. They ordinarily don't go together, but somehow you make it all work.

O Bed! O Breakfast!

You make a great deal of sense."

Mary Dell picked up Rosalie and stroked the toy tenderly. "I appreciate that. And I fully intend to get a real dachshund some day. The two of us will become the gist of one of those eccentric Fort Rosalie tales like the ones Miss Aimee was spinning for us tonight. My flesh and blood Rosalie and I will go for our walk together every morning, and people will say, 'There they go—the Tourist Bureau spinster and her trusty little doggie.'"

Harris looked genuinely surprised. "To borrow your philosophy for a second—you don't really think you'll end up a spinster, do you? You don't see a possible intersection and interaction between the two of us just around the corner?"

Well, there it was again. The Mr. and Mrs. Tourist Bureau thing. Mary Dell considered carefully and said: "Yes, I do see a possible intersection and interaction. Some people refer to that as a commitment, and you and I have to sit down once and for all and decide whether that's where we both want to go."

Before either of them could say anything further, the cleancut reporter who'd handled the Fort Rosalie assignment popped up on the tube, stationed in front of the Casserole Patrol on South Vidal Street, so Mary Dell quickly restored the sound. Channel 12 had at least exercised good judgment in editing out all of Vera Jean's rambling testimonial to society food preparation and had gone straight to the heart of the matter with Megita's interview. Harris sat up straight and stiffened, and Mary Dell gently slipped her hand into his in a show of solidarity as the piece began.

"Is this protest an official function of the Historic Preservation Committee, Mrs. Larose?" the reporter was saying.

Megita leaned into the camera with a lizard-like grin. "No,

it is not. I have simply rounded up our members as private citizens. This is America, and we have every right to assemble and protest, according to the Constitution."

"And what is it you hope to accomplish by this protest?" the reporter continued.

"A greater awareness of morality on the part of the public is what we're after here. So many of these Hollywood stars seem to think the rest of America should applaud their lifestyle choices, no matter how outlandish. They apparently feel that simply because they make millions of dollars in the movie business, they are role-models we should emulate. Miss Cadbury and Mr. Reynaldo have paraded around the country airing their views on living together and having children without benefit of marriage and think there are no consequences to their actions. Everything you do in life, no matter how small, affects somebody in some way. We have just decided, and peacefully I might add, to take a stand in telling Miss Cadbury and Mr. Reynaldo that not everybody welcomes them with open arms here in Fort Rosalie just because they're bringing in huge wads of their Hollywood money."

The reporter then faced the camera for the close. "Harris Lyles, the director of Fort Rosalie's Tourist Bureau, indicated that neither Juliette Cadbury nor Tim Reynaldo would have any comments on the protests. He also made it clear that the views of the Historic Preservation Committee in no way represent those of the Tourist Bureau, which is officially hosting the couple this weekend on a tour of bed-and-breakfast accommodations for the projected filming of *Whispering Dixie* later this year. For Channel 12 News, I'm Brad Watkinson."

Mary Dell shook her head and clicked off the TV. "Well, the cat's out of the bag now."

Harris had worked his mouth into a grim slit. "Ten to one, Horvath will have left a diatribe for me on my answering machine when I get home."

"Maybe he'll have missed it."

"Not likely. But if he does, one of his many lackeys will catch it and call him up. It's inevitable. God, I dread going home to that message."

On an impulse Mary Dell decided to take the plunge, stroking his hand tenderly. "Then stay here tonight. You and I can explore the finer points of the Mr. and Mrs. Tourist Bureau issue."

He took a deep breath, leaned in and kissed her warmly. "I'd like that. Up to now it seems one or the other of us wasn't quite ready. But that philosophy of yours hits the spot. Tonight will be our intersection."

The phone rang, startling them both, and Mary Dell made a face, irritated by the interruption. "You don't think Jim Horvath could possibly track you down here, do you?"

"No way," Harris said, shaking his head emphatically. "He knows nothing about my private life. Go ahead and answer it if you want."

She rose, walked over to the kitchen counter and lifted the receiver with one eye closed and the other eyebrow arched apprehensively. "Hello?"

"Is this Miss Hoskins?" said a thin, nervous voice at the other end.

"Yes, it is. Who is this?"

"My name is Poco McGill, and I don't believe we've ever met. But after that TV coverage I just endured, I think we should get together as soon as possible. I believe I can help you shut down Megita Larose and that ludicrous Casserole Patrol protest. Are you interested in hearing what I have to say? I assure you, it won't be a waste of your time."

"I'd be very, very interested in hearing what you have to say," Mary Dell answered, her body gripped by an immediate adrenaline rush. "When do you want to meet?"

There was a pause, and then Poco said: "How about your office at the Tourist Bureau? Say, eight o'clock in the morning?"

Mary Dell thought on her feet. She could squeeze it in without too much trouble. She and Harris weren't expected at Plum Cottage for breakfast until nine. "Eight it is. Just come to the front door. It'll be unlocked. And thank you very much." She hung up the phone, making a fist for emphasis as she said, "Yes!"

Harris got to his feet. "I take it that wasn't Horvath. So who was it, and what was that all about?"

She rushed over and embraced him with enthusiasm before relating the conversation. "It seems someone's crisscrossing agenda has entered the picture on our behalf," she added at the end.

"Amazing! A demonstration of your marvelous philosophy of life already. I am truly impressed!"

Then they sat down on the sofa again, and she took a deep breath. "Now, where were we? Oh yes, you were going to stay the night, and we were going to work through this Mr. and Mrs. Tourist Bureau business."

"I'm ready," he replied, taking her into his arms. "I think we're both overdue."

O Bed! O Breakfast!

Chapter Eleven

Mary Dell sat by herself in the foyer of the Tourist Bureau anxiously awaiting her eight o'clock appointment with Poco McGill. The silence and emptiness in such a normally hectic place of business was somewhat distracting to her, but she had her very own newly-edited replay of last night's lovemaking with Harris to occupy her time. Their session in bed had been everything she had expected, and he had ended it on a reassuring note by telling her that he wanted to be with her for a long time to come. It had almost sounded like a proposal, but the traditional words never actually appeared. She had chosen not to press, preferring to relish the afterglow by snuggling up to him in kittenish fashion. Nonetheless, she had every reason to believe that a real engagement was well within her grasp.

On a somewhat sour note, however, Harris had decided to tempt fate and retrieve his phone messages while she brewed them some coffee the morning after. She had stood there at her kitchen counter with her arms folded, studying his face closely while he listened to the recording, and she didn't even have to be told the bad news when he finally hung up.

"It's Horvath, isn't it?" she had said.

Harris had grimaced with both eyes shut tightly. "He'll see to it that *Whispering Dixie* is moved to Natchez if we haven't disbanded these protests by tomorrow. I've never heard him so worked up and bent out of shape, screaming and hollering that I'd lied to him—which I more or less did, by the way. Our Poco McGill is going to have to be something on the order of a miracle worker for us." And with that he had headed home to shower and regroup for the breakfast at Plum Cottage.

Mary Dell glanced at the big Tourist Bureau clock mounted over the front door. Three more minutes to the appointment. Less than twenty-four hours before Fort Rosalie lost yet another prestigious booking to Natchez—unless Poco McGill delivered the goods.

The woman arrived precisely at eight, and Mary Dell kept her keen sense of disappointment under wraps as they introduced themselves. This scrawny, sad-faced matron with the fashion sense of an impoverished hausfrau hardly looked like someone who could help them out, but appearances could certainly be deceiving.

"I know what you're probably thinking," Poco began, after they had moved into one of the empty executive offices which sported a comfortable sofa. "I look like a cleaning woman. But I can assure you, I am a full-fledged member of the Historic Preservation Committee—one who will resign shortly after turning an important document over to you."

Mary Dell was intrigued, nodding eagerly. "Yes, your face is familiar to me now. Please go on."

"I should start by saying that I fancy myself the watchdog of the Committee. I grew up with Megita and the Pulliam family, and I've watched her change from an energetic, civic-minded go-getter into a snobbish ogre of the worst sort. Over the years I've been practically the only member of the Committee who has ever questioned anything she's ever done. Most people just bow down and let her have her way. I'm sure Vera Jean Cappelle would gladly be put into the coffin with Megita to keep her company when the time comes."

"I know what you mean," Mary Dell said, surprised by the touch of humor.

"Anyway, I think it's time someone put Megita Pulliam Larose in her place. Only it has to be done the right way. She has to be given the opportunity to do the right thing and save

face, otherwise it will look like Fort Rosalie is just airing its dirty laundry. I don't have to tell you what a field day those ladies in Natchez would have with that."

"You certainly don't."

Poco retrieved a yellowed envelope from her ragged purse and handed it over. "I've had the wherewithal to rein in Megita for many years now but have chosen to exercise restraint until now. Put succinctly, I've had enough, and the letter inside that envelope will give you an ace in the hole—not only now, but forever."

Mary Dell glanced down quickly at the return address:

Leona Pulliam
59 Winchester Street
Fort Rosalie, Miss

The letter was addressed to:

Emma McGill
310 River Avenue
Fort Rosalie, Miss.

"No zip codes," Mary Dell observed. "And a postmark from the 60's."

"It was delivered thirty-seven years ago, to be exact. It's a letter from Megita's mother, Leona, to my mother, Emma, who turned it over to me years later shortly before she died. Those two women were best friends and confidantes, quite unlike Megita and myself. My mother told me she wanted me to have the letter...in case I ever needed it."

"But why give it to me? Why don't you confront Megita yourself?'

Poco rolled her eyes and sniffled a couple of times. "I

thought about doing just that when I refused to participate in the protests initially, but I fell back once again on that sense of restraint my mother had instilled in me. Then I watched my cohorts from a distance yesterday at Plum Cottage so self-absorbed in their silly bridge games and daintily munching their gourmet casseroles and realized what a mockery Megita was making of the Committee and its legitimate mission. That lamentable interview last night on Channel 12 tore it for me."

Mary Dell ran her thumb and forefinger along the top of the envelope and said: "What made you call me instead of Harris?"

"I nearly did call him. But I've been very much aware of your work at the Tourist Bureau since you came here. Your name has come up time and again at Committee meetings—favorably so. After you've read the letter, you'll understand that it was really meant for a woman's eyes—how uncanny its contents really are, how they seem tailor-made for this current controversy. That aside, you and Harris and a great many people in Fort Rosalie who depend upon tourism and the Hollywood dollar for their livelihood are the real players in this. If the threat of exposure came from me, given the fierce rivalry between Megita and myself through the years, she'd interpret it as pure and personal vindictiveness. But if you, as a representative of a public institution, confront her with this revelation, she'll realize that you have no bone to pick with her. She'll have no choice but to exercise restraint for the first time in her life. Above all, she has that queenly reputation and family of hers to protect. I leave the details up to you, but I trust you'll do it up right."

Mary Dell made a soft whistling noise and cocked her head to one side. "God, I feel like I have the secret of the ages within my grasp."

Poco laughed and rose from the sofa. "No, it's nothing like

O Bed! O Breakfast!

that, but the letter may very well blow you away. I'm going to leave you in peace now, but I do suggest you make copies and keep the original in a safe deposit box as I have all these years. You'll want to make it clear to Megita that this document will always be hanging over her head. As for myself, I'm handing in my resignation to the Committee tomorrow. I know Megita and I certainly won't be able to work together after this."

They shook hands, and Mary Dell showed the woman to the front door while thanking her profusely for the help. Then, showing none of Poco's restraint, she yanked the letter out of the envelope and devoured its contents right there in the foyer. When she had finished minutes later, she was overcome by two distinct sensations: guilt for intruding upon such a private confession, and amazement that Poco and her mother had kept this bombshell under wraps all these years.

She staggered to a nearby chair and frowned, turning the letter over and over again in her head. Poco was right. She was going to have to handle Megita gingerly, giving her an out, if at all possible, but she had only a few hours to come up with the right approach. Eventually, she looked up at the big clock and saw that the breakfast hour at Plum Cottage was fast approaching. After making a copy of the letter, she tucked everything into her coat pocket, hurried to the front door, locked it behind her, and headed for South Vidal Street on foot.

A cold front had moved through during the night, lowering the temperature a good ten or twelve degrees, but Mary Dell liked the way the wind blowing against her face seemed to heighten her senses. By the time she had reached the police cordon and identified herself to the officer in charge, she had her plan to save the day completely worked out. The first baby step consisted of wading through the Casserole Patrol's sidewalk bridge tables and drawing Megita aside very discreetly.

"There's something very important I need to discuss with you tonight at the Founders' Club," she explained. "Could I come by after you've wound up your protests at Destiny Manor? Let's say nine or so, after I've finished dinner with the Lurkins?"

Megita looked indignant. "Why can't you say whatever you have to say here and now? I'm not one to play games, my girl."

Mary Dell steeled herself, refusing to let the condescension rattle her. "I'm not playing games, Mrs. Larose. You need to hear what I have to say. That is, if you value your status in this community."

Megita conjured up one of her laser beam stares and said: "That sounds very much like a threat to me. I don't care one bit for the tone of your voice."

"I mean no disrespect. But I do mean business."

"If this is something Harris has put you up to, I have no time for your tricks. I'm sure I'll be very tired tonight after a full day of protesting."

Mary Dell decided that she needed something short and sweet to pique the woman's interest, so she just blurted it out. "All right, then. I have a scoop for you. Poco McGill will be handing in her resignation to you on Monday morning. What I have to say revolves around that little tidbit, for starters."

The ploy seemed to work, and a sly expression crept into Megita's face. "Well, I must admit you've given me some welcome news. I've been trying to get that sourpuss out of my hair for years now."

"Then you'll see me around nine?"

"Very well. But please be brief, and please be punctual. I'll need my sleep for the big rally tomorrow morning."

Mary Dell thanked her, smiled politely and immediately switched gears in her head. Time to focus on Juliette, Tim, and Miss Aimee over Tasmania's delicious breakfast across

O Bed! O Breakfast!

the street. Lord, was she ever earning her salary today!

It had been musk the morning before, but on Sunday, Juliette awoke to the smell of grape jelly. She sat up and smiled at the squat little jar sitting impudently on the night table. It had doled out so much pleasure last night that she halfway expected it to give her a wolfwhistle. Tim had been nothing short of magnificent, leaving her limp and purring, every last drop drained from her. She reached over and grabbed the jar, noting to her amazement that there was still some jelly left in the bottom. Good, that would be excuse enough! She quickly threw on her robe, leaving her snoring prince behind, and headed for the kitchen for more research.

"I wanted to return this," she told Tasmania, after the two had exchanged greetings. "Although I don't recommend that you set it out on the breakfast table with the toast and English muffins this morning."

Tasmania took the jar and dropped it into the nearby trash can without batting an eyelash. "We got plenty more jelly in the cupboard." Then she returned to the stove where she was in the midst of poaching eggs.

"I appreciate your discretion, Tasmania."

"Oh, I don't axe questions around here," she replied. "I just deliver the goods." She paused to pour out a cup of coffee and hand it over to Juliette.

"Thanks. You don't mind me watching you fix breakfast, do you?"

"No, indeed. You free to roam all over and even poke around in the closets if you want. No skeletons in there, far as I know."

Juliette settled back in the breakfast nook with its delicate

lavender curtains at the window and decided to take a more oblique line of questioning than she had with Eola.

"Tell me a little about yourself and your family, Tasmania. Why don't you start with that fascinating name of yours?"

"Long story. You really that interested?"

"Of course I am."

Tasmania turned her back on the little pockets of steam rising from her eggs and began in earnest. "It was my daddy's idea is what it was. Daddy worked all his life here in Fort Rosalie on the barge line, but he had this idea 'bout movin' to Australia someday. My Mama said it was 'cause a' this man he worked with on the barges for a while, name a' Early Cottman, and he was always tellin' Daddy 'bout how good life was down there in Australia where he come from. 'We goin' down under to live with the kangaroos and ol' Early when I save up enough money,' Daddy was always sayin'. Then he sent off for brochures and maps and all like that, and he would read 'em in his spare time. When Mama got pregnant with me, he told her he wanted to name me in honor a' someplace in Australia, just in case he never got down there. Mama told me when I was old enough to understand that one day he just took the map and pointed to that little island off the coast. 'Tasmania I. Johnston!' he said. 'That's what we gonna call her.' 'Well, what's the I. stand for?' my Mama said. And Daddy said: 'I. is for Island, Tasmania Island!'"

Juliette burst out laughing, spewing coffee all over herself. "Oh, look at the mess I've made!"

"That's all right," Tasmania said, handing her a paper towel. "You not the first person that's laughed at that story. Never have used the I. in my name, though. Everybody just calls me Tasmania, 'cept my brother, Hobart. He calls me Tazzie. Daddy named him after the capital of Tasmania, you know. Oh, we quite a pair, me and my little brother—black

O Bed! O Breakfast!

folks livin' here in Fort Rosalie, Mississippi, with our Australian names. Don't know what kinda roots you can make outta that!"

Juliette was delighted with the unexpected twists and turns of the story. Then she remembered her objective. "Do you think your father thought he could find a better life in Australia because of the way things were in the South back then?"

"Never thought about it like that. Maybe it was in his head, maybe not. I do know he worked hard on the river all his life, made decent money and seemed to be fine with that. I never heard him complain about things, 'cept maybe when his back pain would act up. Guess some folks just have to have a crazy dream to keep 'em goin'. Maybe that was his way of keepin' his head on straight."

"So he never got to go to Australia?"

"Lived all his life here in Fort Rosalie right up until the day he died."

"And have either you or your brother gone down under?"

"No, that was Daddy's dream. My dream was to raise my kids right where I am now. My brother, Hobart, feel the same way, still livin' right here and workin' hard as a police officer." Tasmania moved to the kitchen window and pointed to the crowd across the street. "That's him over there right now, keepin' an eye on all that foolishness." Then she turned back to Juliette with a crestfallen expression on her plump little face. "Long as you in here with me like this, I got somethin' I'd like to tell you. Only please don't tell Miss Aimee I told you. This is just between you and me."

Juliette quickly crossed her heart. "No problem."

Tasmania moved back to the stove, quickly checked on her eggs and said: "If Miss Aimee don't win this competition, she flat gonna have to shut down Plum Cottage. She outta money,

plain and simple, so I hope you can find it in your heart to stay with us. Me and my husband make ends meet a whole lot easier with me workin' here all these years. It was always somethin' we could depend on, no matter what. But we could manage without it. Not Miss Aimee, though. I don't know what she'd do without playactin' for her guests all the time."

Juliette was in shock. "It's that serious a situation for her?"

"It's the God's honest truth. But, remember, please don't let on you know. Miss Aimee a very proud woman." Tasmania checked the cuckoo clock on the wall and promptly headed to the refrigerator. "Now, I got me some cantaloupe to cut up for breakfast, if you'll excuse me."

"And I better go get dressed and wake Tim up. It's almost nine."

Back in the bedroom, it took a while for Juliette to rouse her lover, but eventually she prevailed, watching him stagger about trying to dress himself while she rambled on about her recent expedition to the kitchen.

"I can't seem to get any meaty insights for *Whispering Dixie* from the servants or anybody else in this town. Everyone seems so supremely happy and satisfied with their lives. You'd think the Civil War and the civil rights movement were a piece of cake. The big thing that attracted me to this project was the opportunity to project and explore some of the pain the South carries around with it all the time."

Tim interrupted the tug-of-war he was having with his left sock and said: "I'm sure you could find lots of people down here who aren't happy with their lives if you just look in the right places. Hey, I know what Byron Cathcart believes, but maybe the reality is that a lot of people down here, both black and white, have chosen to move on instead of constantly agonizing over the mistakes of the past."

"But there's no conflict or tension in that."

"Not to mention controversy."

"What's wrong with controversy? It makes people think things through and examine their fundamental principles. That's all Byron has tried to do with *Whispering Dixie*," she said, moving to the bathroom mirror to put the finishing touches on her makeup.

A knock at the door prematurely ended their exchange. Tim quickly slipped into his shoes, tucked his shirt into his pants and opened the door to a flushed and breathless Heidi, back at last from her overnight at Betterslie.

"I need to talk to Juliette right away. In private," she said, brushing past him and quickly scanning the bedroom.

"She's in there," he replied, pointing to the bathroom. "And I'm outta here. See you two at breakfast in a few."

From the moment Heidi's reflection appeared in the mirror, Juliette could sense the urgency, and the two of them immediately went out and sat together on the edge of the brass bed, holding hands like girlfriends.

"Now, what's the matter, sweetie? Did something happen last night at Betterslie? I've never seen you so worked up before."

Heidi took a deep breath and swallowed hard. "You bet something happened. Edding actually asked me to marry him. And after I got over the shock, I actually accepted his proposal."

Juliette withdrew her hand, trying to comprehend the words, while the awkward silence brought a frown to Heidi's brow.

"Well, aren't you going to say anything?" Heidi finally asked.

More silence. Then Juliette realized she was creating a scene by refusing to make a fuss. "I'm—I'm overwhelmed. Congratulations, I guess."

"That hardly sounds like a ringing endorsement."

"I'm sorry, sweetie, but it's so sudden. You've only known each other a couple of days. Don't you think you ought to think about this a little longer?"

Heidi eyed her shrewdly. So shrewdly, in fact, that Juliette knew exactly what was coming next, bracing herself mentally for the onslaught. "This from someone who proudly proclaimed to the media and anyone else within shouting distance who would listen that she had fallen in love with the hunky co-stars of each of her first seven films?"

"That was different. I had the inducement of those romantic scripts and intimate scenes with all those men. The line between fantasy and reality can blur so easily under those circumstances. Not to mention the obvious fact that I didn't haul off and get married to any of them like you're proposing to do."

Heidi seemed indignant. "This is no fantasy. Edding and I have discovered that we're kindred souls. I'm exactly what he's been looking for all his life and he's what I've always wanted. He wants to have the wedding at Betterslie when we return for the shoot. That'll give him enough time to plan a genuine Old Fort Rosalie wedding. He's going to give me his mother's wedding ring, which is a family heirloom. He's shown it to me already, and it's unbelievably huge and gorgeous. Imagine me—Heidi Jane Pendleton from Bakersfield, California—becoming Mrs. Edding Denbo, the mistress of Betterslie!"

Juliette rose from the bed and began pacing the floor. She was reluctant to bring up the obvious but felt she must do so for the sake of their friendship. "Please don't take this the wrong way, Heidi, but don't you think it's significant that Edding has coupled the wedding with the shoot? Has the possibility occurred to you that perhaps he's using this as a tactic to get the booking?"

O Bed! O Breakfast!

Heidi bristled and sprang to her feet. "Edding would never do something like that. You're just going to have to take my word for it. We both know what we're doing and this wedding is going to take place and there are things we need to discuss because of it. Such as how much longer I'm going to stay on as your personal assistant. My preference would be to remain through the wedding and the shoot. That will give you plenty of time to find a replacement." Heidi suddenly frowned, sniffing the air. "What's that peculiar odor?"

It took Juliette a few moments because of all the information she was processing, but she was finally able to focus. "Oh. That's grape jelly. Long story." She moved to a rocking chair in the corner of the room and collapsed into it. "A replacement. A replacement." She repeated the word several more times while she rocked back and forth in a trance-like state.

"There are many people who'd jump at the chance to do what I do, Juliette. You shouldn't have any problem attracting a capable person to a high-profile position like this."

"But I consider you irreplaceable. You've been with me from the very beginning. I've always thought the Ten Commandments were handed down on that clipboard of yours."

"That's very funny and flattering, I'm sure. But not entirely the truth. There are plenty of us super-organized and overly-efficient types out there. Take Mary Dell Hoskins, for instance. Look at how smoothly she glides through her job, and it isn't like everything that's happened this weekend has gone according to plan, what with those casserole biddies stalking us."

Juliette stopped rocking immediately. "Mary Dell Hoskins. Of course. You're absolutely right. We'll announce your engagement at breakfast, and then I'll look for the right moment to approach Mary Dell before the weekend is through." Juliette resumed her rocking with a wicked grin. "I can't help but be a little curious, though. How is—I mean, what's Edding like in bed?"

Heidi's eyes widened with what appeared to be remembered pleasure. "Sheer poetry." Then she crossed over, embracing Juliette warmly. "A part of me just can't believe this is happening, and I know it does seem sudden, but this thing has hit Edding and me like a cannon shot. When it happens to you, you'll understand. And I don't want you to take this the wrong way, either, but I certainly hope you'll give serious consideration to staying at Betterslie for the shoot, now that I'm going to be married out there. And, no, Edding didn't ask me to say anything on his behalf. I'm lobbying on my own."

"I'll keep it in mind, sweetie, but I just can't promise anything right now. I have far too much on my mind."

After Heidi had left the room, Juliette continued rocking while she mulled things over. It had been an unsettling morning, every exchange nipping at her peace of mind, her confidence, her determination. It was as if someone had taken a wire whisk to her brain to make a slurry of her thought processes. Tim's incredulous sexual enthusiasm, the validity of Rella Darrow's unrelenting fictional quest, Heidi's overnight courtship and marriage announcement, the possibility of Mary Dell becoming her new personal assistant, Tasmania lobbying for Plum Cottage and Heidi for Betterslie, the constant irritation of those society matrons chanting and picketing in their sneakers. They were all in there swirling around, pressing against the sides of her skull, until she thought her head just might explode.

Tim saved her from such a catastrophe when he came in to announce that Tasmania had just laid breakfast on the table, and she was able to let off a little steam with the revelation of

O Bed! O Breakfast!

Edding's marriage proposal.

"You think he's on the level, Jule?"

"Ulterior motive was my first reaction, too. Heidi insists it's the real thing, though. If by some chance you passed her in the hall, you probably noticed she's on a fuzzy pink cloud somewhere up in the stratosphere."

Tim offered up a genuine smile instead of one of his patented smirks. "I think it's terrific that Heidi's fallen in love. More power to her. More power to anyone, anywhere who falls in love. It's the stuff that keeps us going—not the money, not the fame, not all that other stuff us Hollywood types are supposed to inhale like so many lines of coke."

Juliette eyed him skeptically. "Since when have you basically given a damn about Heidi? I have to beat you off each other with a stick all the time."

"Can't I just be happy for her?"

"You just answered a question with another question, and that's not your style. You've been up to something all weekend. Are you ever going to let me in on it?"

"All in good time," he replied, grabbing her by the arm and pushing her toward the door. "Let's go get some of that enormous breakfast spread. I need to get the taste of grape jelly out of my mouth once and for all."

Elves had apparently visited Plum Cottage's dining room during the night and miraculously freshened all the flowers in the centerpiece to the complete satisfaction of Miss Aimee, who sat at the head of the table in a floral print, purple dress, looking like she was about to grant a roomful of wishes. A diamond-studded tiara crowned her snowy-white head, and she was slowly waving a bejeweled wand directly over her plate.

"Good morning, everyone," she said, as her guests entered and took their places. "This is a figure eight."

"What is a figure eight?" Juliette replied, after taking a sip of her juice.

"This weaving motion I'm making with the wand, dear. It's a horizontal figure eight, and it's the proper way to wave your wand. At least that's what we were taught years and years ago during our wandwaving practices. Perhaps I should start at the beginning. This tiara and wand are all that's left of my costume as Azalea Festival Queen of 1937. The moths have long ago made a meal of my dress, I'm afraid. I was one of the first ones when it all got started, but I wasn't the very first. The year before my mother wheeled and dealed and got me appointed queen, the Festival had an unfortunate experience with gangly Portia Groves, who had to be practically dragged screaming onto the pageant stage. She was quite the tomboy, you see, and the last thing she wanted was to dress up in a hoopskirt and wave a wand at tourists, but her mother evidently thought it would smooth out her rough edges a bit."

"And the opposite happened?" Juliette said.

"Quite the opposite," Miss Aimee continued. "Let me be kind and say that Portia was almost certainly Boris Karloff's inspiration for his interpretation of the Frankenstein monster. I can still see her—stomping around the floor of the auditorium in those clunky saddle oxfords she was wearing underneath her dress and wielding her wand like a psychotic killer in one of those slasher movies the young people fancy so much these days. It was after her dreadful performance in 1936 that the Festival decided to offer wandwaving lessons to all the young ladies so they would know how to greet the tourists in a graceful, feminine fashion. So I thought you all might enjoy observing just what they taught us. Think of a figure eight resting on its side, visualize it in your head and move the wand along the path accordingly,' they told us. And that's just what I'm doing now."

Juliette sprang up from her chair. "May I try it?"

"Of course, dear. That is, provided you don't get so caught up in it that you forget to eat your breakfast. Wandwaving can be such a mesmerizing and powerful tonic for the soul. You begin to believe you can actually perform magic, and perhaps you can."

Juliette retrieved the wand and took her turn, alternately waving it and putting it down for a bite of Tasmania's delicious breakfast. Miss Aimee guided her hand from time to time, and there was even polite applause from Mary Dell, Harris and the others whenever she executed a particularly effective figure eight.

"Oh, I forgot to mention the baby steps," Miss Aimee added a few minutes later. "After all that stomping around Portia did, the Festival also decided to give us lessons on how to walk like a queen. We were to take teensy baby steps while making our figure-eights around the floor. We were not to storm about like the Nazis who were beginning to appear in all the movie newsreels. All told, Portia Groves, who went on to become Fort Rosalie's first large-animal veterinarian, was probably the best thing that ever happened to the Azalea Festival. She ended up helping to create the time-honored style we've become so famous for."

"Oh, let me try the baby steps, too. You never know what bit of business an actress might have to call upon someday," Juliette said, having eaten everything on her plate like a good girl.

"Very well, then," Miss Aimee replied. "I'll supervise you in the parlor after breakfast."

Then Juliette sent shock waves around the breakfast table when she announced Heidi's engagement.

"Have you set a date yet?" Miss Aimee said.

"We think maybe right after the shoot," Heidi replied, blushing and giggling all the while.

The import of the impending engagement was not lost on Miss Aimee, whose tiara seemed to slip slightly to one side. Nevertheless, she confronted the issue head-on. "Will that have any bearing on your decision for accommodations?"

"That's still up in the air," Juliette said, pointing toward the window, where the Casserole Patrol was very much in evidence across the street. "Whether we even return to Fort Rosalie is still up for grabs, for that matter."

"Well, if my vote counts for anything, I think your Plum Cottage is just terrific, Miss Aimee. Best time I ever had with my clothes off," Tim added, while spreading lots of fig preserves on his toast.

After breakfast Miss Aimee was as good as her word, leading Juliette to the parlor to practice her baby steps. "I could even let you try it in an antebellum gown and hoopskirt," she said. "Maybe even the one Elizabeth Taylor gave me, if you'd like."

Juliette nodded enthusiastically. "I'd like."

"Then follow me, dear," said Miss Aimee, pointing the way to her bedroom.

A few minutes later Juliette emerged in the *Raintree County* costume, and Miss Aimee began her instructions. "One, two, dear. Think—one, two. Bitsy, bitsy. One, two. Bitsy, bitsy."

Juliette began shuffling around the parlor while repeating Miss Aimee's mantra, looking slightly embarrassed at first, but soon she was doing her excruciatingly slow laps without missing a beat. "Do I look like a queen yet, Miss Aimee?"

"Worthy of coronation," Miss Aimee replied, handing her the wand again. "Now, try your figure eights while you walk. Get it together, as the young people like to say. One, two, bitsy, bitsy. Figure eight, figure eight. One, two, bitsy, bitsy, figure eight, figure eight."

Juliette was more than equal to the task, and soon everyone was either applauding politely, chanting, giggling or some combination of the three.

"On behalf of Old Fort Rosalie and the Azalea Festival, I officially pronounce you Queen Juliette!" Miss Aimee proclaimed after it was over.

Juliette hesitated as she handed back the wand and the tiara. "I halfway wish I really could wave this thing and make all my problems go away."

"Just think of my little Plum Cottage as your magic wand, dear," Miss Aimee said. "Your home away from home when you return to make your movie." Then she pointed the way to her bedroom. "Now, Tasmania and I will help you out of your costume so that you can return to the twenty-first century and resume your tour."

Miss Aimee may have said her piece calmly, but she was a tangle of nerves on the inside. After she and Tasmania had finished unfastening the hoopskirt and Juliette had left to pack for Destiny Manor, she turned to her housekeeper and said: "Well, what's the verdict? Do you think we stand a chance?"

Tasmania gently patted her employer on the shoulder. "Oh, I think we got us a real good chance. I got a feelin' maybe an angel lookin' after us and put in a good word for us on this one."

"I hope you're right," Miss Aimee said, sighing plaintively. "Because I can't afford to keep Plum Cottage open any longer than one more month."

Tasmania wagged a finger, shaking her head. "Don't you even think that way, Miss Aimee. You'll see. Everything

gonna turn out just fine, or my name ain't Tasmania I. Johnston Evans!"

O Bed! O Breakfast!

Chapter Twelve

Mary Dell sat at the wheel of Harris's Buick, having obtained his permission to drive it during the procession now heading out to Destiny Manor. Although he had balked initially at the request the way some men will do in all matters related to the care and feeding of their cherished cars, he had immediately given in when she had introduced Poco's letter.

"I want you to read it so you'll know where we stand," she had told him as they stood at the curb outside Plum Cottage. "I could hardly contain myself all morning."

So they got into his car, and he slid in on the passenger side and began reading while Mary Dell kept her eyes on the road. Occasionally, she would glance his way, trying to gauge his reaction, but there appeared to be none. Finally, he put the letter down, taking a deep breath and staring straight ahead at the patrol car in front of them.

"So what's our game plan going to be?" he said.

She spoke forthrightly, having rehearsed the conversation in her head all morning during the activities at Plum Cottage. "First, I'd like to be the one to handle this, if you don't mind. I think it needs a woman's touch, and I believe nothing less will work with Megita."

Harris screwed up his mouth, looking thoughtful. "I have to admit, I'd be very uncomfortable talking to her about all this. I'd expect to see an antique vase or two grazing my temple."

"At the very least," Mary Dell replied with a chuckle. Then she grew serious, detailing her strategy as they made their way through downtown Fort Rosalie.

"I think it's our best shot," he said finally. "We'll go with it

and hope for the best." He whistled and shook his head. "Except I have to tell you, this is some lethal dose we'll be dealing out here. I don't think anyone could have dreamed up a godsend like this in a million years. And Poco McGill is certain Megita has no idea this letter exists?"

"None whatsoever."

He continued to shake his head. "I don't want to come off like a coward, but, yeah, you're right. This is a woman-to-woman thing, and maybe the toughest challenge of your entire Tourist Bureau career. But I know you're up to it. You have to be, or we're sunk."

Mary Dell smiled at him, driving on in silence. No, it wasn't going to be easy, but she would pull it off, and he would see without any semblance of a doubt that she deserved to be the better half of that Mr. and Mrs. Tourist Bureau coupling.

Johnny and Terrelle Lurkin made a big to-do of the arrival at Destiny Manor, starting with the formal introduction of the servants in the enormous foyer. Unlike her older counterparts—Eola Griffin and Tasmania Evans, who were casually dressed and laid back in the performance of their duties—Azureen Mazique curtseyed in a French maid's uniform, and the tall and Teutonic Hans Dieterly stood beside her in the traditional white chef's coat and hat, bowing low before his guests.

"We just adore our staff to pieces!" Terrelle said, turning to Juliette and Tim. "And they'll both be pleased as punch to help your chauffeur with all that luggage. You just follow them up the stairs to your rooms, and when you're all settled and freshened up, y'all mosey on down to the cabana in back. Hans has set up a little spread of hors d'ouevres to hold y'all until dinner, and Johnny here has made up a batch of his fabulous juleps. It's right pleasant today out by the pool, so we thought we'd just kinda informally visit with you and Harris and Mary Dell and your assistant for a while, if that sounds good to you."

"Perfect," Juliette replied, following the servants. "We'll look forward to it."

Then the Lurkins led the way to the patio area, where Mary Dell and Harris plopped themselves down on the cast-iron chairs and awaited Johnny's inevitable juleps. After the drinks had been handed out, however, Terrelle lost no time indulging her insecurities.

"If I'm reading the signals right, that Juliette Cadbury seems a mite tense to me, Mary Dell. Do you think it's something I've said or done? Have we gotten too chummy too soon?"

Mary Dell put down her julep cup and said: "Terrelle, you've got to remember that Megita and her crew were right across the street all the time at Plum Cottage, always chanting, making noise, getting on Juliette's nerves. Both Harris and I feel fortunate that she didn't cancel the rest of the tour right then and there."

Terrelle anxiously patted her bulbous hairdo. "It would sure bother the hell outta me, I know that much. Last night in bed, Johnny and I saw the interview with that awful Megita, and it was all I could do to keep from throwin' my pillows at the TV."

"I managed to calm my sweet thing down, though," Johnny said, winking mischievously.

Terrelle was still unsure of herself. "So you don't think it's anything I've said or done so far? Oh, we do wanna make the proper impression."

Mary Dell reached over and patted her hand. "Just be

yourself. Remember that conversation you and I had when I came out to visit. Let them get to know who the real Terrelle and Johnny Lurkin are."

Terrelle managed to calm down, breathing a little easier. Then Juliette, Tim and Heidi finally emerged from the house, and it was time to begin her hostess duties in earnest. She opted for an off-the-cuff remark that reaped huge and unexpected dividends.

"I just adore the color of your hair, Juliette. My mother always loved working with strawberry-blondes in her salon."

"Your mother was a hairdresser, too?" Juliette replied. By then they were all sitting in a semi-circle poolside watching the spouting statuary and sipping Johnny's heady juleps. "My mother was a hairdresser back in Caruthersville, Missouri. How about that?"

Terrelle made Johnny switch chairs so she could sit next to Juliette. "Well, my mother specialized in perms in a little shop called the Permanent Solution down in Beaumont, Texas. Oh, honey, the horror stories she used to tell me about her clients. They'd come in screaming at the top of their lungs with their follicles fried from some bad homemade job and get down on their knees practically begging for a miracle. Needless to say, my mother always came through for 'em. They'd walk outta that salon with a do to die for."

Juliette took a generous swig of her julep, and from that point on, no one else was able to get a word in edgewise between the two hairdressers' daughters.

"Oh, I know just what you're talking about, Terrelle. My mother always told me that the worst clients were the ones that wanted their hair dyed and styled to look like this or that movie star. I think maybe that was when I got the first inkling that a movie star was what I'd like to be. Anyway, she always felt like telling them point-blank, 'Hey, I can dye your hair blonde and sweep it up that way, but with that nose of yours and that terrible complexion, you're never gonna look like Marilyn Monroe or Madonna or whoever in a million years. No miracles today, ma'am. This is not Our Lady of the Blessed Beauty Parlor!"

The others eventually gave up following the exchange and wandered over to the hors d'ouevres table to help themselves to shrimp and veggies and the rest of the appetizers Hans and Azureen were on hand to serve, but Juliette and Terrelle pressed on, fortified by a continuous supply of juleps.

"I'll never forget the way some of those snotty bitches treated my mother sometimes," Juliette continued. "It made me so goddamned mad. I remember promising myself that nobody was ever going to treat me that way. She'd come home in tears. She'd follow their instructions to the letter, and then when the results didn't live up to their absurd fantasies about themselves, they'd rant and rave and take it out on her. I vowed way back then that I'd take my mother away from all that cock and bull one day. And that's just what I've done. I've bought her a house and got her shop sold for a nice profit, and now she's officially retired and living in the lap of luxury in St. Louis, although she still won't go to anyone else to have her hair done."

Terrelle rolled her eyes and swayed back and forth in her chair as the full force of her husband's juleps kicked in. "My mother's the same way. Once a beautician, always a beautician, I guess. It's a good, honest profession, but some people look down their noses at you. Just like some people look down their noses if you move to a fancy old Southern town and restore one of their crumbling houses with your new Texas oil money. Just try that sometime and see where it gets you. It's like everyone in the town who's anybody owns the house except you. Everybody has an opinion that counts except you,

the actual owner. Damndest thing I've ever tried to deal with, I'll tell ya that! You know what I'm talking about, don'tcha, Mary Dell?"

Mary Dell nodded while pointing to the buffet table. "Wouldn't you like a little something to eat now?"

"Yeah," Johnny added. "Let me get you a bite. You know how my juleps do ya?"

Terrelle waved him off, her head bobbing and weaving. "No, I would not like a bite. My friend, Juliette, is discussing the politics of hairdressing and other earthshaking matters. Betcha didn't know that, huh? That hairdressing is fulla politics just like all those folks in Congress. Juliette understands how it works. She's my new best friend. We've found out we have our working class origins in common, even though we happen to be swimming in money now."

Juliette hoisted her cup, and they clinked rims. "You said it, Terrelle, baby. Swimming in money!"

Terrelle stood up, wobbly on her feet, and eyed the swimming pool. "Did you bring a bathing suit, honey? Would you like to go in for a swim? It's heated, ya know, so you won't get chilled."

Juliette looked around, spying Tim at the buffet table where Azureen was loading up his plate for the second time. "I forget," she called out to him. "Did we pack bathing suits for this trip, Tim?"

He shook his head from a distance, but Heidi moved quickly to Juliette's side.

"No, you didn't bring a bathing suit with you," Heidi said, grabbing her firmly by the arm.

Juliette shook her loose. "Ha! I know what you're thinking, Heidi. That time I jumped into that Vegas hotel fountain with all my clothes on and all those reporters snapped all those wet T-shirt pictures of me getting out. That kept the

O Bed! O Breakfast!

tabloids in caviar for three months, didn't it?"

"Yes, it did. And you don't want a repeat of that publicity, do you?"

Juliette scanned the cabana. "What publicity? I don't see any cameras, do you? We're here among friends. Especially my new best friend, Terrelle Lurkin."

"Well, we do have some bathing suits we keep in the changing rooms over there," Terrelle said. "All sizes. Would you like to try one on, honey? I just know we got a couple in your cute little ol' size."

"To hell with that!" Juliette proclaimed, putting her drink down and breaking away from Heidi completely. "Come on, let's go a little crazy!"

Before anyone could blink, Juliette had kicked off her shoes and jumped into the pool, clothes and all, sending a plume of water into the air and more lapping over the sides. She bobbed to the surface with her hair pasted to her forehead and down into her eyes, gasping for a breath and then laughing at the ring of astonished people observing her while she treaded water.

"Come on in, Terrelle. Come in, girlfriend! Don't worry about that hair of yours, either. I can tell you spend a lot of time on it to get it that big. But I have a brilliant idea. Between the two of us, we probably learned all the tricks of the trade by watching our mothers, so later on I'll do your hair and you'll do mine. We'll go up to your room and lock ourselves in and do makeovers and have fun just like girlfriends at a slumber party, and we won't allow any of the boys in. No boys allowed in our clubhouse today!"

Terrelle could hardly resist such a powerful Lorelei song, such overwhelming validation from one of Hollywood's most famous sirens. So she, too, took the plunge, clothes and all. Now there were two people under the influence bobbing

around like corks while the others looked on solicitously.

"You're next," Juliette said, splashing water at Heidi's feet and making her jump back from the edge.

"No!" Heidi shouted, shaking her finger as if Juliette were an unruly pet. "Someone has to stay dry and play lifeguard."

Juliette quickly turned elsewhere, pressing Mary Dell and Harris.

"Thanks, but no thanks," Mary Dell said. "We don't have a change of clothes. We'd have to drive back into town."

"You sure you're all right in there, sweet thing?" Johnny said, kneeling down on the concrete. "You're in the deep end, ya know."

"Oh, stop fretting," Terrelle answered, sending a big splash his way with the palm of her hand. "I may be all wet, but I'm floating on air!"

The two women continued to paddle and spit water out of their mouths while sharing confidences.

"I'm going to tell you something only a few other people know," Juliette began. "It's not really all that big of a secret, though, so why those sleazy, bottom-feeding tabloids haven't gotten a hold of it, I can't begin to fathom. Or maybe they have and I just missed it. When they write about you every day of your life, you're bound to miss a few of their best shots."

Terrelle swam right up and whispered in her left ear. "Something about your hair color? You're not really a redhead? Is that it?"

Juliette snickered. "Hell, no. This really is what God gave me, give or take a few highlights. We all have to have our highlights from time to time. That doesn't count. No, no, no. I'm talking now about my name. My real name. I was born Judy Rae Hamm in Caruthersville. Can you even believe it? All the imagery and glamour of a pork roast, and a real stinker of a moniker if you're going to be an actress!"

O Bed! O Breakfast!

"So how did you come up with Juliette Cadbury? Was it your agent's idea?"

"Hell, no. That slug hasn't come up with anything remotely creative in all the time I've known him, unless you want to count his suggestion that I direct deposit his percentage into his bank account. No, I invented it all by myself, and it was brilliant, really." She paused to push a few strands of hair out of her face. "Took Juliette from Shakespeare and Cadbury from my favorite chocolate bar. Don't you just love that?"

Terrelle began laughing raucously. "I do. I really do. But I think Hershey would have suited you just as well." They were both laughing now, finding every word either of them said to the other a priceless gem, the way inebriated people so often do.

Heidi ventured out to the edge and squatted down. "Don't you think you ought to get your makeover started? You know how long it takes you to do your hair."

"You, too, sweet thing," Johnny said. "Why don't y'all go on upstairs and start on your hairdos and makeup right now?" He extended his big arm to help coax her out, and then Tim did the same for Juliette and finally they were both safely topside, dripping and shaking themselves all over just like a pair of dogs.

"What a blast!" Juliette said, nudging Terrelle with her elbow. "Everybody needs to let off a little steam now and then, or they'll explode. And I'll tell you—I was about to with all that Casserole Patrol foolishness!"

Terrelle gave her a playful shove and guffawed. "Picture it. Pushing Megita Larose into the pool—clothes, string of pearls, big fat mouth, big fat bra and all!"

"Amen to that!"

Then they sloshed over to the changing rooms to towel off while the rest watched in amazement.

"And here I was worried that Terrelle wouldn't be able to let her hair down," Mary Dell told Harris.

"Oh, I think they've definitely bonded," he said, spearing the last morsel of food on his plate.

Johnny waved at his wife solicitously and then approached Mary Dell and Harris. "Hope y'all didn't get splashed too much."

Mary Dell made a cute little face. "Just a drop or two here and there, but nothing that won't evaporate by dinnertime."

"Ostrich steaks tonight, ya know," Johnny said, hitching up his pants. "I already told Tim about it, and he can't hardly wait. Our Hans has gone all out for tonight."

Harris had a pained expression on his face. "Yes, I imagine there's a trick catching an ostrich for dinner."

The highlight of the evening meal a couple of hours later turned out to be something other than the food. Not that the mesquite-grilled ostrich steaks with saffron rice and Caesar salad would fail to offer up an exquisite combination of tastes and draw rave reviews from everyone. But it was the makeover Juliette had done on Terrelle that stole the candlelit show in Destiny Manor's cavernous dining room which Megita Larose had contemptuously dubbed 'that Viking mess hall.'

"She looks absolutely beautiful," Mary Dell whispered to Harris as Terrelle entered the room and everyone took their places.

"I'll go a step further. She doesn't even look like the same person," he whispered back.

Indeed, no thirty-minute infomercial could have rendered more spectacular before and after results. For starters, Juliette had toned down the obvious war paint considerably.

O Bed! O Breakfast!

Then she had softened Terrelle's heavy features by gently framing her face with a spray-free, more casual hairstyle. The hair, itself, actually moved and swayed when Terrelle did. All of it taken together had taken years off her middle-aged appearance, and everyone—including her speechless husband, Johnny—was properly adoring as the meal began.

"Have you ever thought of going into the beauty business yourself?" Mary Dell said. "We're all very impressed with your skills."

Juliette thanked her and then smiled across the table at Terrelle. "We had fun, didn't we, girlfriend? But I don't think we'd really like to have to do it for a living, huh?"

Terrelle put down her fork and shook her new hairdo. "No way. Not after what we saw our mothers go through."

The compliments continued to fly as the meal progressed, but Mary Dell kept an eye on the time throughout each course. After the kiwi-lime pie and cappuccino had been consumed, she rose from the table and delivered the getaway line she and Harris had agreed upon.

"This has been a delightful evening, Terrelle and Johnny, but Harris and I must leave you a little early tonight. Just a little something we need to take care of back at the office."

Terrelle looked disappointed but quickly recovered. "Okay, but don't forget we got eggs benedict, crepes suzette and champagne for breakfast tomorrow around nine-thirty. You don't wanna miss a bite."

Juliette popped up at the last second. "Could you maybe come a half-hour or so early, Mary Dell? We could meet out by the pool, say, around nine? There's something important I wanted to discuss with you."

"That shouldn't be a problem. See you then."

"Well, let me see you to the door," Johnny said, rising from his chair at the head of the table.

"No, please," Mary Dell said. "You stay put and enjoy your cappuccino. We'll duck out the back. Goodnight, one and all."

There was a flurry of farewells, and soon Harris and Mary Dell were comparing notes as they walked through the cabana area on their way to his car.

"I think Juliette had the best time of all out here, if you want my opinion," Harris was saying, squinting to avoid the floodlights shining through all the trees in the backyard. An hour or so earlier, Destiny Manor's outdoor festival of lights had kicked in right on cue.

"Yep. She was just like a little girl splashing around at a swimming party."

"True. But don't forget she was just like a little girl playing with that wand and shuffling around like a geisha this morning at Miss Aimee's."

"Good point," Mary Dell replied, continuing their review and analysis. "She was also in hog heaven being hauled up and down the staircase out at Betterslie. She seems to have an enormous need to revert to childlike behavior at a moment's notice."

They had reached the Buick, and Mary Dell gestured playfully in the direction of the steering wheel. "Back to the natural order of things, sir."

He dangled his keys and smiled, closing her door behind her as she slid in, and they headed back to Fort Rosalie. At the entrance to Destiny Manor, where the Casserole Patrol had long ago wrapped up their Sunday duty, Mary Dell resumed their evaluation of the competition so far.

"Assuming we can work this thing out with Megita and her following, there's something we haven't discussed yet."

"And what's that?"

"Well, it's the fact that two of our B&B owners are going to end up as losers pretty soon. We've been so concerned with

O Bed! O Breakfast!

keeping Juliette and Horvath from moving the production to Natchez that we haven't faced that reality. Two of our 'terrible trio' will soon be screeching like those peacocks out at Destiny Manor." She considered briefly and decided to let Harris know the worst of it. "And if Miss Aimee turns out to be one of the two, Plum Cottage will be 'gone with the wind,' so to speak." Then she told him about Miss Aimee's dire financial straits.

"I can't believe it. Why wouldn't she say anything to me or go to a bank or something?"

Mary Dell gave him a wry grin and arched her eyebrows. "That's not the way a lady was brought up in her generation. To air personal business like that, I mean."

"Speaking of personal business, are you ready for this confrontation with Megita? Are you absolutely certain you don't want me with you?"

"Absolutely certain," she said, reaching over and rubbing his arm gently a couple of times. "Let's stick with the plan. You take me back to my car, and I'll go it alone."

It was in the Tourist Bureau parking lot twenty minutes later that she decided to make a final request. "A sendoff kiss?" she said, gazing into his eyes as he wrapped her up in his arms.

"Granted," he said before acquitting himself masterfully.

She came up for breath and pulled back slightly. "See you at your place in about an hour?"

Then he signed off with the words that made her feel she couldn't possibly lose the battle that lay ahead: "Go get 'em, Mrs. Tourist Bureau!"

Robert Dalby

Chapter Thirteen

The late-Victorian towers of the Founders' Club seemed more foreboding than usual to Mary Dell on this chilly October evening. Once actually used as a funeral home, the building had never really overcome such ghoulish connotations in all the years the Historic Preservation Committee had made it their headquarters, and Mary Dell stood before it at the bottom of the front steps trying her best to keep a whole headful of intimidating images at bay. Finally, she squared her shoulders and marched up the stoop to the showdown.

Megita appeared in the doorway even before she had reached the porch. "Well, it's about time, my girl. I saw you through the window standing there on the sidewalk like some weak-willed Jehovah's Witness. For heaven's sake, get in here and say what you have to say. I need to get home and soak my poor feet."

Mary Dell slipped past her adversary with a perfunctory smile, and the two of them settled in on one of the common room's musty old sofas.

"Well?" Megita said, ferociously staring her down.

Mary Dell reached into her coat pocket and held out a copy of the letter. "This is the reason Poco McGill will be submitting her resignation to you tomorrow. Please read it, and you'll understand everything. It was written many years ago by your mother, Leona, to Poco's mother, Emma. I'm sure you can identify the handwriting and signature to your satisfaction?"

Megita snatched it up, quickly scanning and shuffling the sheets. "So what?"

"Just read, please. Then we'll talk."

Looking thoroughly exasperated, Megita heaved her chest

O Bed! O Breakfast!

and began reading

Mary Dell watched with a perverse sort of gratification as the woman's expression changed from arrogant and annoyed to horrified and disbelieving. Occasionally, Megita would look up, launching daggers with her eyes, but finally she came to the end, letting the sheets go limp in her hand while looking off into a corner of the shadowy room.

Mary Dell gave her a little more time to digest the bombshell and then said: "It is my opinion, Mrs. Larose, that no one else on the face of this earth should ever read that letter or be aware of its contents."

Megita managed to gather herself enough to speak, but her usually-powerful voice was strained, a pale imitation of itself. "Let's get to the point. Why are you here, and what do you want?"

"Harris and I want you to terminate these protests of yours tomorrow, and we want your assurance that if *Whispering Dixie* returns to Fort Rosalie, you and the rest of your members will completely ignore the production. That's all."

"And if I refuse?"

"If you refuse, Harris and I will see to it that this letter is circulated among your loyal following. We doubt very much if many of them will revere you and your family in quite the same way once this true confession has been leaked. You may have a very hard time getting re-elected president of the Historic Preservation Committee with this material tarnishing your sterling silver status in the community. Why, both the Pulliam and Larose clans would never be the same."

Megita recoiled in horror, but then seemed to catch a second wind, reminding Mary Dell of a monstrous cobra getting ready to strike. "You impudent little nothing of a paper-shuffler. I don't give a damn if you are a Hoskins from Wilkins County. How dare you speak to me this way. I'll have your

163

job, my girl!"

Mary Dell swallowed hard, but she knew she was on solid ground. "You'd have to go to Harris to do that, Mrs. Larose, and he and I are in perfect agreement on this."

"Then I'll have his job!"

"I don't think so. To do that, you'd have to go to the mayor, and Harris would have to let His Honor in on the letter and its contents, too. Before everything was said and done, there probably wouldn't be a soul left in Fort Rosalie who didn't know about it. Maybe even some of those ladies you detest so over in Natchez would hear about it. You know what they say about gossip travelling in these parts on the morning dew."

Mary Dell was gaining confidence by the second, surprised to discover she was actually beginning to enjoy the confrontation. After all, like practically everyone else in Fort Rosalie, she had hardly been exempt from Megita's harsh treatment over the years. There had been plenty of insults and mean-spirited slights and the customary condescension to deal with. Watching Megita seething and squirming now was a more than welcome payback.

"I should have strangled that Poco McGill years ago when we were girls in grade school!" Megita proclaimed, obviously still in agony.

"But since you didn't and all this is out in the open now, what do you plan to do?"

"Never mind that. I can't believe you and Harris can justify intruding upon the privacy of my family this way. Have you no sense of propriety?"

Mary Dell reviewed her options quickly and came up with the perfect retort. "I might ask you the same thing regarding the private life of Juliette Cadbury. Now at least you have some idea of how she probably feels having bits and pieces of her personal business scattered about for public consumption

O Bed! O Breakfast!

like so much chicken feed."

"There's no comparison whatsoever. That creature brought it on herself with all of her outrageous press interviews. This letter is a confession of the most intimate nature."

"Agreed," Mary Dell replied, adopting her most serious demeanor. "Harris and I are completely on your side here. It would be cruel and unusual punishment to subject your family to such exposure. All you have to do to guarantee that it will never happen is to call off these protests. Otherwise...well, I've already told you what will happen."

When Megita rose from the sofa and cupped her hands together, Mary Dell knew it was over. The fat lady was about to sing. "Oh, for God's sake. You leave me no choice!"

Mary Dell stood up, slowly shaking her head. "But that's not true, Mrs. Larose. I leave it up to you how you go about shutting down the Casserole Patrol. What you say to the ladies will strictly be your call. Just be certain that you make it very clear to all of us, but particularly Juliette Cadbury and her people, that you won't be pounding the pavement any more."

Megita began thinking out loud while she toyed with her pearls. "Maybe I could do it at the rally tomorrow. But what would the girls think? How could I justify it? What will I say? Oh, I detest you and Harris and Poco for this. No one has ever dared treat me this way!"

"But then no one has ever had the goods on you before," Mary Dell replied, turning to head for the front door. "Just remember. We have this letter safely tucked away for future reference. I suggest you do the right thing tomorrow."

Megita said nothing further as Mary Dell walked out the door and refused to look back until she was well down the street in front of her car. Only then did she really allow herself to breathe. There. It felt good to release the knot in her stomach, despite the fact that it had gone so well and she had held up beautifully through it all.

She checked her watch. Half-past nine. She could hardly wait to get back to Harris and give him the good report. They could celebrate in each other's arms all night, and maybe there would even be a definite proposal this time around.

There had not been much lingering after dinner at Destiny Manor. Obviously still overwhelmed by his wife's new look, Johnny had suggested that everyone retire a bit earlier than usual. That was just fine with Tim, who had been waiting all evening long to implement the third and final phase of his campaign to woo his Juliette to the altar. He sensed he was nearing the promised land, about to make bingo, on the verge of hitting the jackpot, and he could barely contain himself as he entered their bedroom. His Jule would be ripe and ready for the words, he just knew it. He couldn't have misjudged.

"I have another one of my wicked ideas," he told her. "What say we wait a few and then sneak back down to the pool to skinny-dip and maybe make a little love in the water?"

Juliette fell across the bed face-down and groaned. "I've had enough of playing Esther Williams for one day."

"Oh, no, you can't give out on me now." He moved to her side, unzipped the back of her dress and began massaging her shoulders with his fingers. "There's a lot I need to say to you tonight, and I want you in the perfect mood to hear it."

She turned over and propped herself up on her elbows. "So you really have been up to something all weekend."

"I admit it proudly. But first, what about the skinny-dipping?"

"That pool is too damn lit up. Everything's too damn lit up.

It's like a perpetual prison break without the sirens out there. I take it back—the peacocks are the sirens. We'd be putting on quite a show for Hans and Azureen peering out of the servants' quarters."

"Johnny and Terrelle wouldn't be watching?"

She snickered. "I hardly think so. Betcha any amount of money they're up in their bedroom humping and bumping right now. You couldn't possibly have missed that lustful look Johnny had in his eyes all evening after the new, improved Terrelle made her debut—thanks to me, of course."

He lowered himself over her, grazing her lips with his. "What you did for Terrelle today was very thoughtful and very special. You extended the hand of friendship to someone who obviously feels like an outcast here. You let her know you understood because you'd been there and done that. The world needs to see a lot more of that side of you."

"As opposed to?"

He pulled away slightly. "As opposed to the small-town hairdresser's daughter who goes around sticking her tongue out at the world and then gets royally pissed when it refuses to take her seriously. You can't have it both ways, you know."

Juliette sat up straight, looking skeptical. "Is that what you think I'm doing with my life?"

"You've been giving a mean impression. You jump in a Las Vegas fountain with your clothes on, you give the finger to a bunch of misguided but harmless little ol' ladies, you somehow manage to get misquoted every time out with the press. There's a pattern here, Jule, and I was thinking maybe it was time you looked at it straight on and let go of it."

Her skepticism disappeared, turning into irritation. "This is what you wanted to say to me? To criticize every move I make?"

Tim stood up and walked resolutely to the middle of the

room. Then he turned around and steadied himself with a deep breath. "Okay. None of that came out the way I intended. Let me start over."

"Permission granted. Take two."

"What I wanted to say very simply is that I'm in love with you, Jule. I want to marry you, be your husband, give you children. I want us to settle down and make a family together instead of running around the world as the butt of everyone's jokes. I want us to make it legal."

The color seemed to drain from her face. "You really want to get married?"

Her lack of excitement was a disappointment, forcing him to consider the painful possibility that he had misread her, that they weren't on the same page after all.

"The other morning at Betterslie when you jumped out of the limo and confronted those ladies with their scribbled signs, you seemed to wear their slogans like a badge of honor. It was almost like you were thriving on their contempt, that you took pride in the fact you didn't have a ring or hadn't set a date. I remember how it felt when I first hit it big in Hollywood. I thought I could do anything I wanted, and there would be no price to pay. But I'll be thirty-eight next month. I've had my fill of groupies and one-night stands and live-in arrangements for the past fifteen years. It's gotten old, and I'll be getting old before too long. I want something more substantial in my life. Something besides the hype and fluff and nonsense that goes with the movie business. I was kinda hoping you'd want that, too."

She let some time pass before she answered but still seemed unmoved by his words. "I have to be honest and tell you that marriage is the last thing I've had on my mind lately. My career is just now rounding into shape. I have so much on my plate."

O Bed! O Breakfast!

"Yeah, but a lot of it is stuff you've heaped on needlessly," he said, crossing over and kneeling in front of her.

"Such as portraying Rella Darrow?"

"It's like portraying yourself in a way. You don't feel like you're good enough for Hollywood, either, although for different reasons. So you've taken on *Whispering Dixie* to prove yourself once and for all. Look at all the stress you've dealt with this weekend just trying to line up our accommodations. What do you think will happen when we start the actual shoot—whether it's here or in some other town? I know you want to prove yourself as a serious actress, and I'll pitch in and help you every step of the way if that's what you really want. But in the meantime, let me do something else for you—for both of us. Let me give you a ring, and let's set a date. Let's at least remove that obstacle to getting some real stability in our lives, something the sniping of the press can't take away from us." He stood up, dug down into his pocket and pulled out a small black jewelry box.

She got to her feet and took it, opening it slowly and then softly sucking in air. "My God, Tim. This is breathtaking."

It was no conventional wedding band, he had seen to that. Instead of the traditional, showy solitary diamond, he had ordered up a circle of diamonds cut into the shape of small stars and set in a band of gold. "Jewels for my Jule," he said. "You are the star of my heart." He lifted it out gently and worked it down her finger.

She held it up to catch the light, flipping her hand back and forth to view it from every possible angle, and for a while there he was absolutely certain it had done the trick.

"It shoots off sparks, it's so beautiful, but I can't seem to come up with the right words. Line, please?" she said.

"That would be, 'Yes, I'll marry you, Tim.' Just say it, and let's just do it. It'll be the last story those disgusting tabloids ever print about us. After that, we'll just be a respectable old married couple. Nothing newsworthy about that in their stinking, contemptible universe."

But she did not answer him. She did not say yes, no, or anything else. Instead, she collapsed on the bed again, and he quickly sat down beside her, taking her hand in his. "You're not talking to me, Jule."

"The ring is gorgeous beyond my wildest dreams, but you've taken me completely by surprise. All this time I thought you were fine with the way things were."

"That's just it. I don't want to be just another co-star you made it with for a while. I want to be around for a long, long time. We can make movies together or not. I can play Harbaugh Kinsley and you can play Rella Darrow or not, but I want to leave something more of myself behind than a bunch of images shooting out of a projector. A son shooting for the stars, maybe. A daughter who can dress up and shine as pretty as her mother. We'll make beautiful children, Jule. I just know we will."

She remained unenthusiastic, appearing almost stoic. "If this was dialogue from some old studio movie, the audience would say we've got the roles reversed. Isn't the man the one who's supposed to plow straight ahead with his career while the woman makes the case for the warm, fuzzy nest?"

"Yeah, I know. Not exactly living up to my spread-the-seed-around, macho image, am I? But that's all it's become—just an image. It's not what I want, and it's not the real me. I think that's where lots of people in Hollywood get off on the wrong track. They start to believe their press clippings. Hell, I know I'm no great shakes as an actor. I know I'm just a wicked smirk with great abs and a deep tan. But I also know when it's time to pull out of the fantasy and get back to reality."

"Nice speech." Then she abruptly changed the subject.

"Still want to go skinny-dipping?"

"Sure. But what about my proposal? That was more than a nice speech. That was the monologue and the take of my career. A little shy of an Oscar maybe, but don't you think it deserves a reply?"

"Could I sleep on it?"

It was hardly what he wanted to hear, but he decided not to press any further. He had some skinny-dipping to do and some more love to make to his woman, and after all was said and done and they had passed another of their sweaty, athletic nights in bed, maybe—just maybe—he would awake in the morning with an honest-to-God, old-fashioned marriage on his hands.

When Megita walked into the Greek Revival townhouse that the illustrious Pulliam family had called home for four generations, she was a wreck. Fortunately, her husband, Lawrence, had not yet returned from one of his golfing weekends, and the maid had Sunday evenings off as usual, so there was no one there to sniff around, pressing her about her mood. Gradually, the rage Mary Dell had fueled within her burnt itself out as she paced about, and eventually she was left with nothing but the cold reality of the letter. She was not going to be able to shrug it off or sweep it from her memory. She would have to live with this abominable revelation for the rest of her life. And worse. Live with the knowledge that Poco and Mary Dell and Harris knew about it, too.

She opened the library liquor cabinet and downed two straight shots of bourbon, then finally collapsed in her favorite butt-sprung armchair, the one she had mashed into submission over the years while devouring her many press clippings.

The thought of revisiting those awful words was making her ill, but she had to read them again, had to get it through her skull that her perception of the venerable Pulliam legacy had been altered forever, permanently tainted by those shameful paragraphs. This just couldn't be happening to her, the Queen of Old Fort Rosalie. Couldn't have happened to her precious mother, Leona, so many years ago.

She pulled the folded sheets out of her coat pocket and began reading, simultaneously repulsed and mesmerized by each and every word written about events that had taken place light years ago in 1938. That messy, rambling, gut-wrenching, middle stretch in particular:

Emma, it started the last day of my work as an extra. We'd just wound up shooting, and I was happy as a lark to be finished. Two weeks' worth of pay as an extra, and we desperately needed the money. My dear Ben had been laid off for over a year, and we had nothing coming in. 'In Olden Times' seemed like such a godsend. And then something happened. The director's secretary had an attack of appendicitis that last day I was an extra, and they had to whisk her away for an emergency appendectomy right then and there. Victor Favors, the director, needed someone to fill in, and he looked around the set and pointed at me. 'You,' he said. 'I want you. I'll pay you extra.' He had this great booming voice and this way of looking at you that made you think he was undressing you right then and there. He was a fascinating man, and he seemed to have all the answers. You can get that impression if you hang around a movie set too long. I remember thinking how nice it would be if you could only wrap up the real world so neat and tidy at the end of each day.

Anyway, I stayed late helping him do last-minute things, and somehow we got to be alone on the set, and that's when he

O Bed! O Breakfast!

told me he'd had his eyes on me for the past two weeks. That he fancied me. Those were his exact words, can you imagine? He said he'd pay me even more if I would sleep with him, and I told him no at first. But it was the Depression, Emma, and all we had was the family name. We were so far behind with the bills, we were about to lose the car, and Ben had even talked about selling the house, our historic family home. I didn't want to have to give those things up. I wanted our Megita to have her heritage intact.

So I'm ashamed to say I gave in to Mr. Victor Favors from out in Hollywood. I slept with him for the rest of the time they filmed in Fort Rosalie, and I took the money and kept the family's head above water. I told Ben I'd gotten more work as an extra, and I hope and pray to God he never suspected anything or caught on. He certainly never said anything, but you always wonder when you're so filled with guilt. I look back on it all now and I realize we could have found some other way to survive without my whoring. We could have managed somehow. We were flat broke, but we were still Old Fort Rosalie. People would have cut us all the slack we needed.

I just threw that realization to the wind because there must have been a part of me that was flattered. A part of me that liked the thrill of it. The whole community went crazy, as you well remember. Hollywood coming to Fort Rosalie for the first time. It was such a big deal, mostly because we all made it a big deal. It's amazing how people go overboard just because a movie company is in town, what they'll do just to be able to reach out and touch movie stars.

What I've had the most trouble accepting, of course, is that I violated my marriage vows for a few extra bucks and a few weeks of passion. I'm so ashamed of myself, and it's probably wrong of me to burden you with this now, but I just had to let someone know and maybe ask for someone's forgiveness.

Ben's gone now, Megita's grown up, and I don't ever want her to find out. Maybe I can get some sense of forgiveness from you, dear Emma. If it's too much to ask, I'll understand. But I do hope you'll try and that you'll never betray my confidence.

Megita stopped reading and closed her eyes. When she opened them, she was particularly aware of the bourbon racing through her blood and was glad of it. She craved more, hoping it would wipe the slate clean, but she knew better. The reality of what her mother had done would still be there in the morning and the day after and the next and the next, anchored firmly in her brain like a monument to betrayal and bad judgment and making every waking minute an unbearable eternity.

She got up, walked over to the phone and started to call Harris Lyles. Then she thought better of it. Hell, she could work it all out at the rally in front of the Tourist Bureau tomorrow. The bottom line was that she was being made to renounce her mythical throne in this subtle, insidious, behind-the-scenes manner, and she didn't like it one goddamned bit!

Mary Dell sensed the change in Harris the second she waltzed into his kitchen and gave him her best, unbridled hug. It wasn't anything he said, it was the way he seemed to cut the embrace short. Then she looked him straight in the eye and found further puzzlement. He still seemed happy to see her, but something was definitely different about him. There was something in his expression that hadn't been there when he had dispatched her to the Founders' Club with that stirring kiss for good luck.

O Bed! O Breakfast!

"I can tell by your face it went well with Megita," Harris said.

"Yes, it did. Looks like she's going to back down. We'll know for sure tomorrow at the rally," Mary Dell replied, pulling away. "But what's with you? Am I imagining it, or has something else happened? More from Horvath, maybe?"

"Well, yes, as a matter of fact," he explained, helping her with her coat. "He did leave me another message saying he was coming down to Fort Rosalie tomorrow to see for himself if we've shut down the protests." He offered her a chair, and they sat down together at his breakfast table. "But that's not such a big deal now that you say Megita's agreed to cooperate. We can handle Horvath. No, there were a couple of other messages waiting for me when I got home. Maybe the best way to tell you is just to let you listen to them."

She didn't like the way he had phrased that last sentence. There was the vaguest hint of an apology somehow bubbling under those words. Or maybe it was guilt she was hearing. Whatever the case, she braced herself for what apparently would be some unsettling news.

Harris moved to the machine on the kitchen counter, pressed a button and the first message-in-question started playing. It was a friendly, excited female voice, and Harris just stood there, smiling uncomfortably.

"Hi, Daddy!" it began. "It's Christine. I'm calling to let you know that you're gonna be a grandfather. We found out today, and it looks like June on the delivery. Of course, Gary is beside himself and sends you his best. Please call us as soon as you can. I've already called Mama and Sis, and they're both thrilled to pieces. We'll be at home every night this week, so let's talk soon. We love you, Daddy, or should we say, Granddaddy!"

Harris paused the machine. "Can you believe it? I'm gonna

be a grandfather!"

Mary Dell rose quickly and gave him another hug. "Congratulations. How exciting for you!" But she could sense his distraction, that there was more to come, and he did not disappoint her.

"There's another message. I hope you don't mind my playing it."

"Of course not," she replied. But then he played it, and she understood everything.

"Honey!" another excited female voice began. "It's Betsy. Can you believe the news? We're going to become grandparents. Christine and I had such a wonderful talk, and of course I told her I'd be there for her when it's time, but can you believe it? Harris, I'd like to see you soon despite everything—maybe drive up tomorrow and we can talk about it. Things haven't been working out too well lately for me down here in Baton Rouge. Please don't gloat, although maybe I deserve it. Just please call me as soon as you can. Oh, honey, it's a new phase of our lives, don't you think? Call me, okay? Talk to you soon!"

Harris rewound the tape, looking a little sheepish, and Mary Dell could clearly see that he was avoiding her gaze.

"I debated whether to let you hear that or not," he said, once the machine had finished its task. "I thought it might make you feel—well, uncomfortable."

Mary Dell returned to her chair, chewing her lip pensively. "I think it would be more to the point to ask you how that message from Betsy makes you feel. You told me your divorce was a traumatic thing for you. That Betsy put you through quite a lot. How does this announcement affect those feelings?"

He moved to her quickly, gently taking her hand. "All that messiness can never really be undone. It's still here inside, hiding out like some sneak thief, always ready to rob me of any new emotions that come along."

His words knifed straight through to Mary Dell's heart. "Any new emotions meaning me?"

"No, I didn't mean it that way. I meant only that it's been difficult for me to trust the way I once did. You've noticed that I've preferred to take our relationship slow."

She felt a little better, but this business with Betsy had staying power. "Taking things slow has been just fine with me. You've been patient, gentle—everything I've ever wanted. It's just that your ex-wife has me a little worried. Are you going to see her tomorrow?"

He withdrew his hand, and his sheepish look returned. "I've already talked to her, and, yes, I promised her I'd squeeze her into my schedule somehow. I'll listen to what she has to say." Then he sprang up from his chair, flashing a smile. "But let's don't talk about Betsy now. Let's celebrate my grandchild, shall we? I think I have a little brandy in the cabinet over the sink. Will you have one with me?"

Mary Dell nodded without hesitation even though her insides were tumble-drying. "Certainly I will." She watched him puttering around the kitchen, fixing up the snifters, obviously full of himself and his newest accomplishment, and she realized she had no choice other than to go along with his surge of good feeling.

"To my grandchild!" he said, hoisting his glass moments later. "May his or her future be the brightest!"

They clinked rims and sipped, and then she added: "A politically correct toast, to be sure, sir."

"Oh, I'll be happy with whoever comes along, of course. But I have to admit there's a tiny part of me that would like to try my hand interacting with a boy this time around."

She listened to him rambling on, describing some of the things he had always wanted to do with his grandchildren when they came—places to take them, stories to tell them, special toys to buy them—and it was clear to Mary Dell that she was not going to register with him on this particular night. She had reverted to her familiar Tourist Bureau role of sweet-faced sounding board and person to bounce dreams off of and party to lodge complaints with and all the rest. It was frustrating beyond belief.

Finally, he came out of his reverie. "I'm sorry. I've gotten carried away, haven't I?"

"No, I understand. I really do. This is a special time for you."

When they had finished off the brandy, he asked her about staying the night with him, but she did not have to think twice about turning him down.

"I have so much on my mind tonight," she explained further. "And I think maybe we should both be fresh for everything that's going to happen tomorrow."

"You're not upset with me, are you?"

She decided to lie and say no. He had clearly indicated he didn't want to discuss Betsy with her, so there was no point in delving into that. At least not yet.

"Oh, by the way, you'll have to go it alone tomorrow morning at Destiny Manor," he added. "Horvath wants to see me in my office around ten. I'll catch up with you later around noon for the rally."

They fell into each other's arms, but the gesture seemed slightly tentative. "Let's just both get a good night's sleep," she told him after he'd given her a brandy-flavored kiss.

Mary Dell managed to maintain her composure during the farewell at the kitchen door, but once she'd gotten home, she rushed over and collapsed on the sofa, absentmindedly fingering her dachshund toy while she reviewed the tail end of the evening. What was the term? The one she was always

encountering in those pop psych columns in the newspapers. Oh, yes. Emotionally unavailable. Was that the case with Harris now that he was newly-linked with his former life? Or had that actually been the case all along, and she just hadn't wanted to see it?

'Damn the luck!' was the conventional phrase that tried to pop into her head first. But she soon pushed it aside. In her particular philosophy of life, the world was not a place for luck as such. It was a place for people to mingle and mesh and affect each other in a thousand different ways—good and bad. It was a place for a Leona Pulliam to encounter a Victor Favors and create a ripple effect for generations to come. A place for a Megita Larose to meet up with a Terrelle Lurkin and rub her nose in the dirt. A place for a Mary Dell Hoskins to interact with a Harris Lyles and deal with his entire other life that had nothing to do with her. Crisscrossing agendas of every conceivable kind, and luck had nothing to do with any of it.

It was a philosophy that kept Mary Dell grounded for the most part, but it didn't prevent her from tearing up as she drifted off to sleep that night.

Robert Dalby

Chapter Fourteen

It was just an old rock and roll lyric from the late 60's, but it rose with the sun like an anthem over Fort Rosalie the next morning. Vintage stuff, courtesy The Mamas and the Papas.

'Monday, Monday—can't trust that day.'

They all might have been singing or humming the gist of it, running some variation of it through their brains. Tim. Juliette. Mary Dell. Harris. Megita. All the B&B owners. The weekend frivolity with all its jockeying for position was almost over now. It was Monday morning—the day of reckoning for all concerned.

Tim was the first to force a showdown of sorts. He and Juliette were dressing for breakfast, and he waited patiently while she rummaged through her hang up bags for just the right outfit, finally selecting a sweater and skirt in the earth colors of autumn, and then she fussed with her face in the bathroom mirror and spritzed something pungent and suffocating in the general vicinity of her hair and still she hadn't given him an answer to his proposal. This, despite the underwater ballet of love they had choreographed to orgasm the evening before in the heated pool, its surface steaming in the brisk night air even before they had taken the plunge. Despite the silken pillow talk he had whispered to her all through the night. Despite his many heartfelt efforts throughout the weekend, culminating in the soul-stirring presentation of his spectacular golden ring of stars. Despite all those things, there was still no answer.

It was a few minutes before nine, and he was sitting on the edge of the bed with the patchwork quilt puddled on the floor from their nocturnal exertions, feeling vaguely discontented and much-neglected, when her rituals of self-absorption came to an end and her words finally snapped him to attention.

"I've come to a decision," she said. "We need to stay in Fort Rosalie another day."

He didn't make the connection at first, so wired was his brain for a yes or no on the marriage proposal. "What are you talking about? Why do we need to stay here another day?"

She moved across the room and sat down beside him. "Because there are just too many things up for grabs. Those horrible women and their protests out at the gates. I don't even know if I want to return to Fort Rosalie. If we do, I can't seem to decide which B&B to choose. And then I have that meeting in a few minutes with Mary Dell downstairs to ask her about becoming my new personal assistant. I just don't want to rush through any of it. So on the way out I'm going to stop by Heidi's room and tell her to book us a suite at that Hotel Fort Rosalie where the chauffeur's been staying, and then I'm going to ask her to change our plane reservations to Tuesday evening. That way I'll have more time to think things through."

Tim felt the adrenaline surging through his veins. That long, drawn-out recitation of her most pressing concerns, and not the slightest mention of his proposal of marriage. He wondered if she even realized how insulting and demeaning it all was.

"Dammit, Jule! Do you want to marry me or not?"

She held up her hand, casually staring at the ring. "Why can't you understand? I'd rather not cram a major decision like that into such a crowded agenda."

He sprang to his feet and pounded a fist into the palm of his hand. "Geez, Jule—here I am talking about love and marriage, and you sound like a quote from a master's thesis in business management!"

"Oh, stop posturing. Why can't you just let me get all this stuff behind me and then I can give you a decision when we get back to Malibu?"

He sat back down and took her hand, lifting it to his lips, kissing it first and then rubbing it gently. "Because, Jule, love of my life, something tells me that if I don't get a yes out of you now, I'm never gonna get one. There'll always be another deadline or another decision or another project standing in the way. My gut instinct tells me that it's now or never."

She withdrew her hand and stared him down. "What are you saying? If I don't tell you yes right now, we're through?"

"At the very least, I'm through with Fort Rosalie. I'm going back home today. I'm not staying with you at the Hotel Fort Rosalie or anywhere else in this crazy town tonight. Tell Heidi not to change my plane ticket. I'm leaving when we were supposed to leave. If you want me, you'll know where to find me."

She rose and headed toward the door, turning back at the last moment to strike a mannequin-like pose. "You can talk all you want like a bad movie script, but I still have that meeting with Mary Dell and a thousand other things on my mind right now. I had hoped you would be a little more patient and understanding, but evidently that's not in the cards."

Tim didn't feel very good about it, but he had his answer. It was not in the cards. Instead, there had been more temporizing. More excuses. More of the same old, same old. Juliette Cadbury, the darling of the tabloids, was not going to change her spots any time soon. At least now he knew where he stood. He had given it his best shot. There was nothing left to do but pack.

Mary Dell was sitting poolside nursing a glass of orange juice

O Bed! O Breakfast!

when Juliette breezed out onto the patio to join her just past nine. The Lurkins were still inside huddling with the servants about breakfast, so they had all the privacy they needed for their meeting.

"Where's your boss man?" Juliette said, pouring herself a cup of coffee from a nearby table and then dragging one of the cast-iron chairs across the bricks.

"He had an important meeting this morning with the head of the Mississippi Film Commission. We're going to lay this thing with the Casserole Patrol to rest, I assure you. I expect some sort of announcement later today at Megita's rally."

"You're absolutely sure of that? It would relieve at least one of my major concerns."

Mary Dell leaned forward and spoke with confidence. "Trust me on this one."

Juliette looked suddenly smug, even cocky, stretching her arms high above her head as if a great weight had been lifted from her shoulders. "That makes our meeting this morning all the more perfect. I have a proposal for you. As you know, Heidi and Edding will be getting married a few months down the road, and I'll be needing a new personal assistant. I've been admiring your efficiency throughout the weekend and thought I'd just go ahead and ask you if you might be interested in considering becoming Heidi's replacement. You wouldn't have to start right away, of course. Heidi wants to continue through the shoot, right up to the wedding."

Mary Dell took the news in stride, barely registering a sense of surprise. It was that business in the pool yesterday. By some mysterious process, the thoughts she had entertained when Juliette had jumped in with her clothes on seemed to have prepared her for this moment. She had wondered then what it would be like to work for Juliette Cadbury, that Heidi surely had her hands full dealing with her, and now here she

was being given the opportunity to find out for certain. She quickly decided to underplay her hand and remain as calm and collected as possible. That had always worked well for her in the past.

"Could you give me a few more details about salary and duties, that sort of thing?"

"I'd be delighted. For starters, I have no idea what you're making now at the Tourist Bureau, but I'll triple it. And if that's not satisfactory, we can negotiate."

Mary Dell swallowed hard as dollar signs, decimal points and zeroes collided in her head like a school of shiny minnows in a feeding frenzy. She could work the rest of her life at the Bureau and not approach such a figure.

"Triple what I'm making now would be more than generous."

"I thought so. As for your duties—it would probably take less time to list the things my personal assistant doesn't do—but I'll mention just a few of the things Heidi does for me on a regular basis to give you some idea. She makes all travel reservations, answers all invitations and letters, screens all telephone calls, coordinates every meeting, lunch and dinner I take with my slug of an agent, or members of my new production company staff, the bloodsucking press, major and minor producers, trendy and passe directors, A-list and struggling actors, cherished family and so-called friends, not to mention logging my daily agenda onto both my desktop and laptop, ordering out when I want to stay in and eat, picking up dry cleaning and alterations, working out with me in the gym, going to the library to do research for me, and well, a thousand other things. Have I worn you to a frazzle yet?"

Mary Dell gave her best impression of a worldly laugh. "It all sounds like one great big glamorous blur."

"That's where you're wrong. It's hard work, twenty-four

and seven. Even your so-called down time will turn out to be a lot of bother, just like this weekend did." Juliette took a healthy sip of her coffee, and Mary Dell welcomed the lull. It gave her time to gather her thoughts and take the logical next step.

"How soon would you want a decision? I'm sure you can appreciate what an earthshaking effect accepting a position like this would have on my life."

"Earthshaking," Juliette replied with a smile. "Is that a subconscious reference to our California geology? If so, you're wise to bring it up. You'll find that nothing steels your wool like waking up to an earthquake out there. But to answer your question—I'd like your decision by, say, eleven o'clock tomorrow morning at the Tourist Bureau, if at all possible. We're staying over another night at the Hotel Fort Rosalie and flying out Tuesday afternoon so I can have a little more time to make my decision on the B&B. I don't mean to rush you, but if you're not interested in the position, I need to get a search started out in California right away."

"Let me sleep on your offer and get back to you tomorrow," Mary Dell said, forging bravely ahead. Then she decided to shift the focus slightly. "You know, I put myself in your shoes last night when Harris and I were discussing the competition after dinner, and I realized then just how difficult the B&B decision must be for you."

Juliette put down her coffee cup and threw up her hands. "You don't know the half of it. One minute I'm sure I want to stay out here at Destiny Manor with these down-home people and their gorgeous food and sinful swimming pool. I empathize so totally with the way they've been treated by the *noblesse oblige*, and I'd like to support them in any way I can. Then the next minute I'll get a genuine case of the giggles remembering how much fun I had waving that wand and

mincing around the parlor in that costume at dear Miss Aimee's Plum Cottage. And then there's all this pressure Heidi keeps putting on me to select Betterslie because of the wedding. She doesn't think it would look right for us not to stay there, all things considered." She brought her hands together prayerfully in front of her face and lowered her eyes. "I don't suppose you'd be interested in signing on as my assistant right away and making that decision for me? You could even think of it as a training exercise, since there would be times I'd be out of pocket to make decisions affecting various aspects of my career. Heidi acts as my proxy all the time, and I've almost never been disappointed in her judgment. Shall we put yours to the acid test?"

Mary Dell took a cautionary breath, fully cognizant of the fact she was being drawn out into deep water where the sharks liked to circle, astute enough to realize that fording the babbling brook of Fort Rosalie was hardly the same as negotiating the rocky shoals of Hollywood. She must keep her distance, maintain her perspective, make it back to shore without drowning or being devoured.

"That's very tempting, I must admit, but I can't make up my mind about the personal assistant position right this minute, so it wouldn't be fair for me to advise you in any way. As long as I'm a Tourist Bureau executive, I can't appear to be showing any favoritism. I just wouldn't feel right about it."

She was greatly relieved when Juliette flashed one of her dazzling smiles and said: "I like your response. It shows you have integrity and loyalty, and anyone who works for me has to have both."

For some reason a vision of Harris holding Betsy's hand and smiling blissfully at her while they discussed the joys of impending grandparenthood flashed into Mary Dell's head. It was a bond she could neither share nor threaten. All she could do was accept it with one of her sweet-faced smiles, and it made her focus on Juliette's proposal all the more seriously.

"I think I definitely have both," Mary Dell said with a touch of defiance. "You work on the B&B decision, and I'll work on the personal assistant decision, and we'll announce both tomorrow at the Tourist Bureau."

"I still wish there was some way you could help me get off dead center with the bed-and-breakfast thing."

"I'm just curious," said Mary Dell, leaning forward expectantly. "No one has even a slight advantage at this point?"

Juliette's brow furrowed. "Okay. I confess. I have to admit I do want to help that darling Miss Aimee with her financial situation. I don't want to see her go out of business."

"How did you know about that? Did she tell you?"

"Let's just say a certain Australian birdie told me."

Mary Dell was hardly surprised at the revelation. It was one of those things that was difficult to explain in the modern era of political correctness. Tasmania and Miss Aimee. Eola and Edding. Relationships that seemed slightly retro and out-of-date to the casual observer, but they were anything but. Throwing such disparate elements as race, age and gender differences into the blender, they had managed to mix together smoothly because equal parts devotion and respect had been added to the recipe, and those ingredients never went out of style.

"I know that plump little birdie quite well," Mary Dell replied.

"But then there's this business about Heidi's wedding out at Betterslie," Juliette continued. "She really has done wonders for me over the past seven years, so I feel I owe her something, and her request that we stay at Betterslie isn't the least bit unreasonable. I had a marvelous and stimulating time out there. Oh, Edding did push me to the wall on a few things, but I liked that. He has spunk, and so do I. Not to mention that he's very serious about writing a chapter about me in that *O Bed! O Breakfast!* book of his. That's really quite tempting. I would so enjoy the opportunity to get the truth out for once. God, you have no idea how galling it is to have those tabloids nipping at your heels all the time." She paused for a breath. "So I really am torn, and I can't seem to resolve it one way or the other. If you come up with some magical solution between now and tomorrow, give me a call."

"Will do."

Azureen appeared on the patio to summon them to the dining room for eggs benedict, stuffed mushroom caps and champagne, and soon they had joined the others for the sophisticated feast. Although the food was superbly prepared, arranged, and served as usual, the atmosphere at the table was noticeably strained. Mary Dell picked up on a particular lack of eye contact between Tim and Juliette, and Heidi seemed preoccupied—almost certainly with her thoughts of Edding and Betterslie. It was a nervous-looking Terrelle who finally broke through the tension.

"Almost decision-time on the B&B, huh, Juliette?"

Mary Dell quickly intervened. "I know this is going to sound like torture to you, Terrelle, but Juliette has just informed me that she's going to postpone the decision another twenty-four hours. She'll announce it tomorrow around eleven at the Tourist Bureau."

Terrelle slumped noticeably, and Johnny's food went down the wrong pipe, initiating a noisy spate of coughing followed by a couple of sips of water and Azureen rushing over to pat her employer on the back.

"I know you're disappointed," Juliette explained, once the crisis had passed and Johnny's crimson face had faded to pink. "But we're staying over another night so we can work things out exactly right."

Terrelle perked up. "Oh, honey, that's just dandy. Naturally, you're welcome to stay with us."

"I appreciate the offer. But Heidi's already booked a suite at the Hotel Fort Rosalie. It'll keep things on an even keel that way. I'm sure you understand."

It was then that Tim abruptly threw his napkin over his plate, excusing himself curtly, and left the table, having barely made a dent in his breakfast.

"He's not feeling well, honey?" Terrelle said. "He's gobbled up everything we've put in front of him so far. Never have seen such a healthy appetite. Better even than my Johnny's."

"Yes, I'm sure that's it," Juliette said. "Maybe a little upset stomach after all that rich food." Then she, too, excused herself, leaving a half-finished serving.

Terrelle turned to Mary Dell with a look of desperation. "You think it was maybe the ostrich?"

"Just relax, Terrelle. Everything's going to work out fine."

It was her standard soothing Tourist Bureau line, but it was impossible for Mary Dell to apply it to herself at that point. Maybe things would work out fine, maybe not. She had too many things to ponder at once, not the least of which was the personal assistant offer versus her relationship with Harris. She had come to the realization during breakfast that if she chose one, she couldn't possibly have the other.

She had become so mentally entangled in it all that she remembered nothing of her drive back to the Tourist Bureau. Could barely recall standing on the front steps of Destiny Manor thanking Johnny and Terrelle for the gourmet breakfast and the rest of their hospitality. Was not really able to conjure up her parting remarks to Juliette before she headed out, although she thought she had something like, "We'll expect you at the Bureau after you check into the hotel."

What she desperately needed was to resolve her ambiguous feelings regarding this new Harris and Betsy development and to know once and for all where she stood with him.

Harris looked like he had been running on a treadmill or otherwise pushed to the limit when Mary Dell appeared in the doorframe of his office. His hair was disheveled, and his face flushed and sweaty, so she temporarily shelved her concerns about their romantic relationship and quickly adopted her most solicitous demeanor.

"Horvath?" she said, sitting across from him.

"It was a nightmare," he replied, exhaling dramatically and rubbing his forehead with his right hand. "He was a mad hornet from the moment he arrived this morning. He had me drive him out to the gates of Destiny Manor so he could watch the Casserole Patrol in action for himself. He wanted to know why they were still protesting, and I tried to explain that I expected all of that foolishness to be over and done with at the rally later today, but, as you know, I couldn't go into any details concerning Megita and the reasons. He thought I was stalling."

"Where is he now?"

"Downstairs in the meeting room writing a little speech to cover his rear end if the rally doesn't go our way. The gist of it will be that the Film Commission will officially move *Whispering Dixie* to Natchez."

"I can't imagine Megita taking any chances with her reputation," Mary Dell replied. "But in any case Juliette will have the last word, and I assured her in our meeting this morning that I had every reason to believe the Casserole Patrol would soon be a distant memory." Then she remembered Juliette's proposal and decided to tackle the thing head-on. "And something else very interesting came up at that meeting with Juliette out at Destiny Manor. She offered me the position of personal assistant when Heidi leaves. For triple my current salary, by the way."

Harris looked even more bewildered than he had moments before. "And are you going to accept?"

"I honestly don't know yet."

"When will you know?"

"Juliette wants my answer tomorrow here at the Bureau when she announces her B&B decision."

He rose and started pacing, staring at his shoes as he walked, hands stuffed into his pockets. It was Mary Dell's observation that he was never at his best with his strong, beautiful hands hidden away from the world.

"Do you really think you'd enjoy working with her? You've seen her in action. All the crazy emotions, all the immature behaviors from A to Z. Somehow, I just can't picture you being married to a clipboard."

Whatever she had expected of him, it was not this judgmental sarcasm, and it created a backlash of sorts. The image of him rendezvousing and holding hands with Betsy returned full-force, triggering her rarely-seen aggressive mode.

"That's Heidi's style. It doesn't have to be mine. What makes you think I couldn't bring my own unique and stabilizing qualities to the position? I've certainly done that for you here."

Suddenly, they were in the midst of a full-blown argument, the first that had ever taken place between them.

"I can't believe you'd really consider going to work for that spoiled Hollywood brat," he said, taking his hands out of his pockets only to shake his index finger at her.

"She's not a brat. She's a very complex person with a lot of responsibilities and a lot of pressure on her. If a man took on all that she has, you'd probably buy him a few drinks, slap him on the back and hail him as one of your cultural heroes."

"Maybe. But I guarantee you a man wouldn't handle pressure by jumping into a swimming pool with his clothes on. Face the truth, why don't you? Juliette Cadbury is nothing more than an emotional child with a lot of money to burn and too much time on her hands. She's as mixed up as that character she wants to portray."

"Oh, don't be such a stuffed shirt." Then, in a rare display of emotional recklessness, Mary Dell lost it completely. "And you wonder why Betsy left you?"

The words had the chilling effect of a virtual freeze-frame, causing them to stare each other down across the space between them without moving so much as an eyelash. Finally, he managed to trudge across the floor to his desk and collapse into his chair, shattering the stalemate.

"What the hell just happened here?" he said. "It was like two completely different people were here in the room for a while."

"You're right. But I had no business saying that to you about Betsy, Harris. I just lost my temper."

He looked up from his lap, slowly shaking his head. "Does this have anything to do with my seeing Betsy for dinner tonight?"

Mary Dell saw no percentage in holding anything back now. "I'm afraid it does. That whole scene last night with the message from her has really thrown me."

"Well, this job offer from Juliette has thrown me, too. It's not that I want to come off like I'm trying to tell you what to do, but I can't lie about it. I'd really like for you to stay here in Fort Rosalie."

O Bed! O Breakfast!

She eyed him cautiously. "Is that a professional or personal opinion?"

"Both. We were beginning to explore the personal side of it quite nicely, I thought, but there's also no way in hell you're not the best account executive the Bureau's ever had. Juliette Cadbury obviously recognized your abilities from the get-go."

"Yet you think my working for her would be a bad move."

"I think she'd use you up and drive you crazy."

Mary Dell backtracked to Friday afternoon and the first time she had observed Heidi taking notes at the Bureau. How driven, how compulsive she had seemed throughout that entire tension-packed meeting! Harris's last remark was resonating with her strongly now. Perhaps Heidi hadn't started out that way. Perhaps she had once been just a normal, if efficient, person, but working with Juliette seven days a week, twenty-four hours a day, had turned her into that hamster-like creature glued to that clipboard. After all, it appeared she had jumped with dizzying speed at the opportunity to hang her former life out to dry in order to reinvent herself as the mistress of Betterslie.

"I'll admit you've given me something to think about there," Mary Dell said.

"This meeting with Betsy," he began, wincing slightly at the mention of her name. "It's something I owe her. We are going to be grandparents together, regardless of the rest. Don't blow this out of proportion. I know all of Betsy's little tricks and lots of ways around her. You do understand, don't you?"

The small part of her that understood was being crowded out by the rest of her that resented Betsy's intrusion, and she didn't pull her punch. "I understand about the grandparent part. I'm still working on the rest."

He winked at her. "Your jealousy is flattering beyond belief to this old married and divorced warrior." With that, he stood

up, motioned her over to his side, put his arm around her waist and kissed her gently once on the cheek, then lightly twice on the lips. It was exactly what she needed—some sort of physical reinforcement of his availability to quell her doubts for the moment.

Word of Megita's rally in front of the Tourist Bureau had attracted a respectable crowd of onlookers by the time the noon hour arrived, but as usual the Fort Rosalie police department had everyone peacefully separated and the situation fully under control. Mary Dell and Harris were standing before one of the second-story windows monitoring and observing things out on the street, when they were joined by Jim Horvath and Juliette Cadbury.

"I've just made it clear to Ms. Cadbury that she doesn't have to put up with this a minute longer," he told the group. "I've assured her that this is not the way we ordinarily do things here in Mississippi. We fully appreciate the contribution that Hollywood makes to our state's economy."

Mary Dell was pleased to see that Juliette was smiling and appeared to be handling Horvath and his obsequious manner without too much trouble. The man was definitely a pistol. Short, florid, always running his mouth and full of himself, he had some of Edding Denbo's qualities, but what truly defined him was that almighty dollar sign practically branded on his forehead. He was, always had been, and always would be strictly business, and he had no tolerance for anything or anyone that got in the way of his mission to convince every film in Hollywood to come to Mississippi.

"You did notice that there are no signs out there this time, didn't you, Jim?" Mary Dell pointed out. She and Harris had

breathed a bit easier when the Casserole Patrol had arrived without their inflammatory sentiments high above their heads.

Horvath looked puzzled. "So?"

"So they were there at the gates of Destiny Manor this morning," Harris said, finishing off Mary Dell's line of reasoning. "They were obviously told not to bring them to the rally. It's like I tried to explain to you, Jim. Megita Larose will change her spots right before your very eyes in just a few minutes. Shall we go down for the big moment?"

Horvath still seemed skeptical, but they all moved together down the stairs and out the front door, joining the rest of the Tourist Bureau employees who had already assembled there. Then, a curious thing happened. Instead of making some grand speech in front of her troops as everyone fully expected, Megita walked across the street by herself, making a bee line for Juliette Cadbury.

"Miss Cadbury," she said, looking the actress straight in the eye. "It appears I owe you an apology. It appears you were correct. I put far too much faith in one of those supermarket bird cage liners. My organization meant no harm with our protests, although we do not regret the right to exercise such protests, but we realize that we have not achieved the results we sought. We have only succeeded in painting a misleading portrait of our historic city and our great state, and we sincerely hope you will not hold it against us. For our part, we have had our say and will put our Casserole Patrol to rest, saving it for a future and more righteous cause. We mean it sincerely when we say we hope you will return to make your film here in Fort Rosalie."

There was a polite handshake between the two women and then Juliette said: "Apology accepted."

Mary Dell leaned into Harris, squeezing his hand tightly in the excitement of the moment. It could not have gone better,

and she knew there would be more good feeling to follow because of a suggestion she had made to Juliette a few minutes before Horvath had introduced himself and subsequently monopolized her attention.

"Before you go, Mrs. Larose," Juliette added, "I wanted to assure you that I hold no grudges. If any members of your organization would be interested in trying out for parts as extras in my film, they'd be more than welcome. They would just be walk-ons, of course, but we need people with style and energy, and your ladies certainly fit the bill."

Mary Dell beamed as the last of her plan was unveiled. This was the touch that would allow Megita to exit with her dignity and leadership intact, and Juliette had implemented it perfectly.

"Oh," said Megita, appearing to be caught off-guard. Then she drew herself up and managed a smile. "I don't know if anyone would be, but I'll put it to the members when we get back to the Founders' Club."

"Oh, and one more thing," Juliette added. "I couldn't help but notice your organization's catering skills out there over the weekend. Perhaps, some of them would care to make a little extra money and cater for my production company when the time comes?"

This time Megita seemed genuinely impressed. "That's an intriguing offer, I must admit."

Mary Dell was now reasonably certain that Megita would find a way to sugar coat and put the best face on the whole thing for her girls, adding an exclamation point to whatever reasons she had given them for discontinuing their picketing at the rally. More importantly, none of the Casserole Patrol would ever know about any of the machinations that had gone on behind the scenes.

As soon as Megita was out of earshot, Harris turned to

O Bed! O Breakfast!

Horvath and said: "Didn't I tell you everything was going to be just fine?"

Horvath shrugged and then addressed Juliette. "Are you completely satisfied with all of this, Miss Cadbury?"

"Yes, I think so. We have a good faith apology here. I think we can move on to other issues."

"There are other issues?" he said, looking alarmed.

"Relax, Mr. Horvath. Everything else is stuff I have to figure out. A decision on the B&B, for instance."

That appeared to squelch Horvath once and for all, and Mary Dell knew that the crisis had passed. Time to turn her attention to the competition once again. She spent the remainder of the afternoon tied up with paperwork and phone calls to all the owners, setting up the Tuesday morning meeting. In fact, she stayed so busy that she lost track of Harris completely, and thoughts of their relationship never entered her mind.

Mary Dell gave serious consideration to taking the phone off the hook when she got home that evening so she could give the pros and cons of the job offer one last thorough review. She regretted not having done so when it rang just as she was starting dinner. It was Juliette, sounding like she just might be slightly boozed up.

"I'm way up here in this suite on the top floor all by myself," she was saying. "Heidi just left to be with Edding and more of those eternal poems, and you probably don't know it yet, but Tim's completely left. Town, I mean. The chauffeur drove him up to Jackson a few hours ago. He's on the plane by now. Can you come over to the hotel, Mary Dell? I really need a shoulder tonight. That's one of those personal assistant

197

duties I forgot to mention to you this morning. Providing the proverbial shoulder to cry on."

Mary Dell frowned. She was tired. She hadn't eaten dinner. More importantly, she did not feel like holding Juliette Cadbury's hand tonight after more or less babysitting her over an entire weekend. But her Tourist Bureau training and diplomacy rose to the surface. She said yes, she would come, she just needed ten or fifteen minutes. Even though, she neglected to add, it meant microwaving some frozen leftover she would rather not have eaten and then gobbling it down, which she never liked to do.

In the car she had time to reflect further. This was probably going to be a taste of what life would be like for her on a daily basis if she ended up taking the job. Maybe it was providential that she got this preview to keep the temptation of that lucrative salary at bay. As far as she could tell, that was just about the only positive aspect of the position.

"I know I'm probably imposing on you," Juliette said, after ushering her into the hotel's penthouse suite with its breathtaking view of the river, the lights of the city below and the Louisiana suburbs on the other side. "But sometimes I just lose my compass. Don't know where the hell I am or where I'm headed. Do you ever feel like that?"

Mary Dell removed her coat and took a seat at a small table near the window where Juliette had set up shop with various bottles of booze, mixers and ice. "I've been feeling like that all the time lately. I think it comes with being a part of the travel industry."

"Please. Fix yourself a drink. As you can see, I ordered up a small liquor store."

"I think I'll pass. So what are we talking about tonight? Does this have to do with the B&B decision or Tim leaving town?"

O Bed! O Breakfast!

Juliette plopped down into a chair with her clear but obviously potent concoction. She took a healthy swallow and then thrust out her hand, drawing attention to the ring. "This is what we're talking about for starters."

Mary Dell gasped while leaning over to examine it more closely. "My God, Juliette, that's the most gorgeous thing I've ever seen in my life."

"Isn't it, though? It's Tim's idea of an engagement ring. You have to hand it to him. The man has exquisite taste."

"Is this your roundabout way of telling me you're getting married?"

Juliette rattled the ice in her drink and rolled her eyes. "No, it's just one more thing I can't seem to make up my mind about. Tim flew home because I wouldn't give him a straight answer to his marriage proposal. But I just don't know the answer. I like having Tim around, and I appreciate the fact that he's a good lover and all. But I don't know if I want the baggage. Do you know what I mean?"

Mary Dell was momentarily puzzled. Then she thought about her relationship with Harris and the baggage he brought to the table in the form of his ex-wife and daughters and soon-to-be grandchild. They were a part of his life forever, people that would never really go away. On the other hand, she didn't see that Juliette had anything like that to contend with. Tim was free and clear, and what's more, he was definitely in love with her. Any fool could have seen that by watching them together over the weekend.

"If you want my opinion, I think you should marry the guy pronto," Mary Dell offered. "He's a prince, and I'm not saying that just because he's a movie star. Don't you think you and Tim could be happy together?"

Juliette looked away, scanning the lights reflected in the river from the Louisiana horizon.

"I don't know. I just remember how hard my mother had to work to support us in that salon full of curlers and peroxide smells. My father walked out on her when I was just a little girl, and I've been determined ever since not to put myself in her position of helplessness. I like calling the shots in my life, and so far I've been able to do that."

"What about love? What about family and children?"

"That's what Tim says he wants right now, but I don't think I'm ready for it yet. He's in one place, and I'm in another, and the gap seems as wide as the Mississippi River out there."

Mary Dell's sigh was long and plaintive, and she shut her eyes briefly before speaking. "I suppose you realize you're going to break the man's heart."

"Hey. I haven't officially said no yet." She finished off her drink, briefly sucking the lemon wedge nestled at the bottom and then sliding the glass across the table where it clinked against the bottle of expensive vodka she had been steadily draining. "Maybe it's just that I have an aversion to happy endings."

"Let me run something past you," Mary Dell said, trying a different approach, determined to break through the liquor and the lackadaisical attitude. "We've both read *Whispering Dixie*. What really sold you on the project? What do you think made it a national bestseller? Be honest now. I think we both know it can't really have been all the politically-correct posturing. I mean, Rella goes home to root around in her backyard for answers and a quick and easy fix for that guilt-trip she's on but basically comes away with nothing but empty platitudes. What she does manage to straighten out is her personal life. Your man, Cathcart, was crazy like a fox. He knew that what would really put his novel over was to sprinkle it liberally with all those sex scenes. Add a dash or two of honest-to-goodness hot, sizzling passion, and you've got it

O Bed! O Breakfast!

made in the shade these days. The checkout counter romance novelists have known that for generations. If I recall correctly, Rella's lover, Harbaugh Kinsley, nails her in the hayloft, in the rowboat out on the fishpond, in the backseat of that rented convertible at that old abandoned drive-in, and don't let's leave out that marvelous scene where he ends up proposing to her right after they've done it in the hot-air balloon. What's more, she accepts. She at least heads back to Hollywood with her future husband in tow. That's what made *Whispering Dixie* a success, not Rella's long, laborious quest to illuminate the past. End of monologue."

Juliette looked momentarily stunned, but that was soon replaced with supreme amusement as she displayed the ring in front of her face. "I'll be good and damned. It appears my Tim was a very apt pupil, playing Harbaugh Kinsley for real right under my nose all weekend."

"Well, everybody has to get their ideas from somewhere. Looks like he paid more attention to *Whispering Dixie* than you thought."

"That devil. Him and his grape jelly and underwater technique and—"

Mary Dell raised her eyebrows smartly, and Juliette broke off.

"So are you going to tell the man what he wants to hear when you get back?" Mary Dell said.

"Don't rush me, girl. Opening up my eyes a little was a good first step, though." Juliette began to applaud, slowly at first, then more rapidly. "You see how good you are at this? You're not just a shoulder, you're a therapist. Heidi couldn't analyze people at all—just figure out timetables, that sort of thing. I think we'll make a great team, don't you?" She continued to ramble on while fixing herself another drink. "Byron Cathcart is supposed to have the script ready for me when I get back to Malibu, but I think I'll probably have to make some changes now. When I bought the film rights, I insisted on final script approval. You'll realize how important that is when we get into actual production."

Mary Dell suddenly realized that Juliette was talking to her as if she had already accepted the personal assistant position. The possibility of being turned down had evidently not entered her mind. Little wonder. The woman was used to getting her way in everything, but this time she might not get what she wanted. Mary Dell glanced at her watch and stood up in an attempt to extricate herself. It was now or never.

"Well, I definitely think we got something accomplished here, but maybe we should call it a night and try to get some sleep," Mary Dell suggested.

Juliette rose and tugged at her sleeve. "But I'm still not any closer to my B&B decision. You haven't thought of anything yet?"

"Not a thing. Not with everything else that's been going on. Just sleep on it, Juliette. I'm sure you'll come up with the right decision."

It took further skillful maneuvering, but Mary Dell finally managed to slip out of the spotlight and head down the elevator to a late dinner in the hotel restaurant. That cupful of vegetable soup she'd hurriedly slurped up was hardly enough to hold her until morning. She approached the hostess on duty and requested a table in no-smoking, then busied herself scanning the room during the wait. It was on her second pass that she spotted Harris and Betsy in a distant corner, holding hands and looking into each other's eyes like lovers on their honeymoon. She squinted to get a good look. Betsy didn't seem to have changed much. Was still wearing that upswept blonde hairdo and a pair of those long, dangling earrings that were so distracting up close.

O Bed! O Breakfast!

Mary Dell shrank back, knowing they hadn't seen her yet. How could they—locked onto each other that way? Then Betsy leaned over and kissed Harris on the cheek, and that was enough to send Mary Dell to the exits. She had no intention of trying to eat a meal with that sort of floor show for entertainment. Or worse yet—ending up having to go over to their table and make polite conversation through clenched teeth. She would just have to whip up something at home, where perhaps she could get some privacy and time alone at last.

She hated herself for letting doubts about Harris creep back in during the ride home, but she couldn't help it. The session with Juliette had sharpened her sense of paranoia. Ultimately, she saw it as another timely test of her philosophy. More intersections and interactions to deal with. No such thing as good or bad luck. Just that endless, eternal crisscrossing of souls.

Safely back in her kitchen, she tried to settle her mind by making a chef salad. All that chopping and slicing and dicing would be good therapy, allowing her to wield a knife on a variety of inanimate objects that would feel no pain—like veggies and cold cuts. Her strategy began to work. She decided to put Harris up neatly on a little shelf which she designated as things to take down and dust off and polish tomorrow. Then, as she tore apart the iceberg lettuce with gusto, something began to bubble up from her subconscious. Soon, it had activated other key brain cells, and she realized she was on to something. It was a solution to Juliette's B&B quandary, and it had to do with something Miss Aimee had said at her tea party during that initial, illuminating visit to Plum Cottage.

Mary Dell sat down to her salad and worked it all out in her head as she ate. She didn't see any reason Juliette wouldn't go for it, and it certainly didn't compromise her position as a Tourist Bureau executive. It was the perfect solution. Frank

Sinatra. Salad days. That song. Those words. Why hadn't she or Harris suggested it long before now?

Excitedly, she finished up her salad and looked up the Hotel Fort Rosalie's number in the phone book.

"Penthouse suite," she said, moments after dialing and feeling on top of the world.

O Bed! O Breakfast!

Chapter Fifteen

It was ten o'clock Tuesday morning—exactly one hour before Juliette was set to announce her long-anticipated decision to the B&B owners—and Mary Dell had just given Harris the good news behind the closed doors of his office. Juliette had embraced her solution to the booking, and now everything looked like clear sailing.

"Why the hell didn't I think of that?" Harris said, shaking his head.

"I know what you mean. Sometimes the simple and obvious things are the most elusive."

"Well, thanks for stumbling onto the obvious, then."

There was an awkward pause, and Mary Dell had a strong inkling of what was on his mind. But she, too, had something she needed to get off her chest.

"I'm sure you want to know about my decision next," she said. "But there's something I just have to ask you. How did things go last night between you and Betsy?"

He hesitated, looking vaguely uncomfortable. "Okay, I suppose. She's going back to Baton Rouge today. You know how things are between Betsy and myself."

But she wasn't in the mood to let him off the hook. "No, I don't. How are things between you and Betsy? A lot cozier than you've led me to believe, apparently."

"What's that supposed to mean?"

"I mean that I saw you at the table with her last night at the hotel, and it didn't look to me like you were having to slug your way through any sort of wrenching ordeal."

The color rose in his face. "What the hell were you doing? Spying on me?"

"Hardly. I'd been consoling Juliette up in her suite for quite a while and wanted a little bit to eat before bed. I just happened to spot the two of you making eyes at each other when I walked up to be seated. Naturally, I lost my appetite and left quickly."

He took on a sheepish look and said: "You have to know Betsy. She's a touchy-feely sort of person. I didn't see any reason for rancor while discussing our grandchild."

Mary Dell pressed boldly ahead, disturbed by the tinge of guilt she detected in his voice. "And how did your evening end?"

"I don't know that that's any of your business."

"I think it's very much my business when I'm trying to decide whether to stay here in Fort Rosalie or leave for Hollywood."

Harris looked stunned. Finally, he said: "All right. She invited me up to her room after dinner. She said it was just to talk with a little more privacy, and I did go to hear her out. She unloaded her sob story on me—how her studly professor was cheating on her all the time with lots of those shapely LSU co-eds. She claimed she's seen the error of her ways and wants to explore the possibility of a reconciliation with me, especially now that we have our grandparenthood looming on the horizon."

"And do you think a reconciliation is possible?"

He shook his head, but Mary Dell thought the gesture lacked a certain conviction.

"I'm just curious," she said, unable to restrain herself. "Where did you sleep last night?"

She knew what the answer would be when he took so long to speak.

"You have to understand. She conjured up her bucket of tears, and that particular ploy has always gotten to me. I could never stand to see her cry. So, yes, I spent the night with her. I started out on top of the covers, but later on she reached over and touched me, and something happened."

Mary Dell mulled things over, remaining strangely calm. "I thought you knew all the ways around her."

"I thought I did."

"You haven't faced facts, Harris Lyles. You aren't over your ex-wife yet. You still have a thing for her. I suspected it from the moment we started dating, but now here it is, right out in the open, staring us both in the face."

He drew back and held in his breath for a second. "I know in my heart that I could never be happy with Betsy again. Not after what she put me through. I really do want to make a clean start with you. I hope you can believe me, and I hope you'll stay here in Fort Rosalie and give me a chance to prove it."

She stood up resolutely and said: "You'll have my decision at the meeting."

Shortly before eleven, the B&B owners began arriving by twos, as if they were boarding Noah's ark. Miss Aimee, the customary early bird, had brought Tasmania Evans along with her, evidently for moral support. Both women seemed supremely composed, projecting an air of confidence as they solemnly entered the upstairs meeting room. Next, Edding Denbo and Heidi Pendleton drifted in, arm-in-arm, totally preoccupied with each other and taking no notice of anything or anyone else around them. Their gazes were worthy of the sort of photos the tabloids were always running of Juliette and Tim when caught off-guard. And finally, the Lurkins burst through the doorway, striding across the room in that Texas way of theirs

to plop down in their seats. For once there was very little small talk amongst the rivals, making it easy for Juliette to step up to the podium and open the proceedings.

"I hope you'll all bear with me," she began, shuffling the notes that she and Mary Dell had worked on earlier that morning. "I had a very difficult decision to make, and I know you're all just dying to hear it, but first there are some things I just must say to you."

There was the merest hint of groaning, followed once again by an overwhelming, strained silence. "This has been a hectic and memorable few days for all of us, and I'm sure we wouldn't want to go through something like this again anytime soon. But I'm equally sure we've all learned something about the true nature of hospitality in the process. It's more than just a setting of spotless antique china on the table or a vase of fresh-picked purple flowers in the hallway or the smell of clean linen on a big, comfy bed. More than delicious cooking and endlessly-flowing liquor sipped to poetry or a late-night swim in a heated pool in your birthday suit. More than anything else, it seems to me to be a way of sharing part of your life with strangers. Of course, I must confess to each of you that before this past weekend, I had never even stayed in a bed-and-breakfast. Penthouse suites high above the hoi polloi had always been my modus operandi since becoming famous several years back. I felt I deserved the space and God knows I needed the privacy. But this time, for this film, I knew I needed something extra, particularly since I was planning to sink a considerable portion of my own fortune into this project. *Whispering Dixie* is an unusual and controversial book, and, therefore, not everyone's cup of tea or accompaniment to a ladies' club casserole, as was so vividly pointed out to me. I needed to understand more about the motivations behind it so I could interpret my character more realistically and do the job

O Bed! O Breakfast!

I wanted to do."

She paused to turn over a sheet of paper and managed to squeeze in a breath for good measure. "What better way, I told myself, than to dig beneath the surface of all the hospitality and have some real contact with Southerners, asking them the tough questions that everyone always throws at the South. I did just that and probably ruffled a few feathers along the way, but in the end I've concluded that there are no easy answers to what the South is all about, to what makes it so beguiling yet predictable, admirable yet despicable, all at the same time. As a result of this past weekend, each one of you has shed a little light on *Whispering Dixie* for me in a number of meaningful ways. At Betterslie and Plum Cottage I was fully prepared to plumb the depths of stereotyped anger from overworked and exploited servants, but instead found genuine friendship and respect between the races staring me right in the face. It was refreshing to make that discovery, especially after going on what I can only call a fishing expedition with Byron Cathcart's politically-correct bait. Dear Byron and his penchant for propaganda—I must have a few words with him when I return to Malibu. I predict a few changes and a revised outlook for his Rella Darrow before I give my final approval to the script. There is much to celebrate about those who have learned to get along together down here and put the mistakes of the past behind them."

She glanced at Miss Aimee and Tasmania Evans, who were nodding their heads approvingly. It was abundantly clear that these words she and Mary Dell had fashioned together were resplendently truthful and precisely to the point.

"I learned other lessons about the South during my stay here, though. At Destiny Manor I was dealt an uncomfortable reminder of the early wounds I suffered as the child of a single mother who ran a beauty parlor to keep our heads above water. Even today there are some who would probably label that struggling little family unit of ours as nothing more than expendable white trash. There are still far too many people who cannot seem to feel good about themselves unless they are constantly putting other people down. The memories of that period of my life rattled me so much that I had to jump into the Lurkins' swimming pool to drown those lingering bad feelings. Social acceptance in the South, it seems, is not just a matter of race, and Byron Cathcart doesn't even bother to tackle that one in *Whispering Dixie*. The subject bears closer examination because everyone deserves a chance to live out their wildest dreams according to their own definition of propriety."

Juliette could not be sure from a distance, but she thought those just might be tears she saw welling up in Terrelle Lurkin's eyes. Whatever the case, Johnny put a thick arm around his wife, and she soon regained her composure.

Then Juliette honed in on Edding.

"And I must certainly acknowledge the intellectual challenges I was issued by Fort Rosalie's resident poet and his esteemed housekeeper, Eola Griffin. I walked through the front door of Betterslie, marching up that grand staircase armed with Byron Cathcart's published agenda, and left feeling like a warrior whose blade had been dulled by what was finally a fair fight. The other side of the story had finally been presented to me in a most illuminating manner. In short, it's truly impossible to understand the complexities of the South without living down here amidst them, and I am indebted to you in particular, Edding, for helping me to realize that."

"The pleasure was all mine," Edding answered, rising to take a predictable little bow.

Juliette acknowledged him with a nod and rearranged her papers for the last time. "Before I announce and explain my

decision to you, I must also thank Harris Lyles and the Tourist Bureau for the exceptional assistance and guidance shown me throughout this weekend. And last but not least, Mary Dell Hoskins, for all of her handholding, speechwriting and general counsel. Some of the words I've spoken to you are mine, but others were hers or inspired by her during our hectic and impromptu collaboration this morning in her office. She was able to draw some special things out of me, the way a good director can draw an award-winning performance out of an actor."

Juliette took a deep breath and gave them all her best smile. "And now for my decision."

They all straightened up a bit at the mention of that magical phrase. Here at last was the long-awaited bottom line.

"The truth is, I could not see my way clear to staying with any of you."

She paused deliberately for effect, and what an effect she achieved! It was as if everyone seated in front of her had been stabbed clean through the heart. Her histrionic core could not help but savor the momentary mischief, secretly amused by all those faces frozen in horror and disbelief. Then she finally put them out of their misery.

"Unless," she continued, "I could stay with all of you. I followed through on a suggestion from Mary Dell that made me realize I could have it all. She mentioned a song that Miss Aimee fancied—'All Or Nothing At All'—made famous by the late Frank Sinatra. My decision didn't have to be a zero sum game. All of you could be the winners, and all of you are."

She drew herself up for the stretch run. "So here's the way I'm going to divvy it up. For my own special reasons I will rent both of Miss Aimee's rooms at Plum Cottage for myself for the entire three months. I'll probably use one of them just for storing and trying on my costumes. Hey, if it was good enough

for Elizabeth Taylor during *Raintree County*, it's good enough for me."

Miss Aimee and Tasmania clasped their hands together and then hugged each other tightly.

"Thank you so much, my dear!" Miss Aimee exclaimed. "We can hardly wait!"

"Then, since my trusted personal assistant, Heidi Pendleton, is going to be married to Fort Rosalie's own Edding Denbo right after the shoot, I think it only fair that she gets to stay out at Betterslie during the production. Her room there will be included in my overall production budget, and I will make time to give you all the inside gossip you need for your new book, Edding."

Heidi was a diminutive blur, jumping up and rushing over to Juliette to give her a quick hug, while Edding stood up and bowed once again. "On behalf of Mr. and Mrs. Edding Denbo of Betterslie, Fort Rosalie, Mississippi, we thank you," he said.

"And now for my wonderful friends out at Destiny Manor," Juliette continued, turning to the Lurkins. "Since you have eight rooms available, I have decided to treat the members of my production company to deluxe accommodations rather than the usual hotel or motel rooms. We'll fill your lovely home with laughter and good times for three straight months. They'll adore your pool and your peacocks, and you'll adore them. They're a hard-working bunch, but they certainly know how to unwind."

Terrelle dabbed at her eyes and stepped up to the podium. "Oh, this is such a relief. I was so worried we were out of it because I thought Hans's ostrich steaks had upset Tim's stomach. You have no idea how happy you've made me and Johnny. It feels like we've been vindicated somehow."

The atmosphere in the meeting room remained congenial, as the 'terrible trio' mixed and mingled without a trace of their storied competitiveness. For what had to be a first, they genuinely seemed happy for one another. Then Mary Dell stepped up to the podium to address the group.

"If I could have your attention, please." She had to repeat the sentence before everyone began calming down, but eventually she had the floor. "I have an announcement of my own to make. While you all know that Edding and Heidi are going to be married in a few months, you may not know that Juliette has very kindly offered me the position of personal assistant once Heidi leaves. I've been contemplating this offer seriously for a day or so, and I've gone back and forth about it several times, but I'm very pleased to announce to all of you now that I'm going to accept the offer."

While Juliette and the others gasped and rushed forward to embrace and congratulate her, Harris quickly left the room, his hands jammed into his pockets. It took a good ten or fifteen minutes for the excitement to die down and all the goodbyes to be said and for the meeting room to clear out, but eventually Juliette and Mary Dell were left alone.

"My instincts were dead wrong, you know," Juliette said to her newest employee. "After you left my suite last night, I would have bet my career you were going to stay right here in Fort Rosalie. That was one of my most miserable performances in years, thanks to all that booze I guzzled. To be honest with you, I'm still feeling it a little bit even now. Don't know how I got through that long-winded speech I just gave, except I kept telling myself it was good practice for the Oscar I just know I'm going to win someday. I plan to give the longest acceptance speech on record. Anyway, I clearly remember going to sleep thinking I had probably turned you off but good. Am I right about that?"

They sat down next to each other, and Mary Dell said: "Yeah, you're right. I had pretty much decided against you at that point."

"So what changed your mind?"

"Let's just say that I ultimately decided in favor of less baggage."

Juliette was puzzled but reached across and squeezed her hand anyway. "That's pretty cryptic, but I'll take it. Now, I'll want you to get together with Heidi whenever you can spare the time in the months ahead. You can ask questions galore, observe and learn from her as the shoot progresses. I just know it's all going to work out fine. Later on, we can iron out the details of your living arrangements when you finally come to Malibu." She checked her watch and sprang to her feet. "Oh, look at the time. Heidi and I have that plane to catch in Jackson in a few hours, so I best get back to the hotel and see that everything's in order, including tracking Heidi down. It's not going to be easy prying her away from Edding at this stage."

Mary Dell frowned. "You haven't mentioned Tim in all of this. I got the impression he might not even be coming back to make the film."

Juliette waved her off. "Oh, I can't make up my mind about him right now."

"Look. If I'm going to be your assistant, I'm going to have to speak my mind from time to time, so now's as good a time as any. You need to think about why it is that although you have a great many things to do twenty-four and seven, you manage to make the time for everything and everyone except Tim. He's the one thing you keep putting off—the ultimate afterthought. Think about balance in your life. Think about all the thousands of ordinary nights that will inevitably precede and follow that one Oscar night of glory you may or may not get. Give the long haul a pause."

"You're quite the philosopher, aren't you?" Juliette replied, wrinkling up her nose. "That's just fine as long as you maintain your practical, efficient side. Would it make you feel any better if I promise to think about Tim on the flight over a martini or two?"

Mary Dell looked resigned. "I suppose it'll have to do for now."

Then they made their way down the stairs together, past all the gawking secretaries and account executives and out the front door to the parking lot and the awaiting limo. Just as the chauffeur had opened the door and Juliette was about to slip into the back seat, a sturdy-looking black police officer approached from the sidewalk, waving a piece of paper above his head.

"Miss Cadbury!" he called out, catching up to her. "I hope I'm not bothering you to ask, but could I maybe get your autograph for my kids? They've been after me all weekend, ever since they found out I was gonna be part of your escort detail."

"I thought you looked familiar. I'd be delighted, of course," she said, taking the paper and pen he offered. "Especially now that I know you led the way in your patrol car, keeping those casserole-eating hordes at bay. What's your name, officer?"

The man beamed, puffing out his chest. "I'm Hobart Johnston, and my sister is Tasmania Evans. You sampled her good cooking at Plum Cottage. Tazzie phoned me and told me all about your stay there. Said you even asked all about our crazy family and such as that. Said you were just about the nicest guest they ever had there. Just thought you might like to hear that. They get all kinds, you know—some of 'em pretty rude and stuck-up—but they thought you were just the best ol' time they ever had inside those purple walls."

Juliette inhaled his compliments like her favorite perfume. "Well, the feeling was mutual, Officer Hobart Johnston, and I'll be returning to Plum Cottage very soon. Now, is there anything special you want me to write on this little ol' piece of paper here?" She was having fun with it, playing around with her spur-of-the-moment Southern accent.

"My wife's name is Sharla—that's S-H-A-R-L-A—and my kids are Sharlette—that's E-T-T-E—and Keesha—that's K-E-E-S-H-A. We all been to a good many a' your movies."

Juliette looked around for a suitable surface and shrugged. "Where's Heidi's clipboard when you really need it? Isn't that the way of the world?" She settled for pressing the paper against the limo window, then handed the paper back. "Read it aloud. I like to hear my best lines repeated."

He ran his eyes over it quickly and drew himself up proudly. "To Officer Hobart Johnston, my protector, and the beautiful women in his life—Sharla, Sharlette and Keesha—Thanks, Juliette Cadbury." He extended his hand, and she shook it warmly. "And thank you, Miss Cadbury. I'm gonna have to scrape my girls off the walls tonight."

"This isn't goodbye, of course. I'll be back right after Thanksgiving to start production of the movie, so you tell Tasmania I. Johnston Evans to pull out all the stops on those menus, and you be sure and get yourself assigned to my escort detail again."

"Will do on both counts," he replied, waving as he walked away.

"You do autographs rather well," Mary Dell said, once he was out of earshot.

"It just occurred to me that that's the first one I've been asked to sign all weekend. No wonder, with those protests keeping my public at arm's length. Come to think of it, though, I really didn't miss all the hassle and the bother. Too much contact with the public gets real old real fast, and it usually ends up getting me into lots of trouble."

Mary Dell pointed to her watch. "The time. The hotel.

Heidi. The plane flight. You need to get going."

The reminder sent Juliette climbing quickly into the backseat of the limo. "Rattled off in rapid fire sequence like a true personal assistant. I'll be talking to you in a day or so. Many, many thanks for an unforgettable weekend, sweetie. You really pulled it off for me from start to finish, and we'll be back before you know it for the shoot. That's when the fun really starts."

"I owe you an apology," Harris said, gazing directly into Mary Dell's eyes as she stood before him at his desk. He had summoned her to his office to take one last stab at convincing her to stay. "I was wrong about Juliette. Those comments I made about her being an emotional child, I mean. That was quite an impressive speech she made today. She revealed her maturity to me for the first time, and I regret misjudging her now. She's obviously much more in control of her life than I thought she was. That's the first thing I wanted to get out of the way."

He tried to gauge her reaction and detected a softening of attitude, so he proceeded with a bit more self-assurance. "The second thing I wanted to say was that I fully appreciated your input in that speech. She couldn't possibly have pulled that off alone. She had them all eating out of her hand at the end there. Those three relentless rivals of ours were carrying on with each other like they'd always been the best of friends. Big ol' Johnny thumping little bitty Edding on the back like they were fraternity brothers or hunting buddies or something. Miss Aimee and Tasmania discussing their menus for the upcoming shoot with Terrelle. Never thought those contentious women would end up comparing their most treasured recipes. What a real breakthrough for all of them, and what an accomplishment for you, it goes without saying."

"I appreciate the compliments and apologies, Harris, but I know where you're going with this. I've made up my mind. I've decided to go to work for Juliette Cadbury just as soon as the shoot is over."

"If that's what you really want, then so be it. I just wanted to add that I'm sure it will be a great help to both the Tourist Bureau and the production company if you act as the official liaison for both throughout the shoot. The continuity will be perfect for your transition to personal assistant full-time."

"Your support will mean a lot to me, of course."

He hesitated, then decided to go for it. "There's always a place for you here. Nobody does it like you." He wanted to add a more personal note, make a more emotional appeal, but he couldn't seem to find the words, and before he knew it, she had thanked him, excused herself and left the room.

He watched her go, feeling the hurt building inside his chest. Maybe he should never have crossed the line and removed the barrier between supervisor and employee in the first place. All the manuals advised against it, yet he had done it anyway.

At any rate, it was too late to undo it now. He had to deal with the results, with such things as attention to detail in matters romantic. Little things that swayed yearning hearts in a big way. He had lost his touch and his edge. He had botched the thing with Mary Dell big time in the way he had handled things with Betsy. More to the point, when Mary Dell had announced she intended to accept Juliette's offer, his heart had sunk to the soles of his shoes. It was then that he began to realize just how deeply in love with her he had fallen in the space of the last few days. Maybe it was all the confidences they had kept during the hectic weekend, but he felt closer to her than he ever had to Betsy. Was there nothing he could

O Bed! O Breakfast!

do now to prevent Mary Dell from walking out of his life and perhaps making a disaster of her own in the Hollywood fast-lane?

He tried to change the subject in his head, drumming his fingers on the desk while projecting himself as a grandfather. Okay—he could handle that. A cherub-faced little boy or girl who would call him by some cutesy name and give him a hug around the neck and look up into his eyes adoringly. That particular image was just fine with him. That kind of love was a good thing, and he had reached the age when it was appropriate for him to experience it. But it was hardly a substitute for the other kind of love—the love of a woman looking into his eyes adoringly, and he knew beyond any shadow of a doubt, particularly after this recent pity coupling of theirs, that Betsy could not and would not be the woman ever again. Even after the grandchild came, he would see to it that she remained largely a voice after the beep on his answering machine.

What he wanted now was to make a fresh start with Mary Dell, to make her understand that he could put her first in his life where it really counted. But how to do that? There just had to be something he could do to turn her around.

He decided to walk down to the Bluff after work by himself. Maybe something would come to him along the way. He reached the Bandstand and surveyed the expanse of brown water two-hundred feet below. There was a big barge tow heading upstream and fighting the current, and he almost had to laugh. He was in a similar fix—struggling to spawn like the crusty and feisty old salmon that he was—and he just stood there, leaning against the railing until the tow had rounded the bend and disappeared from sight. It was a beneficial thing for him to watch—the tow eventually prevailing against that incredible onrushing force generated by the Mississippi River. It gave him exactly the boost and the inspiration he needed.

The idea that came to him was certainly non-confrontational. It had the element of surprise. And to borrow from Mary Dell's cherished philosophy, it even involved an interaction and intersection or two.

What the hell! He had nothing to lose.

O Bed! O Breakfast!

Chapter Sixteen

Thanksgiving was just a day away, but Fort Rosalie could barely focus on the holiday, itself. Instead, everyone was preparing for the return of Juliette Cadbury and the rest of her *Whispering Dixie* entourage. Filming was to begin over Thanksgiving weekend, and the town was acting almost as if it had never hosted a location shoot before, which was certainly far from the case. Perhaps the preponderance of tabloid media types checking into all those rooms in the Hotel Fort Rosalie had a little something to do with it. They had a way of stirring things up and keeping people agitated, making for the outrageous photos and scandalous copy which kept their bread buttered. After all, Juliette Cadbury was going to be hanging around for quite a while, and it didn't get any better than that.

For her part, Mary Dell remained calm and composed, handling her duties as the Tourist Bureau's official liaison to the production company like the professional she was. But it was the way Harris had so cleverly and adroitly come at her out of left field that had changed her focus so radically—almost overnight, really—and in a way practically everyone in Fort Rosalie could not help but notice.

"I have some advice for you, dear. You'd better be careful," Miss Aimee was saying to Mary Dell as they sat together in the front parlor of Plum Cottage having another tea party. They had nearly finished reviewing a last-minute list of things to do before Juliette's impending arrival. "You're fast becoming one of Fort Rosalie's living legends with those lunchtime walks of yours. Tasmania and I look forward so to pulling back the curtains and peeking out the window when you all come down the dead end here."

Mary Dell put down her cup and grinned. "And I look forward to waving to you, too."

"Now what's your little dachshund's name again? I keep forgetting."

"Rosalie. In honor of our illustrious city, of course."

"Oh, yes, How old is she now?"

"Four months, although I've only had her for a few weeks. She's been a dream dog to handle, since Harris shopped around and ordered her up pedigreed and housebroken. You have no idea what a huge difference that last part makes. I have absolutely no patience for cleaning up messes. The way I look at it, newspapers are strictly for reading. Still and all, I can't possibly describe how much this adorable little black and tan creature has changed my life."

Miss Aimee stirred her tea and picked up a buttered biscuit. "As I said, people all over town are starting to call you the Lunchtime Dachshund Lady. It reminds me of the way they started calling me the Purple Dress Lady years and years ago when I decided it was high time I made a name for myself. You just have to be consistent with your eccentric gimmick over a long enough period of time, and people will fall right in line."

"Well, people can call me whatever they like, but I wouldn't give up my walks with Rosalie for anything. It's wonderful exercise for both of us, and the whole universe just seems like a better place to be after we've made our rounds. I work out all my problems in my head, and I know it's just what the vet ordered for Rosalie, since she's cooped up most of the day waiting for me to come home."

Miss Aimee was chewing a bite of biscuit thoughtfully. "Enough about your delightful puppy. Tell me how things are going between you and Harris these days. And don't bother to deny that the two of you are an item. I have my reliable sources, you know."

"I have no intention of denying anything. We're taking it slow and easy—that's the way we both want it. Oh, that ex-wife keeps leaving calculating messages on his answering machine at all hours, trying to weasel her way back in, but I know now that Harris is up to the task. When I opened my apartment door that memorable morning and saw him standing there with that whimpering, wiggling, delicious little doggie handful, I melted to the floor. I knew then that he really wanted to be a part of my life and that I had been wrong to worry and fret about anyone or anything from that other life he used to lead. When he delivered Rosalie to my doorstep, he proved to me right then and there that he'd been listening closely to my daydreams and paying attention to my ambitions. It wasn't too long after that I decided to renege on my commitment to Juliette. At that point I knew where I really belonged."

"And how did she take that bit of news?"

"As you can imagine, she waxed very dramatic for about five minutes, but eventually she calmed down. She needs an actual script and some competent direction to carry on any longer than that. Believe me, there are plenty of people out there in Hollywood who will be more than willing to audition for that job, and she knows it. I just happened to be a known quantity that more or less fell into her lap for a little while due to extenuating circumstances which no longer exist."

Miss Aimee finished her biscuit, gently clearing her throat. "What's the latest on her relationship with that dashing Mr. Reynaldo? My God, what I wouldn't give to be a few decades younger!"

Mary Dell was counting the flurry of phone calls from Malibu in her head. "The last time I talked to her, she said Tim refuses to play Harbaugh Kinsley unless she marries him,

and at this point it doesn't look like that's going to happen."

"I can't believe it," said Miss Aimee, nervously rearranging things on the coffee table. "What on earth is wrong with the woman? They make such a handsome and energetic couple, and I have to confess I got a vicarious thrill or two just having them stay under my roof."

"Juliette has a will of iron, as you well know. But then so does Tim. I'm not so sure they would stay together very long even if they did get married."

"So who will she get for her leading man?"

Mary Dell laughed. "Are you kidding? She's got actors lined up from one end of the country to the other testing for the part right now. Meanwhile, they'll shoot around Harbaugh Kinsley's scenes until the new guy arrives."

"I hope that young woman knows what she's giving up," said Miss Aimee, shaking her head. "I know I would have given anything at any time in my life to have had someone fall in love with me the way that young man was obviously in love with her."

"Well, at least Edding and Heidi are still on."

Miss Aimee chuckled richly. "Indeed, they are. Eola Griffin called up the other day and gave Tasmania all the wedding details. It seems our Edding has already composed an original ceremony for the auspicious occasion. Part prose, part poetry, but all Edding, I hear. Those nuptials of his will likely be the longest in the history of the South, not to mention that he has in mind making that poor Heidi risk her neck descending his staircase with a mile-long train gliding behind her. Meanwhile, he will be safely waiting for her below at the bottom of the stairs in his full, miniature-adult regalia. Can't you just picture it?"

Tasmania appeared in the doorway, her smile aimed straight at Mary Dell. "Excuse the interruption, but I just got

O Bed! O Breakfast!

off the phone with my brother, Hobart, and he said for you to be sure and tell Miss Cadbury that he got that escort detail assignment again. He really enjoyed himself last time. Everybody in his neighborhood thinks he's some kinda celebrity now just because he drove his patrol car all around the county in front of her limousine that weekend. Is that some kinda foolishness or what?"

"Oh, let your brother have his moment, Tasmania," Mary Dell replied. "It's not every day a policeman flashes for a movie star, so to speak, and gets applauded for a job well-done. I'm sure Juliette will be delighted to hear the news." Mary Dell checked her watch and made a face. "It's almost four. I'm supposed to meet Harris at the Hotel Fort Rosalie bar. He promised me he'd have his mind made up about some very important matters."

Miss Aimee made a soft cooing noise, and there was a naughty twinkle in her eye. "Ooh! Do I hear wedding bells?"

"Too soon for that. But maybe another step on the road to Mr. and Mrs. Tourist Bureau." Mary Dell rose and headed for the front door, turning at the last moment to give both Miss Aimee and Tasmania a hug. "I think we've been very thorough with our checklist. Plum Cottage is ready to take center stage, as far as I can tell."

"And it will stay that way for years to come, thanks to Juliette Cadbury," Miss Aimee added at the last second.

On the walk to the hotel, Mary Dell enjoyed the attention she received as a result of her walks with Rosalie. There was that rotund lady sitting on her front porch who liked to wave at her when she passed by every weekday with her puppy straining at the bit and sniffing indiscriminately at whatever captivated her nose. In the next block—those two little girls in pigtails who sometimes pressed their own noses against their living room window, both of them busy this afternoon playing

a frenzied game of swinging statue in their front yard and giggling behind their hands the moment they spied her approaching.

"Where's your wiener dog puppy, lady?" one of them called out, emerging from her contortions. "I never seen you walk by here without your wiener dog puppy. Nothin's happened to her, has it?"

"No, indeed. She's at home in my apartment being a good girl, I hope. We'll be taking our walks again regular as clockwork right after the holidays, though," Mary Dell replied as she walked by. Her lunchtime routine had truly drawn people out of the woodwork, making her feel so much more a part of the fabric of Fort Rosalie than she ever had before. Miss Aimee had nailed it. She was making a name for herself, well on her way to becoming an institution, and she liked that very much.

Harris was waiting for her at his favorite corner table, nursing a martini and munching on a pretzel. "How did it go with our purple people?" he said, rising to pull out her chair.

"We were on the same page all the way down the line. Everything's ready for Juliette's arrival." An overly made-up cocktail waitress came over and took her white wine order, and then Mary Dell continued. "I can't believe the production company arrives this weekend. All our hard work is finally coming to fruition."

"Not our hard work—your hard work. You know very well you rescued this thing time and time again when it looked for all the world like it was going to turn into a runaway train."

When the wine arrived, Mary Dell lifted her glass, intending to make a toast. Then she put it down again, eyeing Harris warily. "I started to propose something, but first I need those answers I've been waiting for all week."

"Two questions, right?" He forsook his drink to place both hands on the table. "Okay, here goes. Yes, the Board of

O Bed! O Breakfast!

Aldermen approved your raise at the afternoon meeting, and it officially goes into effect next month, just in time for all that Christmas shopping you're planning to do. It's no Juliette Cadbury-triple-the-money-raise, but the most substantial we've ever given."

"Excellent. And?"

"And—yes, I will drive down to your family home in Wilkins County with you and Rosalie tomorrow to meet and have a scrumptious Thanksgiving dinner with you and your lovely parents, both of whom you insist are just dying to meet me. Is that what you wanted to hear from these veteran lips?"

She reached across and placed her hands atop his. "I couldn't have written a more appropriate script myself." Then she raised her glass in earnest. "Here's to respectable raises and Thanksgiving dinner with lovely parents. Or is it lovely raises and Thanksgiving dinner with respectable parents?"

They laughed, clinked rims and sipped.

"And you still insist your lovely, respectable parents won't think I'm a tad bit too old for you?" he said.

"Stop bringing that up," she answered, playfully rapping his knuckles. "All I've ever done for years is write them glowing letters about you and how wonderful you were to work with. By now, they think you practically invented the entire concept of tourism. Don't worry. When they see how we are together, they'll be very pleased."

"An intersection and interaction of unparalleled portent."

She smiled in spite of herself. "Pontificate all you like, but I do think you and I were put through the wringer on more than one occasion. The good news is—we were able to stay connected."

"Yeah. I almost let you get away. But I don't intend to let that happen ever again."

Mary Dell settled back in her chair and let his words filter

down to the bottom of her soul. It was everything to know who she was and where she fit in and that someone truly loved her for those things besides. And on the eve of Thanksgiving, that was truly a lot to be thankful for.

The End

O Bed! O Breakfast!

Robert Dalby

O Bed! O Breakfast!

ABOUT THE AUTHOR

Robert Dalby, a native of Natchez, MS, currently living in Tupelo, is a graduate of the University of the South; his previously published work was GOD OF THE DOOR.

Robert Dalby